DAVID

Also by Mary Hoffman
Troubadour
The Falconer's Knot

The Stravaganza Series
City of Masks
City of Stars
City of Flowers
City of Secrets
City of Ships

DAVID

MARY HOFFMAN

BLOOMSBURY

NEW YORK BERLIN LONDON SYDNEY

First published in Great Britain in July 2011 by Bloomsbury Publishing Plc
Published in the United States of America in October 2011 by Bloomsbury Books for Young Readers
www.bloomsburyteens.com

For information about permission to reproduce selections from this book, write to
Permissions, Bloomsbury BFYR, 175 Fifth Avenue, New York, New York 10010

Library of Congress Cataloging-in-Publication Data
Hoffman, Mary.
David / Mary Hoffman. — 1st ed.
        p.   cm.
Summary: An eighteen-year-old stonecutter who is caught in the middle of political conflict in
Florence, Italy, in the early 1500s, must flee for his life in disguise because his has become the best-
known face and figure in Florence.
ISBN 978-1-59990-700-0 (hardcover)
[1. Michelangelo Buonarroti, 1475–1564. David—Fiction. 2. Artists—Italy—History—
16th century—Fiction. 3. Florence (Italy)—History—1421–1737—Fiction. 4. Italy—
History—1492–1559—Fiction.] I. Title.
PZ7.H67562Dav 2011   [Fic]—dc22   2011006287

Typeset by Hewer Text UK Ltd, Edinburgh
Printed in the U.S.A. by Quad/Graphics, Fairfield, Pennsylvania
2 4 6 8 10 9 7 5 3 1

For Toby Sharp, a Giant fan

'David with his sling, I with my bow.'

Michelangelo (fragment)

Contents

CHAPTER ONE

Blood and Milk

y brother died last month. No one bothered to tell me. But then, there is no one left alive who knows my real relationship with him. Of those who remember me in Florence, some say he was my master – which he was for a while, even though he didn't normally take apprentices. Others think I was his paramour, which is another way of saying they never knew him or us.

But when his nephew brought his body back to Florence, word reached me here in Settignano.

My dear brother was nearly eighty-nine. It would have been his birthday last week. So eighty-one and a half years since I came into the world and he was waiting to greet me. And to look after me.

And sixty years since that time when everyone in Florence knew who I was.

'David!' they would call, from every street corner and tavern. But that was not my real name.

Those three and a half years were the only ones in my life when I had what you might call adventures. It wasn't what I was expecting when I left our home in Settignano to find my brother and make my fortune in Florence.

I knew nothing of politics or the fads and fancies of great people like dukes and princes. Nothing about life at court or the ways of grand ladies. But I was a quick learner and I soon found myself at the heart of conspiracies, plots and murders.

Now that he's gone, I can tell my story and I'll tell it like a proper story, even though there will be no 'once upon a time' and not exactly a 'happy ever after' either. But it's my story and no one else can tell it.

Florence, March 1501

The first thing I knew about life in the city was a knife at my throat and three ruffians at my back. I was tall and well-made then and could easily have fought them off if it hadn't been for the knife. First the prick of it drawing blood from my Adam's apple and then a swift slash that separated the pouch containing my small store of money from my belt. Then the three ran off laughing, leaving me like the stupid country boy I was, standing gawping down at the dangling leather purse strings.

'Welcome to the city, bumpkin!' one of them shouted and then they were far away.

I had set out on foot from Settignano later than I had meant. First there was my mother, with her endless messages and packages for my brother, then my five big sisters all smothering me with kisses and wailing that the family's baby was leaving home.

Baby! I was eighteen and a half years old and I had a girl waiting to waylay me on the dusty southern road out of the village. It took longer to disentangle myself from Rosalia than from any of the women in my family. And, truth to tell, I didn't really want to disentangle myself all that quickly. Rosalia was fifteen, plump and as rosy as her name, even though her hair and eyes were dark.

'Don't leave me, Gabriele,' she murmured when I eventually sat up and brushed the grass from my hair. 'I shall miss you so.' (I told you my name wasn't David.)

'I'm not leaving you,' I protested. 'I am going to the city to make my fortune. I'll be back in a year or so and then we can be married.'

'You'll forget me,' she said, sniffing a bit, 'once you've seen those grand ladies in the city, with their silks and velvets and precious jewels.'

'Not many of those left after the Mad Monk had his way,' I told her but she didn't really understand. She'd been a little girl of twelve when Savonarola built his bonfire of all the rich and luxurious goods he could make people yield up in the city. And only a year older when the Friar himself had burned in the same place.

If I knew little of city politics, Rosalia grasped even less.

She was so sure that I would meet a rich woman who would want to steal me from her that I felt touched. Before her, the only females who had told me I was handsome were my mother and sisters and I had no idea what was waiting for me in the big city. Rosalia turned out to be right in a way, but I didn't forget her completely – even though there were many temptations.

I thought about Rosalia, as I stood destitute in the shadow of the great cathedral that first night. There was nothing I could do except try to find my brother and I didn't even know if he would be there.

I had been to the city only a few times in my life and I wasn't sure how to get to where my brother lived. There hadn't really been a proper plan in my head when I set out and I was

beginning to realise how foolish this had been. I had made for
the cathedral as the one landmark I remembered; you could
see it from anywhere in the city.

That was another mistake because I had been gazing up at
the huge cupola when those three villains jumped me. Now I
trailed round to the front of the building and sat on the steps
with my back to the rough facade. There was some bread and
cheese in my bag and a leather bottle with a bit of wine left
in it. At least I still had my bag. As well as a few changes of
underwear and a spare shirt, it held my stonecutting tools and
without them I wouldn't have a chance of earning any money.

But the plan, such as it was, had been to pay for a few
nights' lodging to give me time to find news of my brother.
And now I had nothing but a meagre supper and no money.
So I sat on the steps and munched on my crust and watched
the fashionable people parading between the Duomo and the
Baptistery, cursing my stupidity and ill luck.

Gradually, I noticed that people were staring at me, both
men and women. I supposed I looked a comical rustic figure
sitting eating my humble meal in front of the grandest building
in Europe. I began to blush and feel uncomfortable. Hastily, I
stood up and brushed the crumbs off my jerkin, feeling I must
move on, even though I had no idea where I might go to spend
the night.

And then a young girl – a servant I supposed even though
my Rosalia would have died to wear clothes of that quality –
came up to me and whispered that I was sent for.

'Sent for?' I said. My first thought was that she bore a
message from my brother but how would he have known I
was there?

'My mistress sent me,' said the girl, pointing to a palazzo
overlooking the cathedral square. There was a veiled figure at

a window on the first floor, from which she would have been able to watch me eating my bread and cheese.

'But what does she want with me?' I asked.

The girl smirked even though she was hardly more than a child. I felt myself blushing even more than before; Rosalia had been right. The women of the city were clearly without shame.

On the other hand, if this girl's mistress had taken a fancy to me, I would at least get shelter for the night – maybe even a little money to tide me over till I could find my brother.

I was innocent but not so innocent as not to understand what would be required of me in return. I followed the girl and let her lead me through in the grand wooden doors that formed the entrance to her mistress's palazzo.

Clarice de' Buonvicini turned out to be a young widow with two small daughters. She wasn't beautiful but she was very gracious and within a few minutes I felt like a coarse peasant with a dirty mind.

'I saw you alone and lost on the cathedral steps,' she said, 'and I wondered if you needed help.'

So I told her the whole story of my misadventure. She gave me sweet wine and biscuits and listened most sympathetically to my woes. And she was really interested when I told her about my brother.

'I didn't think he was in Florence at present,' said Clarice. 'But I have seen his wonderful crucifix in the church of Santo Spirito, and his fame reaches us from Rome.'

'He's not my blood brother,' I explained. I didn't want her to think I was claiming any tie with the Canossa family; I was clearly no aristocrat. 'We are milk-brothers only.'

'Ah,' was all she said to that.

She asked if I would dine with her and, since I was always hungry and the bread and cheese hadn't made much of a dent in my appetite, I accepted. But I was acutely aware of my rough clothes and my working man's hands, which seemed big and clumsy holding the stem of one of her wine glasses.

I swear she read my mind because she asked, hesitantly, with great delicacy, if I would like to wash, and change my clothes after my journey, then added since I had been robbed, would I care to wear something of her late husband's – we were much of a height, she said.

The maid, who was beginning to annoy me a bit with her knowing looks, laid out fine white silk hose and red velvet breeches and doublet on a bed in a chamber she led me to. Then she was back with a basin and ewer of hot water while I was still sitting on the bed in my undershirt, feeling the brocaded coverlet with my callused hands. She smirked again, looking at my bare legs.

I sent her on her way and was then glad of that hot, scented water. Once I was dressed in my borrowed finery I could almost believe myself worthy to sit at the lady's dinner table, if it hadn't been for my hands.

I nearly got lost trying to find my way from the chamber to the room where the lady was dining. I could have waited for the impudent servant to fetch me but I'd had enough of her. And my luck held: Clarice was in the second room whose door I tried.

She jumped up rather quickly when she saw me and put her hand to her heart as if I had startled her. Maybe I reminded her of her late husband, all dressed up in the dead man's clothes?

They seemed to be having an effect on me too, since I hurried to pick up her napkin and pull out her chair for her. We sat and ate together, talking of sculpture and marble and quarries and she was so interested in every detail of my life that what could have been an awkward evening passed off very smoothly.

We were waited on by liveried menservants and I was sure that one in particular was giving me nasty looks. Every time he poured me more wine or offered me a dish, I tried to hide my hands under my napkin. I was certain that he had the same vile thoughts about me as the lady's maid entertained.

But Clarice had been nothing but courteous to me. After dinner, she asked if I would do her the honour of accepting shelter under her roof for the night. In the morning she would send out to see if my brother could be found. When I nodded, she rang a bell and the maid came with a candlestick and showed me back to the chamber where I had changed my clothes.

I had drunk a lot of wine by then and fell on to the soft mattress with relief, discarding my fine clothes on the floor like a lout. I fell asleep almost immediately, thinking what a tale I would have to tell Rosalia and how she had been quite wrong about Florentine ladies.

But I had been asleep only a short time before I found myself having the most delicious dream. It was a warm night and I felt myself wrapped round by cool limbs. It was a heavenly embrace and I responded in my sleep like any healthy eighteen-year-old. It took some minutes before I realised that this was not a dream at all and the stately, elegant lady I had dined with had slipped naked into my bed.

Next morning she was gone and I wondered again if I had imagined the whole thing; had it been a wine-induced vision? I woke late, as I could tell from the angle of the sun shining through my shutters. I stood at the window wrapped in the brocade coverlet and saw that it gave on to an enclosed court-yard, not the cathedral square.

Down below, servants were hanging out washing, chopping herbs and gossiping. I imagined that several of them pointed up at the window and cackled with laughter. I jumped back quickly lest they see me. I looked round for my old clothes but they had gone; there was nothing for me to put on but yesterday's finery, which looked tawdry and ridiculous to me in the light of day.

How was I to escape? I still had no money and nowhere certain to stay in the city. I was now feeling very uncomfortable indeed and ashamed that I had betrayed Rosalia on my first night in the city.

There was a knock on my door and the maid came in with more hot water and my work clothes, washed and brushed, over her arm. I was so relieved that, firstly, I was not still naked and, secondly, I could change back into the stonecutter I was that I took no notice of her expression.

After changing my clothes, I tried to creep unobtrusively down the stairs but my lady came out of a room on the first floor and beckoned me to her. She gave me a very nice smile and she seemed altogether younger and more lively this morning. There could be only one reason for that and I had no idea how to speak to her or behave towards her.

Clarice, on the contrary, was completely composed.

'Good morning, Gabriele,' she said. 'I have some news for you.'

9

She beckoned me into her parlour and indicated a chair. I sat down awkwardly, once again very conscious of my rough clothes against the velvet upholstery.

'While you've been sleeping,' she said, 'my people have been out searching for information about the sculptor.'

I noticed she didn't refer to him as my brother. Perhaps she didn't take our relationship seriously now that I had explained it? Blood is thicker than milk, I suppose.

'And they have found that he is not currently in the city,' she continued.

My expression must have betrayed me because she touched my shoulder sympathetically. 'But he is expected any day,' she said. 'He has written to his father to say he is leaving Rome because of an expected commission here.'

My relief must have shown as clearly as my earlier disappointment. I had no ability to suppress my emotions at all – I was still too inexperienced to pretend.

'So you see,' she was saying, 'you can continue to stay with me until we hear he has arrived.'

I must have babbled something about not wanting to be a nuisance, but before I knew it the lady was in my lap kissing me, and I knew that she would have me stay, even if it meant stealing my clothes to keep me there.

There is a very efficient communication system in Florence between ladies of a certain rank. It operates through their servants and if men were anything like as well organised, then the city's politics would progress a lot more smoothly.

Women called at ladies' houses – to collect their laundry, curl and colour their hair, measure their waists for clothes they were making, bring headdresses to sell them, and for many other reasons. And during their visits they talked, not so much with the ladies, who were reasonably discreet, but with their servants, who were anything but. And then their gossip passed from the servants to their mistresses.

I don't know how I knew it but I was sure that the ladies of Clarice de' Buonvicini's circle knew all about me and what I was doing in her palazzo. The maid – whose name turned out to be Vanna – would have told the laundress, who would have told a maid in another lady's house, who would have passed it on to a visiting hairdresser, and so on. And since it was only the very richest ladies in the grandest palazzos that had a specialist in to do their hair instead of leaving it to their maids, my name was soon being bandied about in the highest social circles.

At the time, I didn't know about the underground gossip network; I learned it much later from a servant-girl who was much more to my taste than Clarice's pert maid.

These ladies, who had been so starved of gossip as well as finery during the years when the Friar Savonarola preached against all the things that made their lives bearable, then began probing their sources of information and drawing their own conclusions. Clarice started to receive a lot of visitors.

At first, I was kept well out of their way and in fact time lay heavily on my hands. I was used to work – hard, physical work cutting stone and heaving huge blocks of it. My callused hands were a badge of my trade. But spending the days lounging in my lady's chamber was making them almost as soft as hers.

If I thought about the softness of my lady's hands, I was soon riddled with guilt about what they had been doing very recently, and in my idleness had too many moments in which

11

to think about my infidelity to Rosalia. so it was almost a relief to be summoned to meet Clarice's friends.

She insisted on my wearing her late husband's clothes all the time now. I didn't even know where my working clothes were.

I don't know how she explained my presence to her grand friends, but I was becoming more confident about handling a wine glass or a silver fork. And I didn't pretend to be a gentleman. If they asked, I told them my trade. But mostly they didn't talk to me; they talked about me. In whispers, to my lady and to each other.

And it was in her parlour that I first heard murmurs that I would make a good artist's model. It wasn't the work I had come to Florence to do; I wouldn't have been so conceited about my looks. But several of these aristocratic ladies said they would like to own my portrait and I was becoming bold enough to think that some of them at least would have liked to possess the original.

I was getting better at suppressing my blushes but I was quite sure there would be more honour in posing for a great artist than in being handed from lady to lady like a lapdog.

And perhaps that was the beginning of the process that would end, three years later, in my becoming the best-known face and figure in Florence.

CHAPTER TWO

The Old Block

It was two more weeks before I heard anything of my brother and by then I was deep in sin. Not in adultery, since my lady's husband was dead, but treachery to my Rosalia. Even then I knew that if I ever did get back to Settignano and marry her, I would not say a word about my exploits in the city. But infidelity to a girlfriend is not a sin you have to confess to the priest – though fornication is. I decided to say nothing about either and on my one visit to the confessional while I was with Clarice I kept my counsel about both.

Then one day my lady sent for me when I was helping in the kitchen. In spite of my new fine clothes, I was often in the kitchen or courtyard lending a hand by cutting wood or lighting fires or even carrying barrels and boxes for the cook. I ran lightly up the stairs to her chamber – oh, if only I could take stairs at such a pace now! – and found Clarice looking rather sad.

She smiled when she saw me, as she always did, but I thought I saw her brush away some tears.

'Bad news, my lady?'

'No, not at all,' she said. 'Good news – for you at least! The sculptor is back in Florence. Shall I send a message to him for you?'

'No!' I said too eagerly. 'Just tell me how to find his house and I'll go myself.'

13

'You will be happy to leave me, I think, Gabriele,' she said.

Looking at her sad face, I knew then what I needed to say and do, but, still, a few hours later, I left the palazzo in my stonecutter's clothes, carrying my canvas bag and it was as if I had just arrived in the city and the last few weeks had been but a dream. One difference was that I now knew to keep my purse thrust deep inside my jerkin and it was a lot heavier than when I left Settignano.

My step was light, as I headed towards the river, where my brother's home was. It felt like a fresh start, though at the back of my mind I knew I'd be seeing Clarice de' Buonvicini again. I squared my shoulders, tried to ignore the curious glances people were giving me, and walked away from the protective bulk of the cathedral, past the Bargello and then towards Santa Croce church.

It was beginning to get dark – my lady had been so reluctant to let me go – and as I searched for my brother's house, a feeling of unease lowered my mood. There were a lot of people about, small knots of young men talking together and giving other groups evil looks. I patted my jerkin to make sure my money was safe.

But these were not like the ruffians who had robbed me on my first night. They were well dressed and well fed, more like Clarice's circle of friends than robbers. Not that I had met any of her male friends, if she had any. These bravos were more like rival gangs of young aristocrats. But that didn't make them any less dangerous: I saw steel glinting at several belts.

I wanted very much to be indoors among friends; life at Clarice's must have made me soft.

'If you are going to walk the streets at night, you'd better know whose side you are on,' said a familiar gruff voice behind me.

I turned to grin at the face of my milk-brother before answering, 'I'm not on anyone's side.'

'Not possible in Florence,' he said, giving me a bear hug. 'We'd better get you out of the way before you get into trouble.'

We were soon sitting in his father's house toasting each other with rough red wine, no better than I used to drink in Settignano. There was no sign of his father, old Lodovico, however, or any of his brothers. I looked at him with satisfaction. No one could have called my brother a handsome man, though he might have been passable if a young friend of his hadn't broken his nose when they were just boys. But he took no account of appearances and was careless about his clothes.

All the years I knew him, my brother moved in a sort of cloud of white dust. It made me feel right at home. It was partly that he worked all day on his sculpture but mainly because he hardly ever changed his clothes.

He was looking just as closely at me.

'Gabriele,' he said, 'you've grown. You are a man now.'

'Not much of a one yet,' I said. Next to him I felt like a boy.

'But a very good-looking one,' he said. 'You'll have to be careful.'

I couldn't help it; I blushed. My brother narrowed his eyes.

'I don't mean that high-born lady who's been playing with you for these last weeks,' he said. 'That's only to be expected. I mean men. There are a lot in Florence who would pay you to be their toy.'

This wasn't a conversation likely to restore my composure. It was true I had been looked at by as many men as women when I was sitting in front of the cathedral, eating my bread and cheese, before my lady rescued me.

'I have never been with a man,' I said. 'That is not the way my inclinations lie.'

15

He gave a short, barking laugh. 'It might not be your inclinations that would be consulted,' he said. Then he looked at me, appraising me, as if I were a block of marble. 'Beauty like yours doesn't last long,' he said at last. 'You might be tempted to make the most of it.'

'Stop it, Angelo,' I said. 'I am willing to be a model for artists, if that's what you mean, but nothing else. And I'd far rather earn my money cutting stone. That's why I came, to see if there was any work to be had in the city.'

'Plenty of work for a stonecutter,' he said. 'If that's what you really want. But you'd better learn to protect yourself.'

He handed me a wicked-looking dagger.

'Take this,' he said. 'And keep it with you always – just in case.'

Then he seemed to relax, as if I had passed some sort of test. He poured us both some more of the rough wine.

'It's good to see you,' he said. 'Tell me about your mamma.'

When Angelo – which is what we called him in the family – had been born, his mother, Francesca, sent him to my mother to be nursed. Not straight away, because they had been away from Florence when the baby was born. Francesca already had a two-year-old son and I think she might have liked to carry on suckling this new babe herself but her husband had grand ideas; he thought that their remote connection with the aristocratic Canossa family meant it would be demeaning for his wife to put milk in her own child's mouth. So off went little Angelo to my mother, who had a baby girl – my sister Giulia – about the same age.

It was a funny thing: my mother had five daughters before I was born and Angelo's mamma had five sons before she died.

16

It's like that with some women. But when Signora Buonarroti breathed her last after the birth of her fifth son, Angelo was still living with us. He was only six and I don't know what happened to his four brothers; the new baby must have needed a nurse but it wasn't Mamma. Angelo was pining and old Lodovico, his father, was at his wits' end, so he let him stay with us.

I say 'us' but I wasn't born then. My mother claims that I was conceived the very night Francesca died. That's why they gave me my name.

'She left your brother, named for the archangel Michael, with us and straight away a boy leapt in my womb,' she would say. 'So we called you Gabriele.'

It was embarrassing. And a bit blasphemous.

But my parents had been desperate for a son after five girls. My father was a stonecutter and he hoped to have sons to follow him into the trade. As it turned out, he got just the one. And that one was born nine months after little Angelo became a permanent part of the family.

Angelo was a stonecutter too! But in a much grander way. He was a sculptor who worked in marble. He always said he'd drunk his love of stone in with my mother's milk. And he was no archangel, in spite of his name, but he was like a brother to me and I loved him. He lived with us for another four years until his father took him back and sent him to school. My earliest memory is of Angelo drawing pictures in the earth for me with a sharpened stick.

'Wake up, sleepyhead!' said my brother, squeezing cold drops of water on my face from a cloth held high above me. 'The sun and I have been awake for hours.'

I came to, spluttering. 'Sorry,' I said.

'You got into soft ways at Signora de' Buonvicini's,' he teased. 'You never slept in like this in Settignano, I'll wager.'

'Wasn't allowed to,' I admitted.

'Why did you come to Florence?' he asked suddenly. 'Wasn't there enough work for you back home?'

'Ay, enough, but only boring work,' I said. 'I wanted to be where you could see the cut stone turning into beautiful buildings.'

It was true. Half the reason I'd been so easily robbed that first night was because I was staring like a booby at the white, green and pink marble inlaid in the walls of the cathedral. Everyone knew in Settignano about this pattern and where the stone had come from – Carrara for the white, Prato for the green and Siena for the pink – but this was the first time I had seen it up close.

Angelo cuffed me gently round the head.

'You're too much of a dreamer to be a *picchiapietre* all your life,' he said. 'Maybe you should be a sculptor like me?'

'I don't think so, brother.' I shook my head. 'I might be a dreamer but I'm no artist.'

'We shall see,' he said. 'Now eat a crust of bread and I'll take you to see a real piece of stone.'

He wasn't a man to spend long sprucing himself up before going out into the world in the morning so I had to hurry to keep up with him. Literally a crust to eat, after all those delicacies at my lady's, and five minutes to splash my face with more water and drag my fingers through my hair, and then he was striding off back towards the cathedral.

I was a bit nervous about coming so close to Clarice's palazzo again so soon after leaving it but my brother skirted up the other side of the cathedral and towards its works' building.

He was obviously well known there, by all the greetings he got on the way in. But he merely grunted in reply or lifted a hand. He was a man with a purpose. And when he'd reached what he wanted to show me, I saw why.

It was a block of old marble lying on its side in a court-yard. It must have been nine *braccia* or so long – about the size of three men lying end to end. The surface of it had my hands itching, it was so pitted and full of holes. Someone had botched a job of turning it into something – or somebody.

'Carrara,' said my brother, tapping the block with his toe.

'How old is it?'

'It's been lying around here nearly forty years.'

'What was it going to be?'

'A giant for the cathedral.'

'Didn't get very far, did he – whoever he was?'

My brother shrugged. I could see he wasn't interested in whatever had happened to this block of stone in the past. The gleam in his eye told me that he was thinking only of its future.

'You want it, don't you?' I said.

'Maybe,' he said. 'I think I can get it. They want to get rid of it.'

'I should think so too, if they've been tripping over it for forty years!'

'I'm not the only one after it, though,' said my brother. 'Someone else wants it as a present.'

'A present?'

'I'm going to charge them well for what I make of it,' he said, 'but it will be worth it.'

I could see that he thought this big ugly block was a challenge. I knew he was a great man now with a reputation that had travelled north from Rome but I really doubted

19

he could make anything worth looking at out of such a monstrosity.

'Come on!' he said. 'We're going to measure it.'

By July negotiations were going on for Angelo to have the block of marble. He now had to make a model to convince the Operai del Duomo, those exacting men who oversaw the art of the cathedral, that he could really do something with it. I had never seen him so excited, but then I'd never seen him work before either. Whenever he had come to visit us at home, he had been on holiday.

But Angelo had also signed a contract to make fifteen figures for Cardinal Piccolomini in Siena; he had boasted about it. I couldn't see how he was going to make those if he got the Duomo's old block to sculpt. He told me he'd promised the Cardinal not to undertake any other work till the Sienese commission was finished, but I could see he didn't intend to keep his word if he got hold of that block.

I was still staying with him at his father's house; it wasn't comfortable but it was convenient and I felt safe there. I hardly saw Lodovico but he was willing enough to have me in his home. It was obvious that money was a bit tight. Angelo never took any notice of home comforts – he was a bit like a monk in that way – and I'm ashamed to say I often sloped off back to Clarice's in search of some better wine and more plentiful food. Yes, and other comforts too.

And I enjoyed playing with her two little daughters, Benedetta and Carolina. They knew me now and, for want of a father perhaps, they looked forward to my visits. They were sweet-natured, like their mother. I knew nothing of their father, save that he had died eighteen months earlier in a riding accident.

Angelo never said anything about my absences – just gave me a quizzical look when I came back smelling of perfume. He had found me work in a stonemasons' workshop near the great cathedral, which kept me close to the big block of marble and to my lady's palazzo. If I stayed overnight with Clarice, I could stumble out in the morning and into work, but when we broke off at midday I always found my footsteps taking me to the Opera del Duomo; that block was beginning to fascinate me almost as much as it did my brother.

He had started calling it 'David'.

'I can make something of this,' he would mutter, walking round and round the block and making the odd mark here and there on the surface.

It was as if he were boring into it with his eyes, trying to find something inside it that was trapped, frozen in the marble like a fish in a block of ice. But it wasn't a fish he was trawling for; it was a man.

One night back at the house he asked me to pose for him. He wanted me to strip and there's no other man I would have done it for. I trusted him completely, but I was a bit nervous that some other member of the family might walk in. He wasn't satisfied with my position until he had got me standing with my weight on my right leg, my body pivoted on that hip and my head turned to the left. My right arm was to hang down loose, but with my left – bent up towards the shoulder – I had to pretend to hold a slingshot. My left foot was raised – resting on a cauliflower!

'Is that Goliath's head?' I asked.

Angelo just grunted.

I found it very difficult to hold the pose and I was embarrassed to have him gazing so intently at my naked body.

'You're frowning, Gabriele,' he said, rapidly sketching in fast fluid lines.

'Sorry,' I said.

'No,' he said. 'It's good. It's how David would have looked.'

Over the next few weeks I got more used to standing with my clothes off while Angelo circled round me sketching me from every angle. There were sheets and sheets of drawings: my head, my arms, my back and my buttocks.

I thought I'd stopped frowning but there it still was in all the drawings of my face.

'Do you need all these?' I asked him one day, as casually as I could.

'Huh,' he grunted. 'You want one for your lady love, don't you?'

I blushed at being so transparent, but he gave me a handful of the drawings he didn't want. It seemed to make him decide on what he did want, because the next day he said he was ready to make a wax model for the statue.

Clarice was delighted with the few sketches I gave her.

'I will have this one framed and hang it in my bedchamber where none but I will be able to see it,' she said.

And your servants, I thought, uneasy about that little maid Vanna looking at me with no clothes on.

I stowed the rest of the drawings away carefully. I don't know why. I certainly had no idea then how famous this David would be. Or how dangerous it would be for me to look like him.

My brother was now completely absorbed in the wax model he was making, based on those drawings. It was less than life-sized, being smaller than me, let alone than that huge old block. I looked at the progress of the wax model every day, drawn by this manikin who had my body and face. No one else was allowed in the workshop, even though the Operai were very interested in what he was doing. He was much too secretive to let them in or show them anything till the model was finished.

But then my lady hit me with news that put all thoughts of my other self out of my mind.

We had just finished eating a good dinner at her house and the servants had withdrawn when she chose to tell me.

'Gabriele, dear,' she began. 'I'm afraid these lovely evenings of ours are coming to an end.'

I just gawped like a ninny. 'Why?' I asked stupidly. It should have been obvious that she had tired of me.

'I am getting married again,' she said simply.

My face must have shown my dismay and disbelief. She had never mentioned another man's name all the times we had been together.

'Antonello de' Altobiondi has been courting me for some time,' she said. 'And I have a reason now to accept him.'

You'll hardly believe that I still had no idea what she was talking about.

'Innocent boy,' she sighed, taking my face in her hand and squeezing it. She released me with a little shake. 'I am expecting a child – and that is somewhat disapproved of in a widow.'

A child! She was carrying my child and this Antonello de' Altobiondi was going to be its father.

CHAPTER THREE

After the Sweet, the Bitter

On our rare days off work my brother took me round the city showing me what he thought were the best works of art. He called it 'taking me to school'.

A favourite place of his was Santa Maria del Carmine across the river. It was a short walk from the cathedral and it felt as if we were going out into the countryside but there was the church with its chapel devoted to the life of Saint Peter.

'I used to come here every day when I was a boy – younger than you,' said my brother. 'My old master sent me to copy the frescoes – it's where I got my nose broken as a matter of fact.'

The atmosphere inside the chapel was so serene I couldn't imagine any violence happening there. Small groups of young men, obviously apprentices in other artists' workshops, were sitting diligently drawing.

I had never seen anything like those paintings on the wall.

'Who did them?' I whispered.

'Big Tom,' said my brother, grinning. 'He was supposed to be helping Little Tom, who was older than him, but Big Bad Tom ran rings round him.'

'Did you know him?' I asked, surprised by his familiar tone. There was so much about my clever brother's life I knew nothing about.

'No,' he said. 'These were painted long before I was born

– nearly eighty years ago. But everyone saw straight away that the younger painter was the greater artist.'

I looked at the fresco of Adam and Eve being driven out of the Garden of Eden. She was howling with grief and trying to cover her nakedness with her hands. But Adam had his hands over his face and looked inconsolable.

It made me feel very uncomfortable and set me thinking about my situation with Clarice. She hadn't for one moment considered marrying me and I suppose I couldn't blame her for that; aristocratic ladies don't marry stonecutters, except in old fables. But it was the way she had kept the news of the baby to herself up till now and made this life-changing decision on her own that made me feel sore. As if it had been a women's issue and I – or even Altobiondi – just pawns in a game where she was queen.

But my brother was pointing out another picture to me. Saint Peter was baptising some new converts – some of the first Christians ever – and there was a queue waiting to be initiated into the new religion.

'That's the one that got me my new nose,' he said. 'See that young man waiting to be baptised?'

Indeed my eyes had already been drawn to this figure. He stood stripped to his underwear, hugging himself with his arms to stop from shivering, just waiting to step into the river and be born anew. You could feel how cold and nervous he was.

'Torrigiani started moaning about how Big Tom was an incompetent draughtsman,' my brother continued. 'The arms were "too small", the anatomy "not accurate", he said.'

I thought I could see where this was going but I had never heard the full story of the broken nose before.

'What did you do?' I asked.

25

'Nothing,' he said innocently. 'I just told him he was wrong. In a certain amount of detail.' He was grinning as if the incident were taking place right now before his eyes.

'And Torrigiani didn't like being wrong so he hit me – a great single punch in the face. We both heard my nose break. And the blood was pouring out in a flood – ruined the drawing I'd just made.'

'What happened?'

'Well, Torrigiani legged it and I went back to the sculpture garden.'

'What did Lorenzo de' Medici say?' I asked, though I felt shy at even mentioning the great man's name. I knew that my brother had caught the eye of this illustrious patron when he was just a boy. Lorenzo de' Medici had taken him to live in his house and eat at his table alongside his own children. And put him to study in the sculpture garden up by San Marco. This was ten years ago or more and it didn't last long; Lorenzo had died in 1492.

'He was very angry with Torrigiani,' said my brother, his strange horn-coloured eyes looking into the distance as if he could still see the remembered scene. 'It must have looked worse than it was – me all covered in blood. Lorenzo called me in to give an account of what happened. I think he was pleased I had defended a great artist against a piffling student like Pietro Torrigiani.'

'What happened to Pietro?'

'Oh, he left town soon after,' said my brother, smiling. 'It taught him not to show disrespect of his betters.'

'What was he like?' I asked.

'Torrigiani?'

'No. Lorenzo.'

He looked round as if there might be listeners behind every pillar.

26

'Come on,' he said. 'There's a tavern nearby. Looking at great art always makes me thirsty.'

We left the chapel and were soon sitting with two generous flagons of *vernaccia*. It was a warm August evening and I'd been in the city nearly five months but I still felt there was so much about it I didn't know or understand.

'You said you weren't on anyone's side when you arrived,' said my brother. 'Do you still feel the same?'

'I don't want to have anything to do with politics,' I said quickly.

He snorted over his wine. 'That's what people say who don't understand what the word means. And it's very dangerous to stay ignorant in Florence – you might not stay alive very long.'

'But what has a stonecutter to do with politics? How can I affect anything that goes on in government rooms and grand buildings?'

'I might have thought that once, but I lived among the great men of the city when I was just a boy and that shaped my thinking.'

'So you are a Medici man through and through?'

Again, he looked round cautiously as if the very walls might have ears.

'I *was*,' he said. 'I was Lorenzo's man, heart and soul. There was never anyone to touch him. But when he died and his son Piero took over, he was a bitter disappointment – nothing like his father.'

He seemed lost in thought.

'Lorenzo gave me marble to work in. Piero gave me snow.'

'Snow?' It seemed impossible, a cruel joke.

'It was the winter of '94,' he said. 'Do you remember it? You'd have been – what? – twelve? It snowed in Florence, in January.'

'I remember,' I said, thinking of snowball fights with my friends in Settignano. It was the only time in my life I had ever seen deep snow.

'Piero asked me to make a snowman,' said my brother. 'And I did. And it was a good piece of sculpture. But in a few days it was just a puddle. That's the sort of man Piero was. I still have the marble reliefs I made for Lorenzo and I expect to have them till I die. I'll show them to you.'

'So you are a republican now?'

My brother called for more wine; he had a real stone-worker's thirst and so did I. You never really seem to get the dust out of your throat.

'I am all in favour of a single ruler if that ruler can be a Lorenzo de' Medici,' he said at last. 'But there are few men like him. Even his own son had none of his quality. So in general, yes, I'm now a republican.'

'Then I am too,' I said.

He laughed his short barking laugh, a stonecutter's cough.

'You can't just say you're a republican because I'm one.'

'I'm not. I'm saying it because you've explained it and I agree with you. I'd like to see those reliefs, by the way.'

'That's right,' he said. 'You stick to stone and things you understand. But be careful. We may be republicans and that's the faction with the upper hand in Florence now. But there are still lots of Medici supporters who would bring the family back. And the two sides hate each other. I can't do that. I can't hate the family that made me what I am. But until another Lorenzo is born, I'll stay a republican, even if I don't take an active part in the city's politics – just enough to keep me alive.'

It was not long after this conversation that Angelo decided to change the stance of the David and I had to pose for a whole lot of new sketches. We had got through a lot of cabbages and cauliflowers, much to the housekeeper's annoyance, before my brother suddenly said one night that he had changed his mind.

'Everyone shows David when the fight is over,' he said. 'But wouldn't it be more interesting to depict the young shepherd before he knows he's going to win?'

I hadn't thought about this. In fact, I hadn't thought about the subject of the statue at all. I knew that in the Bible, David was a young boy who looked after his father's sheep and had lots of older brothers. I knew lots of youths like him in my village home. But the one in the Bible killed a massive Philistine called Goliath with a shot from his sling, even though the enemy giant was armed to the teeth.

'I see what you mean, I think,' I said. 'He goes out armed only with the slingshot he'd normally use on wolves and suchlike.'

'And the Philistine is a huge monster of a man in full armour,' said Angelo, 'while David has no more than a rough loincloth to protect him. Not even a shield.'

'Oh, he will have a loincloth?' I asked.

'No, not in my statue,' said Angelo. 'I shall show him naked to emphasise his vulnerability. I must get into his face – your face – all his determination and strength together with his nervousness and fear.'

'That's a tall order to put in one statue,' I said.

'It is. And it must send other messages too. This is a work to please the Republic. It must represent how Florence herself, even when seeming vulnerable to attack, is determined to beat any superior force, with the power of her proud history.'

If anyone could do all that, it would be my brother.

We abandoned the vegetables and I stood with all the weight on my right leg and my left leg lightly bent. I tried to look warlike and apprehensive at the same time, which caused my brother to laugh so much that he begged me just to concentrate and leave the expression to him.

I'd stopped going to see Clarice but I hadn't stopped thinking about her. I didn't love her but I was fond of her and it irked me that she was carrying my first child and had so casually decided to give it a different father. I decided I would find out everything I could about this usurper Altobiondi.

Antonello de' Altobiondi was a dyed-in-the-wool Medici supporter and I got my information from an unexpected quarter: my brother's father, Lodovico.

Lodovico didn't approve of Angelo's profession, thinking sculpture only one small step up from painting, which he saw as an artisan's work, like dyeing or tanning. His oldest son, Lionardo, was a Dominican friar and had been a fanatical follower of Savonarola, that friar who had endured the same fate as all the fripperies he disapproved of – burned on a bonfire in the piazza before the government building.

The three younger boys were still at home though and Lodovico's second wife, Lucrezia, had been dead a few years; it was a very male household, with no one minding too much about washing or changing their clothes very often. The old housekeeper did the best she could to put food on the table with the stingy amount Lodovico gave her but it was a struggle, with four hungry young men in the house. And now five, with me there.

Now that I couldn't supplement my diet with trips to Clarice's better-provisioned table, I was famished most of the time. Lodovico wouldn't accept any of my wages, though I'd offered straight away. His pride was too great to take money from the child of his son's wet nurse!

But he seemed to like having me there.

'You bring a flavour of the country to my house,' he had said graciously when I first arrived. 'Tell me what news of my farm in Settignano. I don't get there as often as I should – has the harvest been good?'

And in return for news of the countryside he enjoyed telling me about life in the city. After I'd had that conversation about politics with my brother, I began cautiously to pump old Lodovico for information about the rival factions in Florence.

I didn't even have to raise the name Altobiondi before he mentioned it.

'No one understands my position,' he said. 'We are distantly related to the de' Medici – through my first wife, you know. She was a Rucellai through her mother and a Tornabuoni through other connections. Lorenzo the Magnificent's mother was a Tornabuoni, of course. Yes, a fine woman of a noble family.' He seemed to be drifting off into reminiscence.

'So some people assume,' he continued, 'that I and all my family are Medici men! And yet at least three of my boys were followers of Savonarola and he was a bitter enemy of the de' Medici, even though he visited Lorenzo on his deathbed.'

'Three?' I said. I had known only about Lionardo.

'Oh yes,' he said. 'Lionardo, who lives as a religious in San Marco to this day. But not just him. Michelangelo and Buonarroto too. And I wouldn't wonder if the others weren't followers, except that they were a bit young to be influenced by his preaching.'

Lodovico never called my brother Angelo, as he was known in our family; he always gave him the full name of the archangel: Michelangelo. Angelo hadn't told me he had been a follower of the Friar's. I'd have to ask him about it. Certainly, you couldn't be a Medici man and a Savonarola man at the same time.

'So the *arrabbiati* expect me to side with them and yet I have at least three *piagnoni* in my family!' said Lodovico.

Lodovico explained that the *arrabbiati* were the 'enraged ones' who were violently opposed to Savonarola, the fanatical friar. And the *piagnoni* were sneeringly called the 'weepers', people who had been moved to tears by the preaching of Savonarola, though they themselves preferred to be called *frateschi* he told me, which meant 'followers of the Friar'.

'The *arrabbiati* have gone underground now we have the Republic,' Lodovico said, 'but they are still active and dangerous. And then there are the *compagnacci*. There are only about a hundred and fifty of them but they are even fiercer than the *arrabbiati* and are at daggers drawn with the *frateschi*.'

All these words made my head reel and I decided to make a note of them. Politics in Florence was a much more complicated thing than even my conversation with Angelo had taught me.

'Men like Antonello de' Altobiondi won't stay quiet for long,' Lodovico was saying. I pricked up my ears at my rival's name. 'I shouldn't like to be in Gonfaloniere Soderini's shoes when they rise up against him.'

'Altobiondi?' I prompted him.

'Yes, Antonello. He's the current head of his family and leader of the *compagnacci* – they are all Medici supporters, of course. They've decided we are not, because of my sons, so we are in danger from them. You must watch your step. Don't talk politics in public.'

I wondered if he knew about Angelo's advice.

'What's this Antonello like?' I asked.

'Oh, he's a bit of a blusterer. Proud of his family's connections but there's nothing wrong with that.'

'What sort of age and appearance?' I asked as casually as I could. 'So that I know how to avoid him.'

'Well, he's about thirty,' said Lodovico, frowning. 'And pleasant-looking enough.'

I was disappointed. I was hoping he'd be at least fifty with a wart on his nose.

'Well-made but a bit short.' Lodovico was warming to his theme. 'Dark hair, big nose. Oh, and here's another thing, he's going to marry the widow Buonvicini. Very hastily. There's gossip that he's got her with child already, because the wedding ceremony is being held very soon.'

It hurt to hear it, even though I already knew. What would old Lodovico say if he knew the baby the widow Buonvicini was carrying was mine? He clearly had no idea of my connection with her.

'Purple and green,' Lodovico was saying.

'Sorry?'

'The colours of his house – the de' Altobiondi,' he said. 'His followers and a lot of the other *arrabbiati* have adopted purple and green as their colours.'

That should make them easier to avoid.

'But isn't it dangerous for them to display their affiliations publicly like that?'

'Ha, my boy!' said Lodovico. 'You can tell you haven't spent much time in the city! When have Florentines ever been sensible about their affiliations?'

'And the others, the *frateschi*?'

'Black,' said Lodovico. 'Always in black.'

So I was now armed with a lot of useful information, even though I couldn't quite believe that all the warring factions in Florence would wear identifying colours. But thinking back to my first night when I was robbed and the feeling of danger in the air when I walked to the San Procolo district to find my brother, I did remember that some of the groups of young men were dressed alike. I hadn't noticed the colours then — only the air of hostility between them.

And the very next day, I saw Antonello de' Altobiondi for the first time. I was walking from my *bottega* to Angelo's workshop at lunchtime, so I could eat my bread and cheese with him, when I saw a short, big-nosed man with black hair, dressed in purple and green velvet, coming out of Clarice's house.

I can't tell you how it hurt to see him. My mind immediately put him between the sheets with Clarice and a burning jealousy started to eat at my insides.

He didn't see me at all. He walked right past me and I, all dusty in my stonecutter's clothes, made no more impression on him than if he'd walked past a horse. Less perhaps, since he might have been more interested in a bit of horseflesh.

I suppose I should have been grateful that he didn't register me; it meant he didn't share the widespread Florentine preference of men for men. But that meant he was as keen a lover of women as I was.

The day would come when he knew well enough what I looked like and who I was. But that was still in the future. For now the only comfort I could hug to myself was that it was my picture Clarice had hanging in her chamber. Or perhaps hidden under clothes in her *cassone* now that Antonello might be sharing her bed.

'What's the matter?' my brother asked when I walked into his workshop with a face like thunder.

'I've just seen an enemy,' I said.

'I didn't think you had any enemies,' he said.

'It's Antonello de' Altobiondi,' I said. 'He's going to marry Clarice.'

'Uh-oh!' said my brother. 'Then you have made a very dangerous enemy indeed!'

CHAPTER FOUR

Followers of the Friar

The wax model had done its job and in August it got my brother his commission from the Operai for the marble, but it wasn't enough to act as a pattern for the sculpture, which he had two years to make. Besides, the wax was beginning to melt in the late summer heat, so Angelo made a cast of it in two halves and filled them with gesso. He pounded some good marble from Volterra into chips and mixed up such a fine plaster that when he stuck the two halves together and broke the cast after the plaster had dried, the figure shone almost like a finished statue.

He grunted with satisfaction as he tidied up the gesso model with a fine chisel.

'It's me,' I said, staring at the plaster model. I remembered all those evenings – the awkward position I had to maintain till my muscles ached. I could see them straining in the chest and abdomen of the little model.

'The left leg's not right,' he said, frowning. 'I'll never get that out of the block.'

'I think I must have got it wrong when we gave up the cauliflowers while you were sketching.'

'Not your fault,' he said absently. He was never interested in what had caused problems, only in how to solve them.

It was much more embarrassing looking at my nude self in the round than it was seeing his sketches. And he had made such an elaborate decorative pattern of my pubic hair! It matched the curls on my head.

Looking at the model was like seeing my life from the outside and I didn't like how it made me feel.

It was the day after I had first seen Altobiondi and I was feeling frustrated. It was all right as long as I was wielding my tools in the *bottega* but whenever I had idle time I found my fists clenching. I spent whole hours wanting to hit someone.

Angelo had built a workshop now in the Opera, the walls set up around the block and roofed over, so that he could work undisturbed. The old 'David' block was now propped at an angle, ready for my brother to start carving but the new model was being built up on a wooden trestle, standing upright. My brother was looking at the model as intently as I was – and back and forth between it and the big old marble block. It was hard to believe that he would make anything like as powerful a figure out of that botched block as he had created in gesso.

I opened and closed my fists thinking that I felt more like a botched block than the athletic and well-muscled man my brother had shown in the model. Was the real me somewhere inside that hulking ugly lump of marble? If only I could be as without emotion as the stone.

There was no getting any conversation out of Angelo while he was in this concentrated mood so I wandered away from his workshop with another hour left before I needed to go back to work. Most workmen found somewhere to sleep after their midday meal but I was young and fizzing with pent-up energy.

I hadn't seen Clarice for over a week and I'm sorry to say I was probably suffering from pent-up lust as well. You forget about these things when you are as old as I am now but I was a healthy eighteen-year-old man, who had been satisfying his desires – and hers – daily for weeks so it was hardly surprising I was frustrated.

I drifted listlessly round the cathedral. There was a group of young men dressed in black on the steps talking animatedly. My ears pricked up. Were these *piagnoni*, the followers of Savonarola? One of them was looking directly at me, his gaze burning into me.

He detached himself from the group and came over to me.

'You're a friend of the sculptor, aren't you?'

I nearly laughed. There were so many sculptors in Florence that was like asking me if I knew any bakers. But I knew who was meant.

'Yes,' I said. 'If you mean Michelangelo. I have known him all my life.' I was proud that this was true but I wasn't going to say he was my brother till I knew who this was and why he wanted to know.

'So where does he stand?' asked the man in black. He was shorter than me but still reasonably tall and well-made.

I bit back a facetious reply.

'He means whose side is he on?' said another man from the group, smaller, with fair hair.

'Who wants to know?' I asked.

'We know he was taken up by the Medici,' said the first man. 'That sensualist and libertine Lorenzo was his patron.'

'That is no secret,' I said. Though the way my brother talked about Lorenzo had made him seem of a quite different character.

'But what about now?' said the little fair one. 'Is he still in contact with the family?'

'I don't think so,' I said. 'He was disappointed in Piero.'

This seemed to be a good answer. The men exchanged smiles.

'So he is for the Republic?' asked the first man.

'Yes,' I said. It didn't seem to me that there was any harm in agreeing to that. 'Can I go now?'

'What about you?' said the little one. He was looking up at me unafraid, though I towered over him. I wondered if he was armed. It was broad daylight and I wasn't really scared of being attacked, even though there were six or seven of them.

'What about me?' I hedged.

'Whom do you support? Are you a Medici man?'

'I am a republican,' I said.

They seemed to relax and the taller one clapped me on the arm.

'Good fellow!' he said. 'We could use muscles like yours. Come and meet the others.'

And that was how I became a follower of Savonarola, even though I had never seen him and he had been dead three years.

The first of the black-clad young men who had spoken to me was Daniele – the *frateschi* did not use surnames. And Daniele told me that if I wanted to be one of them I had to use the more respectful term for the followers of the friar Savonarola. His small fair friend was Gianbattista, who invited me to his house up near the San Marco monastery that evening. Since I had nothing better to do, I went. There I met Paolo, a Dominican friar who had known Savonarola in person, and brothers called Giulio and Donato, who were alike as twins but with two years between them.

'This is Gabriele del Lauro,' said Daniele, introducing me to them one by one, and then Gianbattista poured me some wine and before I knew it I was one of the group.

You'd better know what side you are on, my brother had told me. Now it seemed I was on the side not just of the Republic but people who were violently opposed to the de' Medici and plotting to make sure that family never returned to the city.

But they didn't discuss plots in any detail that night. They just drank and talked like any other group of young men. The only difference was the presence of a religious in their midst, the Dominican, Fra Paolo, though that didn't seem to restrain the others. Fra Paolo was the only one there who had known Savonarola personally but the others had all been present when the Friar had been executed three years before.

'It was horrible,' said Gianbattista, putting a hand to his eyes as if he could see the scene right in front of him. 'They had tortured him for weeks. Then they left him a month and tortured him again. He knew what to expect the second time and that made his suffering all the worse.'

I felt a ghoulish interest in hearing an eyewitness account of the execution. Even in Settignano we knew about the Mad Monk and his doings in the city. He was a powerful preacher – Angelo had told me that – and the people who heard him preach in the great cathedral were swayed by what he thundered out to them from the pulpit.

These sermons and Savonarola's ugly death were as fresh to my new friends as if they had happened yesterday.

'They hanged him and two other friars,' said Daniele.

'I thought he had been burned,' I said. That's what we'd been told in Settignano.

'That was afterwards,' said Gianbattista. 'As soon as the three men stopped twitching, the fire was lit under them – so that there should be no trace left of their bodies.'

'And they even took the ashes away in carts so that no one should collect them and treat them as precious relics,' said Donato. He clearly still felt very sore about it.

'But some women did get a few and the guards caught them and smashed the vases they had put them in,' added his brother Giulio.

They painted such a vivid picture of the scene as the evening wore on that I felt in the end as if I had been there myself – the huge crowds of Savonarola's enemies and supporters, the dangling men, the smell of scorched flesh. Only Fra Paolo said little, but when he did speak it was clear that the bitterness was as strong in him as in the younger men.

'They punished us up at San Marco too,' he said. 'They took away our bell – the Weeping Lady, *La Piagnone*, and said we couldn't have her back for fifty years. Fifty years! Which of us will be alive in 1548?'

I didn't know then that I would be. I wonder if San Marco ever got its bell back? I suppose I'll never find out now. And Fra Paolo must be long dead. Not many in that room that night would live even another ten years but I didn't know that then.

I staggered back to Lodovico's house well pleased with my new friends. I was rather too full of drink and not full enough of food and I had a terrible head the next morning. It took several hours of hard work and frequent splashing of my head under the water-pump before my brain cleared. And then I thought, who were the 'they' that killed the man my friends wanted me to accept as my dead leader?

It couldn't have been the Medici – Piero had been chased out four years earlier, after my brother went to Rome. Florence had become a Republic then so it must have been republicans who killed Savonarola. But I was a republican and so was my brother – as were the *frateschi* who were so keen to recruit me to their cause.

Did I say my head was clear? The more the effects of the wine wore off the more I realised I was still a babe in arms as far as Florentine politics were concerned. And I wondered if I had got in with the wrong lot.

That day I saw Clarice again. She was coming out of the cathedral, arm in arm with Antonello de' Altobiondi and they were attended by a group of fashionably dressed friends. Clarice had flowers in her hair and was wearing a gown of gold brocade. She had been getting married.

As the party swept past me near the Baptistery, Altobiondi looked through me as he had done before but Clarice caught my eye. Did I imagine her glance of sympathy? And was I the only one who could detect the swelling under her gold sash?

I wondered if she would possibly get away with her deceit of her new husband, but a feeling of despair washed over me. How could any man withstand the trickery and guile of women? She would bamboozle him about dates and the early arrival of the baby that was mine. And she had probably been sleeping with him since accepting his proposal. That thought did not console me.

Sick at heart, I went to see my brother.

Just for once he was not working; he was sitting gazing at the block, but when he saw my face he snapped out of his meditation and jumped up.

'What's the matter?' he asked.

'I've just seen Clarice and her new husband,' I managed to say.

'Well, you knew it was going to happen,' he said.

'But she's carrying my child,' I said. I couldn't keep the burden of it to myself any longer.

My brother gave a great breath out, making a noise like a bellows. Then he put his hand, all dusty as usual, on my arm.

'Gabriele,' he said, 'I'm sorry.' He paused for a long while, looking into my eyes. 'Can I give you some advice?'

He had never offered to do so before. I was surprised and nodded. I could feel tears building up behind my eyelids and I didn't want to weep, not in front of my brother.

'It's not a good idea to waste your energy on physical love,' he said eventually. 'It saps your strength and distracts you from your purpose.'

'That's all very well for you,' I said and I could hear myself sounding truculent, like a child. 'You have a purpose – you're a great artist. What do I have to save my strength for? I'm just a stonecutter.'

I felt the full force of this truth overwhelm me even as I said it. What was my purpose in life?

'Then marry,' said my brother. 'Find a nice healthy girl and settle down.'

I thought of Rosalia waiting for me back in Settignano. How long would she wait? And was I supposed to live like a monk until I returned home? I was a *fratesco* in name only.

'You see,' said my brother. 'All this has just made you unhappy.'

'Do you follow your own advice, brother?' I dared to ask.

He frowned and I wondered if I had gone too far and roused his famous temper. But he did give me my answer.

'A long time ago,' he said, 'I decided there was too much pain in love. Since then I've put everything I feel into my work.'

I could see he was telling the truth; something very bad must have happened to him at some time in the past, something he wouldn't have told his family in Settignano or Florence.

'So you will not do what you advise me and take a wife?'

He gave me a very strange look then, half frown and half grin. 'No, Gabriele, I shall not take a wife.'

I had reason to think of this conversation many times in the coming years. But for now I was comforted to know that he too had been unhappy in love. I sat and ate my lunch with him in silence but it was a companionable silence. Gradually, the ache I had been feeling round my heart started to subside.

I didn't blame Clarice for her decision; it was just the way she had made it without me. And I had never before experienced physical jealousy the way I did towards her new husband. Now I felt as if I were growing up: no longer the baby of the family but a man – with a man's problems. I decided to do my best to forget about Clarice and to concentrate on my work and save the money to go home and marry Rosalia – if she'd still have me.

To keep my mind off women, I spent more and more of my evenings with Daniele and the other *frateschi*. We usually met at Gianbattista's house near San Marco and as time went by I met more of their associates. After that first night, the wine was brought by a young woman, who turned out to be Gianbattista's sister. I wondered why she would demean herself to wait on a group of young men but gradually I learned that she had been a follower of Savonarola's too.

'We like to keep our meetings secret,' Gianbattista told me. 'It's better not to have servants gossiping about us. And we can trust Simonetta – she is one of us.'

Simonetta was as different from Clarice as you could imagine. She kept her luxuriant dark hair fiercely constrained in the plainest of snoods and wore dark austere dresses with no ornament. But she was a beauty for all that. Nothing could conceal her luminous pale skin and her huge dark eyes. I shouldn't have noticed, with my new decision to avoid women, but I did.

I was noticing altogether too much. It was clear from the house they lived in that Gianbattista and Simonetta were from a noble family but I never saw their parents or learned their surname. But I did wonder what they and their friends expected of me; I was the only working man among them.

All the men wore black, as I'd noticed before, and they wore their hair cut short. I stood out among them in my working clothes with my unruly curls unshorn. But they didn't ask me to change how I looked.

'We could use muscles like yours,' Daniele had said at our first meeting and it seemed that was what they prized – my youth and strength.

It was weeks before I felt comfortable enough to ask what had bothered me after that first meeting.

'Who were the people who got rid of your leader? I thought the city was republican by then so why would the government be against someone who spoke out against the Medici?'

'You have much to learn,' said Fra Paolo sternly.

But Gianbattista defended my ignorance.

'We are so sensitive to all the factions here in Florence,' he said. 'But you can't expect a country boy to know about that. His question is quite reasonable. And if you are to be one of us, Gabriele, we need to answer you.'

'Savonarola had angered the Pope by his preaching,' said Daniele. 'His Holiness thought our leader had too much

45

power in the city. And there were citizens who were against him too. Not just the *arrabbiati*, but all those who loved luxury and display.'

'The *compagnacci* was what they were called!' said Gianbattista. 'It means "rude companions". They were young men like us, of noble birth, who conspired against him. The ones who call de' Altobiondi their leader.'

Altobiondi again!

'And they are republicans?' I asked, trying to remember my conversation with Lodovico but still confused.

'No, they are pro-Medici all right,' said Daniele. 'They live lives of luxury and indulge themselves in the dining room and the bedchamber. They didn't want to give up their velvets and laces and perfumes and rich food.'

'You can tell them by their purple and green livery,' said Donato. 'They have adopted the heraldic colours of the Altobiondi family to show their allegiance.'

As I had thought before, if everyone was going to show what they believed by wearing distinctive colours, I would be all right! I wondered if I'd have to start wearing pure black.

CHAPTER FIVE

The Furious Ones

In September I had my first birthday ever away from home. There wasn't a great deal of fuss but I was sure that being nineteen years old meant I was much more grown up than when I was a mere boy of eighteen.

My brother had made the first cut in the block of marble in the middle of the month. This was a significant moment. Before that, all he had done was knock off a sort of lump in the region of where the Giant's chest would be.

'Some sort of knot or clasp on the shepherd's cloak, probably,' he said. When it came to sculpture, he had a fine disdain for other people's ideas.

But now he had stopped squaring and walking round the model roughing out the outline with charcoal on the stone, and was really sculpting, in a hail of marble chips. I was still the only one allowed into his improvised workshop and that made me proud. Though there was not much to see yet.

There was a big old sink in the corner of the workshop and I wondered about it at first, since my brother was not a great one for washing. Then one day he asked me to lower the gesso model into the sink! At first I was astonished, but after we laid it on its back, he filled the sink from the pump until the whole of the body was submerged.

I felt sorry for myself, lying there on my back with the water above my face. I was a drowned man.

The sink had a hole in it and Angelo released the plug so that just a little water ran out of it into a channel that led out into a drain.

'You see?' asked Angelo.

What I saw was a knee.

It was my left leg, sticking up out of the water.

'It shows me how much to cut away from the block,' he explained. 'I'll let out a little water every day, as I work on the block, then I can check all the angles and details on the statue.'

And that was the last I heard from him for some time.

He never talked much and he said even less when he was in the thick of his work. This was the first time I had been with him while he was working in marble and I soon learned to slip in and munch my bread and cheese quietly while he worked.

I had a lot to think about. I was worried that at the rate I was earning in the stonemasons' *bottega*, it would be years before I could save up enough to go home and marry Rosalia. I'm now ashamed to admit that it never once crossed my mind that she might not wait for me. After my humiliation over Clarice's marriage, once I made up my mind to return to Rosalia, I just assumed that I would be able to take up my first love where I had left off.

But that didn't mean I had no eyes for other women.

Early one morning, crossing the great square in front of the government building, I saw a group of women behaving strangely. They were glancing all around them and then moving swiftly away from the spot where they had been standing, as if running away. I saw they had dropped flowers on the spot which I guessed was the place where Savonarola had died. One of the women was Simonetta.

There was a shout and a city official rushed over to snatch up the flowers and looked about him. I hurried over to the group of women and gave Simonetta my arm; the other two seemed to melt away. She was trembling and leaning so heavily on me for support that I felt the weight of her breast pressing against my arm.

'Are you all right?' I asked and she could only nod. 'That was a risky thing to do,' I whispered.

'You saw me?' she asked, her big brown eyes full of alarm.

'Well, yes. It is broad daylight.'

I was horrified to see that she was quietly weeping. Two big tears spilled out of her eyes and she let them splash on the red tiles of the piazza without wiping her face.

'We cannot go out after dark when we might be safer from the officials,' she said. 'It is scarcely safe to be out on our own in the daytime. But we grieve so for our leader that we take the risk.'

'Let me escort you home,' I said. 'You are upset and have been in some danger.'

I knew it was strictly against the laws of the city to show any reverence for the place of Savonarola's death or anything associated with him. I would be late for work but there was pleasure to be had in seeing Simonetta safely home, as well as following my conscience.

At their house, which was quite out of my way, Simonetta offered me wine and I took it. I thought again of how different she was from Clarice, as she poured my drink for me. My lady was always exquisitely dressed and her elegance and style made up for the fact that her features were quite unremarkable. But Simonetta always wore the plain, dark colours recommended by her leader, without lace or frills or any other ornament and yet she was lovely in her simplicity.

49

I had some very unworthy thoughts as her hand brushed mine when she passed me the cup.

'Wait here a minute,' she said and left the room. When she returned, she was carrying a plain wooden casket.

She opened the lid and showed me a sort of greasy dust inside. I was too stupid to guess what it was.

'They hanged him and burned him,' she said, 'and then they took the ashes away and threw them in the river.'

I didn't like to say that there must have been wood ash and the grisly remnants of the other two executed friars mixed in with Savonarola's remains. She was clearly showing me what she considered to be a sacred relic.

'But some of our people waded into the river further down and rescued what they could,' she continued. 'Only the most loyal *frateschi* have any.'

I suppose I was a loyal *fratesco* by then. I was certainly falling under the spell of this devout young woman, even though I couldn't really share her veneration for the dead man whose ashes she believed she was holding. She was like a nun – someone who should have been out of the reach of human passions – but I couldn't help imagining her naked in my arms. I had to get out of that house quickly, before I did something that would set her brother and the other *frateschi* against me.

I thanked her for the wine and for the honour of the glimpse of what was in the casket and left hurriedly. I ran all the way to my workshop, pleading a stomach upset as a reason for my lateness. And certainly I arrived feverish and trembling and could not concentrate properly on my work that morning. My brother had been right; the lusts of the flesh brought nothing but trouble.

Angelo showed me his marble reliefs as he had promised. There were two, both made from marble given to him by Lorenzo the Magnificent at the time this remarkable man had been my brother's patron.

And the two couldn't have been more different.

'This was the first real work I did,' he said, unwrapping the bundle of cloth that protected the first relief. 'You can see it's the work of a young and inexperienced sculptor.'

I couldn't see that: to me it was beautiful. There was a Madonna, sitting on the corner of a flight of stairs that disappeared away into the distance on the left. She was a sturdy peasant women, like my own mother, veiling her breast with a piece of cloth; the equally sturdy Christ child seemed to have just left off from drinking her milk.

The whole was of a beautiful ivory colour, polished to a very high shine. I could have looked at it for hours.

'How about this one?' he asked, unwrapping another bundle. 'I think it's more successful.'

It was certainly very different – a mass of writhing naked male bodies, standing out from the background in contorted poses.

'Who are they all?' I asked.

'It is a classical story,' he said. 'The Battle of the Centaurs and Lapiths.'

'Centaurs are mythical beasts, I know,' I said. 'But what are Lapiths?'

'Just men like you and me,' he said. 'They were celebrating the wedding of their king when the centaurs, who had been invited to join them, got drunk. One of them attempted to carry the bride off and then all hell broke loose.'

I could see that. There was such a tangle of limbs and muscles. It wouldn't be the last time that a fight broke out at a wedding because too much wine had been consumed, and I thought Angelo had captured the moment wonderfully well.

He was pleased by my praise, I could tell.

I was spending more and more time with the *frateschi* at Gianbattista's house. If I'm honest, it was as much because of the appeal of his sister as any attraction to their political views. Gianbattista didn't seem to mind that Simonetta had shown me the sacred relic. She had told him of my protection after the incident in the Piazza della Signoria and he obviously approved.

I had passed a further test and been admitted into the inner circle. Whenever I went to one of their meetings, I lived in hope of a glimpse or a touch from the unobtainable sister. I didn't fool myself that her family would ever consider me as a possible suitor and I didn't even know if I wanted to be one. But putting her in the forefront of my mind blotted out the image of Clarice with her new husband and helped me to forget how long it would be before I could be back with Rosalia.

'We need to find out just what they're planning,' said Daniele one evening.

'Who?' I answered absently, looking at Simonetta.

'The *compagnacci*, of course,' said Fra Paolo, looking at me as if he thought I was the village idiot. He usually did look at me that way; I wasn't his idea of an aristocratic *fratesco* at all.

'We think they are plotting to bring back Piero de' Medici,' said Donato.

'But didn't they try that once before?' I asked. I remembered that Angelo had told me something about an attempt on the city gate some years ago.

'What a botch that was!' said Gianbattista. 'It was in '97. Piero brought a small army to one of the city gates in the south.'

'What happened?' I asked.

'The government took all his followers hostage in the city,' said Donato. 'More than fifty high-born *compagnacci*. He didn't dare risk their lives – it would have wiped out his power base completely – so he slunk away.'

'By August the five main conspirators were executed,' said Daniele. 'And one of them was the *gonfaloniere* of the city!'

'Beheaded in the Bargello in the early hours of the morning,' said Fra Paolo. 'They say it took five blows of the axe to get old Gonfaloniere Nero's head off.'

I thought he was taking rather a ghoulish delight in the facts of the case.

'The *compagnacci* and the *arrabbiati* have never forgiven the city for what it did to those five,' said Gianbattista. 'And we believe they are planning another attempt to reinstate Piero – better organised this time.'

'*Arrabbiati* is the right name for them,' said Donato. 'They are literally enraged by the idea that anyone would want to get rid of the de' Medici.'

'Why do they think so highly of the family?' I asked. I'd never really understood.

'Money,' said Fra Paolo. 'The de' Medici made their fortune first through wool and then through banking, till they had a stranglehold on the city.'

'My . . . friend, the sculptor,' I said cautiously, 'thought very highly of Lorenzo.'

'He did some good things,' said Daniele. 'But he was like the rest of them in one way – he thought he had a right to rule the city.'

53

'And Florence is a republic!' said Giulio. 'It had the right idea when it first pushed Cosimo out nearly a hundred years ago. They should never have let him back in. It's not right to buy influence with money.'

They were beginning to whip themselves up into a sort of frenzy. Then suddenly Daniele turned to me with a serious look.

'You could find out what they're plotting.'

'Me?'

'Yes. You could be our spy in the pro-Medici camp.'

'But how?' I protested. 'I'm not even an aristocrat.'

'But you know de' Altobiondi,' said Gianbattista quietly. 'At least, you know his wife.'

I jumped as if stung by a bee. Was this why these men had befriended me in the first place? But if they knew what my relationship with Clarice had been, they must also know how unwelcome I would be in her husband's house? And did Simonetta know too? I didn't dare look at her.

'I see we are right,' said Daniele. 'And we could give you the right clothes. Your face would do the rest.'

I was still fretting about my new task the next day and wondering how I could get out of my role as spy. So I was not expecting the young woman waiting for me outside my *bottega*. She was dressed as a servant and at first I thought she might have come from Clarice, but she would have sent Vanna, the impudent maid who had first summoned me to my lady's house nearly six months earlier.

This one was a comely full-figured young woman of about my own age. She cast her eyes down modestly enough but I had caught a glimpse of her frank appraising stare when she called my name as I came out of the building, slapping the stone dust from my hands.

'My master desires that you should visit him,' she said, giving me a slip of paper with a name and address on it.

'Why?' I said. 'And who is he?'

'I don't know, sir,' she said. 'Andrea Visdomini merely told me to bring the message to Gabriele del Lauro at the stone-cutters' in Via del Proconsolo.'

'And how did you know that was me?'

'I was told . . .' she hesitated. 'He said . . . the young, good-looking one.'

We were both embarrassed now.

'What's your name?' I asked.

'Grazia, sir,' she said. I swear she almost curtsied.

'Call me Gabriele,' I said. 'Does he want me to come now?' I was feeling in need of a wash and hungry for my lunch.

'After work would be soon enough, my master said,' said Grazia. 'Do you know the way?'

It was on the tip of my tongue to say I'd need her to come back and lead me there but I decided against it; my love life was complicated enough without pretty Grazia.

I said goodbye to her, quite reluctantly, and went to see my brother at work. He grunted when I entered to let me know he knew I was there.

I took a ladle of water and poured it over my dusty curls and whitened hands. Angelo laughed – a low rusty sound.

'Soon no one will be able to tell the difference between you and David,' he said.

How many times did I think of that remark in the future!

But I just munched my bread and cheese and I asked him if he had ever heard of Andrea Visdomini.

'What do you have to do with him?' he asked.

'He wants to see me. I don't know why.'

'Well, he is a wealthy man,' said my brother. 'And a patron too. Maybe it was me he wanted?'

'He told his servant to ask for me by name at the stonecutters.'

'Well, are you going?'

'I suppose I must,' I said. 'But I'd like to know whose side he is on.'

'Now you sound like a proper Florentine.'

I went just as I was, after work, carrying my bag of tools and as dusty as I always was at the end of any working day. *Whatever he wants with me, he'll see me as I am*, I thought. Just another working man in the big city.

A manservant answered the door; no sign of luscious Grazia. He led me to a room on the *piano nobile* and told me to wait. My brother had been right. There were bronzes and marbles in the room that showed me Visdomini was both rich and a man of taste. I was pretty sure he would be a Medici supporter.

But the man who came into the room with a light step was not much older than me. He did not look like a wealthy patron. He was finely dressed, with lace at his wrists and a surcoat of purple brocade but he was slightly built, with long light brown hair and a pleasant high voice.

'Ah, Gabriele!' he said, coming forward to shake my hand as if it were as clean as his and as if he had known me all my life; he didn't flinch at the dust.

'But where are my manners?' he said. 'You must be thirsty. Your work must make you very dry, cutting stone all day.' He sent his servant for wine and told him to bring a ewer of warm water too.

I was glad of both and somehow it didn't feel awkward to wash and dry my hands and face in front of this rather foppish youth, even though he looked at me hungrily the whole time, as if he were a starving man and I a tasty round of cheese.

It wasn't till the servant had taken away the water and the master himself poured me a goblet of wine that he spoke again.

'You are an artist of some sort?' he asked.

A feeling of disappointment settled on me; it was my brother he wanted after all.

'Not me, sir,' I said. 'I just cut stone according to other men's patterns. It is my . . . friend, Michelangelo, who is the artist.'

'You live in his house, I believe,' said Visdomini.

'In his father Lodovico's house,' I corrected him. 'Ser Buonarroti has a farm in Settignano where I come from. And a quarry. He has been good to my family.'

'Ah, so you have a patron?'

I did not know what to answer. Was this man wishing to become my patron? And what would he want in return?

'You must be wondering why I sent for you,' he continued. 'I have not long come into my late father's fortune.'

I noticed he was not in mourning.

'He was a patron and a collector of beautiful things, a friend of the late Lorenzo de' Medici.'

Ah, I thought. *I guessed right.*

'I want to continue in his footsteps. Buying beautiful things, I mean. But I think painting is the future. Not religious paintings, although we have those in our chapel, of course. I mean the kind you can stand on an easel and display in your own home.'

I couldn't see where he was going with this. Neither I nor my brother could paint a picture for him.

'More wine?' He refilled my goblet. I was trying hard not to relax too much but the combination of his excellent wine and being able to rest after a day of using all my muscles was undermining my will.

'Do you have a painter that you, er, help?' I asked.

'Yes, I do,' said Visdomini. 'Another young man. He's called Leone. He's a wonderful artist. But he needs a subject.'

At last I felt I might have some idea what he wanted me for.

'Would you be willing to pose for Leone?' he asked.

I felt flustered and didn't know what to answer. Would I be paid? Would I be able to keep my clothes on? Standing naked in front of my brother was one thing, but I didn't want an unknown painter – or his patron – ogling me in the nude.

'You have such a fine physique,' said Visdomini. 'I hope it doesn't embarrass you to hear it said? You must have had it remarked on before. And that face! You could be Hercules, or Perseus or any Greek god. And, of course, you'd be well rewarded.'

Suddenly, I realised that if I came to this man's house, I might be able to find out what the *frateschi* wanted to know without ever going near Altobiondi and his wife.

'Would I be doing it here, sir?' I asked.

'Why, yes, if you were agreeable,' he said. 'I have set Leone up with his own workshop in my courtyard. If you would be willing to pose for him two evenings a week, I would pay you . . .'

And he mentioned a sum that far exceeded what I earned at the stonecutters' *bottega*. It would more than double my income and I could put all this extra money into my savings.

If I could, at the same time, find out information that would satisfy my republican friends, it seemed to me that I had nothing to lose.

'All right,' I said, then realised that sounded a bit ungracious. 'I mean I would be happy to oblige you.'

He looked at me with his pale hazel eyes. I couldn't make out what he was thinking.

But he was smiling and shaking my hand again.

'Excellent, excellent,' he said. 'Come tomorrow night if you can start so soon. You will get a good supper when your work is done.'

I thought about the meagre table at Lodovico's and calculated I could eat in their house before leaving for Visdomini's on my evenings as an artist's model. That would supplement my diet without digging into my savings.

What could possibly be said against such an arrangement?

CHAPTER SIX

Mothers

The day after my first meeting with Andrea Visdomini I was astonished to find two other people in my brother's workshop. They weren't looking at the emerging statue; that was behind sheets. But it was still an unusual event to meet anyone else there.

'Ha!' said my brother. 'Here he is – my little model.'

The two men smiled as they took my hand. I loomed over them and Angelo.

They were introduced to me as brothers, both architects, known as 'da Sangallo' because of a famous commission the older one had completed years before. This Giuliano, ten years older than his brother Antonio, had been another artist favoured by the great Lorenzo, and Angelo had met him as a boy at his patron's table.

Giuliano had an intelligent beardless face, with a quick bright expression. He had come from where he was working on a new palazzo for the Gondi family. His younger brother looked a lot like him and they both seemed to be old friends of my brother. To me they were just a pair of nice old men but I could tell that Angelo thought highly of them – and that wasn't true of many people.

'It's a big day today, Gabriele,' he said. 'We're going to turn him over.'

It took me a while to realise that he meant the statue. That meant he had already finished the front face of it to the point he was ready to work on the back.

I suppressed a smile. My brother knew I'd be there at lunchtime with willing muscles to put to the task but he had invited only two other people to help us and the older one must have been nearly fifty!

God forgive me that I thought fifty such a great age then! But I was still a boy, only months past my nineteenth birthday and fifty seemed an unimaginable distant landmark, a bit like the Pantheon in Rome – something I had heard talked about but never imagined seeing.

I knew that Angelo had invited the Sangallo brothers for their loyalty and discretion, not their strength. He was already taking down the sheets and the brothers were rolling up their sleeves.

But all three of us were dumbstruck when we saw what Angelo had done so far. Of course, I had seen the model – had posed for it – but this was something different. Out of the marble a giant was thrusting his way. His face was mine but turned to one side, with a fixed frown that I didn't realise I'd had. His left leg was sticking forward while the right was going to bear his weight. My brother had made clever use of the gap already roughly chipped out by an earlier hand that showed where the division between the legs would come.

As I looked at this giant image of myself, I could easily believe that the rest of him was waiting inside the marble for my brother to come along and chip him out. He looked like an outsize man who had been trapped by a flood of molten stone and only half released.

I had no idea how much progress he had made in a few weeks and that the figure would be ready for turning so soon. But I think I knew even then that it would never be placed far up on high where people would see only the front of it. Angelo was going to make this a statue you could walk round and marvel at from all angles.

'You have caught his likeness exactly,' said Giuliano, gesturing towards me. 'There will be no doubt in the city who your model is.'

'You will be called David,' said Antonio, 'and it will be an honour.'

He was right about the first prediction – but not about the second.

The four of us took most of my lunch break to wrestle that old block with its half-formed giant breaking out of it, till it was turned on to its white marble stomach and the rough surface was ready for my brother's chisels. Then he broke out the wine he had brought – far superior to what we usually drank at his father's house.

I drank deeply because I had taken most of the strain of the weight, even though we had used ropes and an ingenious pulley system that my brother told me Antonio had shown him how to make. And as far as I know Angelo used it ever afterwards for his upright figures in the round.

When I left to go back to my workshop, the three men were contemplating the block with satisfaction. I was glad to be warmed by the red wine and the exercise, because it was winter now and I had to wear a woollen jacket over my canvas shirt. I tugged it around me as I passed by Clarice's old house.

She had moved to live with Altobiondi on the Via Tornabuoni; I knew that. Her old palazzo had to my fanciful eyes a sad, deserted look. Though, of course, stone cannot show its feelings. I was the one who felt abandoned.

My first evening at Ser Visdomini's house was unthreatening enough. I bolted down my evening meal at Lodovico's even less ceremoniously than usual and turned up on the Via dei Servi promptly. But the evenings had been drawing in for some time and it was already dark. I was used to roaming the streets of Florence now and always kept an ear open for footsteps behind me and a keen eye for glimpses of anyone trying to spy on me.

I was surprised when I got to his house to be introduced not only to the painter Leone but also to Visdomini's wife. I was actually more surprised that he *had* a wife. She was a slight pretty young girl, with fair hair and a trace of a lisp; Andrea treated her as if she were his younger sister.

Leone was a burly young man with a snub nose and arm muscles like a wrestler. I was glad he wasn't going to be an enemy. Visdomini led us to Leone's workshop in the courtyard, leaving his pale, insubstantial wife in their grand reception room.

I couldn't believe my eyes when I saw how completely fitted out the artist's studio was. I caught his glance and saw that he realised just how lucky he had been to secure such a rich and discerning patron. There were low wooden tables with all that was needed to make his pigments and even an urchin to do the grinding. The boy was sitting dozing on a three-legged stool but jumped up when we came in.

And as well as canvas and paints, the room, which had both a large window and a skylight, was furnished with a velvet sofa and rich hangings and cloths for the painter to use as props. A brass ewer and bowl for water, a pewter jug of wine and a bowl of fruit completed what could have easily been a study for a *natura morta* painting.

Lucky Leone.

The room was well lit with candles in sconces but I could see that the winter evenings were not going to be the best times for sketching or painting. I hadn't thought of that before. Perhaps Visdomini's offer wasn't what it seemed after all?

He soon left me with the painter and the little apprentice, who was allowed to go to bed on a straw mattress under one of the tables. Leone would not need any pigments tonight. It appeared that all he wanted to do was draw some preliminary sketches of my head.

'You're good at staying still,' he said.

So I explained about posing for the little model of David. Leone was immediately fascinated.

'You stood for the great Michelangelo?' he said.

'Yes, but I live in his father's house so it was quite natural for him to ask me.'

I was quite pleased that Leone had such a high opinion of my brother. He sketched for about two hours and it wasn't difficult to hold the pose; I could even sit while he worked. It was going to get more difficult in sessions to come but for now I was earning my money easily.

When the time was up, Leone rang a little bell and – to my delight – Grazia brought us our supper. There were meats and bread and olives and vegetables *sott'olio*, and another jug of good wine.

'Stay and talk with us,' said Leone, exactly what I should have liked to ask her.

'My master sends you this,' said Grazia, handing me a purse.

She sat down on the apprentice's stool and even accepted a little wine.

'Gabriele is the perfect model,' said Leone and I was glad he had used my name in front of her, just in case she had forgotten it.

'Can I see?' she asked, putting out her hand for the sketches.

This was another good move, because it meant she looked from the papers to me and back again. Leone had drawn me from at least three angles.

'Who is he supposed to be?' she asked. She seemed very friendly tonight.

'Hercules,' said the painter. 'He has the physique for it, don't you think?'

Grazia was admiring my figure, which was very pleasant, when we had an unexpected visitor. I knew it only because Grazia jumped up, spilling her drink.

'My lady!' she said.

'It's all right, Grazia,' said Signora Visdomini. 'I just came to see that everything had gone well. My husband wanted me to make sure that Gabriele had been paid and given his supper. He has had to go out.'

'Thank you, my lady,' I said. 'Your servant has been looking after me well.'

Then she asked to see the drawings, just as Grazia had. I wondered if she had really been asked to come and check on me or was just curious. But I didn't mind at all that a second nice-looking woman was appraising my features.

I went home well pleased with my evening's work and hid my money under my mattress. Being an artist's model was much easier work than squaring and dressing stone.

Saint Nicholas's Day was on a Monday and so I had two days off work in a row. I had to go and pose for Leone that night but I was pleased when Angelo asked if I would like to go to church with him; we didn't spend much time together when he wasn't working.

Santa Croce was the nearest big church to Lodovico's home and the one his family most often attended, but after the service I found there was another reason to go there on this day. All the brothers were there, with their widowed father, and went to the graveyard to stand by a simple headstone.

FRANCESCA DI NERI DEL MINIATO DI SIENA

was the name on the stone.

1455–1481
MOGLIE BEN AMATA DI
LODOVICO DI LIONARDO DI
BUONARROTI SIMONI

We were here to pay our respects to Angelo's mother.

'Twenty years ago today,' he said to me under his breath. 'That's when she died.'

The date soon after which I had been conceived according to my own mother. That thought made me feel so peculiar that I studied the dates on the stone to take my mind off it.

'She was only twenty-six?' I asked, *sotto voce*, because Lodovico was within earshot. He seemed so old to have had such a wife.

'That's right,' said Angelo. 'The same age I am now. Only she will be just twenty-six years old for ever.'

I didn't know what to say; I had never seen Francesca but Angelo had often talked about her. He had spent too little of his six years with her before she died, he said, but I knew she was his ideal woman. He told me once that the Madonna in the statue in Rome, that had brought him so much fame, had his own mother's face. If that were true, Francesca di Neri had a far finer monument than the one in Santa Croce's churchyard.

'She was worn out by bearing children,' he whispered fiercely. 'Five sons in eight years! And that's just the ones that lived. It was having Gismondo that killed her in the end.'

He was looking at his father with a sort of bitterness.

'Animal lusts,' he growled. 'I told you – best to steer clear.'

'But if we all did that, the world would soon be empty,' I dared to say. 'Besides, you told me to marry.'

He rubbed his hands over his eyes. 'You're right. Don't take any notice of me. I just wish she had lived longer – to see what I could do.'

Lodovico and his other sons were moving away from the graveside so I thought I'd leave Angelo on his own to pay his respects. But he didn't want that.

Instead, he took my arm and said, 'Come on. We'll go and see a living mother now.'

I realised he intended us to walk to Settignano and my heart leapt.

My home village had never looked more lovely to me as I tramped into it along the dusty road with my milk-brother. It was a cold, crisp day and I knew we would be chilled to the bone walking back after dark but it felt so good to see my childhood home, modest as it was.

My mother did not know what to do with herself and which of us to kiss first. My father clapped us both on the shoulders. My sisters were sent for and arrived in a bustle of giggles, shrieks and young children, my little nephews and nieces.

After the first flurry of welcome, my mother was concerned about having enough food to give us all a sufficient Saint Nicholas's Day dinner. I was mortified to have brought no presents for anyone but Angelo's suggestion had been so sudden and there had been no time to go back to his house for money.

He, however, had brought a bag of silver coins, which he passed to my father and then he set to whittling wooden toys for the children, something I could help with. I wonder if they still have those wolves and bears and lions and dogs, original woodcarvings by the hand of Michelangelo? I've never asked but they would be worth a fortune now.

After the feast my mother provided, restlessness took me out of the house and off to find Rosalia. Now that the moment had come I felt very unsure of my welcome but I needn't have worried.

As soon as she saw me through the window, she squealed and ran out to meet me. We had both had birthdays in the nine months I had been away and she was now a sixteen-year-old in full bloom. How I longed to be alone with her, but her family were all around her on this saint's day and very interested to hear about my adventures in the city.

I had to give them all an expurgated version, of course, and all too soon it was dusk and I had to start the long walk back. Rosalia came with me to my parents' house.

'It's too cruel,' she said, 'to see you for only one hour after you've been away so long.' There were tears and I think disappointment that I had brought her no Saint Nicholas's Day present. I felt that I was a very poor lover.

And holding Rosalia in my arms to kiss her goodbye I felt worse than that – a rat and a worm, who had betrayed her simple and honest love.

When we set off back to the city, I was in a whirl of emotions. Angelo by contrast seemed almost serene.

'You have a good family,' he said.

I just grunted.

'And if that pretty girl is your sweetheart, you are a lucky devil,' he added. 'Are you serious about her?'

'I am,' I said, though I felt pretty miserable about Rosalia at that precise moment.

He looked sideways at me. We were striding out with our cloaks over our faces, walking into the wind, but I knew he was assessing my sincerity.

'Don't agonise about it,' he said kindly. 'I know you've been up to some unwise games in Florence but your Settignano girl need never know. Save your money, come back and marry her and be true to her ever after and there will be no great harm done.'

He was right. If only I could have taken his advice sooner.

There was time for only the briefest of bites to eat at Lodovico's house. The older Buonarroti was in a foul mood because he had wanted to spend the whole day with all his sons, remembering their mother; he was angry that Angelo had deserted them without a word.

I escaped to Visdomini's house as soon as I could and was a little late.

My head was full of images of mothers – my own living one and Angelo's dead one. And of Rosalia, who I wanted to be the mother of my own children. And that sent me back to thinking of Clarice, who must be big with my child by now. It seemed to me that I had made an awful mess of my life in just nine months.

Grazia let me into Leone's studio and gave me a nice smile. I smiled back. Maybe life was not so bad after all.

Leone wanted me to pose without my clothes and to hold a piece of cloth that he would transform into a lion's skin in his painting. There was a fire in a small brazier and a stack of wood beside it and the little apprentice was staying awake to feed it so that I should not catch cold.

The painter had not got far with his sketch when the door opened behind me. I longed to snatch the cloth around my loins but did not dare move. There was a swish of some rich cloth on the stone flags of the floor and Andrea Visdomini came into view. He circled me and then went to look at what Leone was doing.

I was glad of the candlelight and firelight so that the lord would not see the colour of my face. He was examining me and the drawing as if he would like to buy me. I suppose in a sense he had.

I was just wondering if I should stop coming to this house when I heard the door open again. A muffled noise told me that the newcomer was female. This time I covered my nakedness with the cloth and turned to see Grazia in the doorway, her hand to her mouth. Visdomini looked highly amused.

'What is it, girl?' he asked. 'Can't you see I am busy?'

'I'm sorry, my lord,' she stammered. 'But you have visitors. Ser Altobiondi and his friends are here.'

I grabbed my clothes and ran. Tonight I would go without payment or any supper.

CHAPTER SEVEN

Beginnings and Endings

I thought I had burned all my boats at Visdomini's but there was no way I could have borne any more evenings of people walking in on my nakedness without warning. I cursed my prudishness as I walked to work next day, not only because of the money and the extra food, but because Grazia's announcement of the visitors confirmed my suspicions that Visdomini was in deep with the pro-Medici plotters. I might have lost my best chance to help the *frateschi*.

But I need not have worried. Visdomini himself was waiting outside my *bottega*, early though it was. He came towards me with both hands open and a penitent expression.

'Gabriele!' he said. 'I am so sorry about last night. Please forgive us and come back to Leone for your next sitting.'

It was a strange new experience having a rich man humble himself to me and I wasn't sure if I liked it.

Visdomini fished out a bag of money, larger than my usual fee and thrust it into my hand, continuing to apologise.

'I am having a bolt installed on the inside of Leone's studio door,' he said. 'Everyone who comes when you are there – including me – must knock and wait for admittance while you make yourself, er, comfortable.'

He did seem genuinely sorry and yet I was the one who had broken our agreement and run away.

'It is I who must apologise, my lord,' I said. 'I should not have left with my work undone. I was merely startled.'

'Understandably, and I promise it will not happen again. Please say you will come back. Leone is fearful that his Hercules will not be finished.'

What could I say? Visdomini insisted on my taking the money, even though I hadn't earned it, and as soon as I had finished work, I went and bought a little cameo ring for Rosalia, which used all he had given me. Later that week, I entrusted it to a carter in a little packet addressed to my sweetheart. And before Our Lord's birthday, I was rewarded with a letter written by a scribe in Settignano, in which she thanked me so artlessly and with such joy at having a memento from me, that I forgot my new patron's eyes assessing the body of his Hercules.

He had been as good as his word and from then on, Grazia would knock at the door when she brought my payment and supper, and Leone would make her wait while I hurriedly dressed myself. He and I fell into the habit of eating our supper together. Sometimes Grazia stayed and drank with us; sometimes if she had urgent duties to attend to she left the two of us together.

Leone was painting now and his Hercules was emerging out of a greenish-brown background, his muscles glowing bronze, like the tawny lion's skin.

The evenings that I was not posing, I was with the *frateschi* up near San Marco. I told them that I was now practically a member of the household of a prominent pro-Medicean and they didn't again suggest that I should infiltrate de' Altobiondi's circle.

But after the night of my embarrassment, when I knew there had been conspirators at Visdomini's house, I hadn't heard any more about them. I was beginning to feel that although I was in one way an insider, in another I was further from finding out what was going on in his *salone* than if I spent my evenings in the street watching the comings and goings at his front door.

My chance to find out more didn't come until the year had turned and then I am afraid it was baser instincts that led to my greater knowledge.

One evening, when I had been posing less than half an hour, there came an urgent knocking at the studio door.

'Curses!' said Leone. 'Who is this interrupting my work now?'

I scrambled into my clothes.

It was much too early for our supper but it was Grazia, with an urgent message from her master.

'He wants to bring his friends in to see the painting,' she explained. 'They are on their way down.'

Leone grumbled a bit; like most painters he didn't want people to see his work before it was finished but what could he do about it? His patron housed, fed and clothed him and paid for all his materials and would buy the painting from him at the end. That left Leone no rights in the matter. And I had the strongest feeling that Visdomini had commissioned his Hercules because he wanted me to be the subject, rather than having searched for an appropriate human model for an idea he or Leone wished to see completed.

Chief among the friends who came crowding into the studio was de' Altobiondi. For the first time, he registered my existence.

'Your painter has caught the likeness well,' he told Visdomini, looking at me and the canvas by turns. 'But where did you find such a Hercules in our inferior times?'

'In the Via del Proconsolo,' said my patron, laughing. 'See, he has the muscles to kill a lion with his bare hands. Show him, Gabriele.'

He made me roll up my sleeves and make fists to show off my arm muscles. I burned with the humiliation but put all my anger into clenching my fists with a realism that came from the desire to smash them into Altobiondi's face.

'A magnificent specimen,' said Altobiondi, just as if his friend had shown him a new hunting dog or hawk.

'Your wife certainly thought so' was on the tip of my tongue, but I had no desire to be run through by the blade Altobiondi carried openly on his belt, so I kept quiet.

They didn't stay long. Visdomini had been keen to show off his pet painter, the handsomely equipped studio and his tame Hercules, but once his friends had shown they were sufficiently impressed, they were keen to get back to whatever business they had upstairs.

'Nobles!' said Leone, hefting the coins the departing visitors had pressed on him.

I had come in for my share of largesse as well and it was all going to go into my stock under the mattress – my wedding fund, as I was beginning to think of it.

But we both gave a bit to Grazia, who was surprised and thankful.

'You don't have to,' she said. 'I do only what I get paid for.'

'So do we,' said Leone, and I saw for the first time that he was as much a servant as was the waiting-girl or the artist's model. 'They make me sick, with their fancy clothes and their airs and graces and their belief that God put them on the earth to get others to do their will.'

These were revolutionary thoughts. I looked round to check that none of Visdomini's friends had lingered behind to ogle the pretty servant – or me – but we were safe.

74

'Are you against the noble families then?' I asked in a low voice.

'I don't know why any working man would think differently,' he said, looking at me disapprovingly. 'Even though I am dependent on their patronage.'

'I feel the same,' I said, the coin that Altobiondi had almost thrown at me burning in my palm. 'I am a republican.'

'But your friends in San Procolo are Medici men,' said Leone.

We seemed to have stopped work and Grazia was listening to us intently.

'The sculptor had a patron too,' I said. 'Lorenzo de' Medici. And he had good cause to be grateful to him. But he became a supporter of Savonarola and so did at least two of his brothers. Indeed the oldest one is still a friar at San Marco.'

The name had been said. Leone looked round as if the walls might have ears.

'What about you?' he asked. 'Are you a *piagnone?*'

I nodded. The painter came and clasped my hand.

'We will not talk more of it here,' he said. 'But it gladdens my heart to know that you and I are on the same side.'

He glanced at Grazia. 'You will keep our secret?' he asked her. 'Working people should stick together.'

'Then you should know what's going on upstairs,' she said. 'I hear things as I bring them their wine. Which I must go and do now. The master won't like me to linger down here with you two when rich men might need food or drink.'

'What is going on upstairs?' I asked. 'What have you heard?'

'They want the de' Medici back,' she said.

'Everyone knows that,' said Leone. 'They think the return of the family means the return of wealth to their pockets.'

'But what are they doing about it?' I asked. This was my chance to find out the details of the plot.

A bell rang in the distance and Grazia jumped up, flustered.

'I must go,' she said. 'Tomorrow I have a half-day free in honour of Saint Remigius. Meet me at the Baptistery at midday and I'll tell you what I know.'

And then she was gone. Leone looked at me with a half-smile.

'I notice she didn't offer to tell me,' he said, as he bolted the door again. 'Come on, get your clothes off. Neither of us is being paid to chat.'

I was outside the Baptistery as the bell in the campanile tolled the midday hour. And yet I almost missed Grazia. She had changed into her best dress, a mossy green velvet one that I somehow knew had once belonged to her mistress. It was only half covered by her russet cloak, so I knew she wanted to show it off. And in her hair she had twined a crimson ribbon. She wore no jewels – I doubt she possessed any – but she looked as charming as any lady could on this cold January day.

There were few places in the city where a young man might take a young woman to be warm in winter – especially on a saint's day. But I knew of a bakery nearby, where the ovens would be fired up even on a holiday and the baker had befriended me some months before, for the sake of my close-ness to the Buonarroti family. He had a very beautiful wife of good birth and was always talking about having her portrait painted. I think he liked to be on friendly terms with artists.

So I took Grazia to Gandini the baker's and bought us hot soft rolls to eat as we sat in a corner of his *paneficio*. It wasn't really open to the public but a few of the baker's regulars were there and his wife gave us cups of hot spiced wine in honour of Saint Remigius, she said.

Grazia and I were sitting cosily in a corner and I realised that we looked like any other couple of the common people, enjoying some rare time away from work. *I must tell her about Rosalia,* I thought.

But she started to talk in a low and urgent voice about the conspirators at Visdomini's house. It was clear that she didn't think of our meeting as any kind of tryst.

'They are supporting more than one member of the de' Medici family,' she said. 'Piero, as before, but I think they have no high hopes of him after last time. So now they are talking about Giovanni – the one who is a cardinal in Rome. And another one . . . Giuliano? No, Giulio. He is the bastard son of Lorenzo's brother.'

That made me jump a bit and I thought of Clarice for the first time for weeks. It seemed as if nobles could father children outside marriage and their offspring still find a superior place in society. But not men like me.

Still, this was a useful titbit to take back to the *frateschi*.

'Do you know anything about when they are expecting to bring the de' Medici back into the city?' I asked. It was very intimate, sitting so close together that our faces were almost touching, keeping warm in the bakery while the streets outside were rimed with frost.

'No,' said Grazia. 'I hear only snippets. It has taken weeks to understand as much as I have told you.'

'It's very helpful to me,' I said. 'But I don't want to get you into any trouble.'

'Why does it help you?' she asked. 'How does it?'

'You know I am not sympathetic to the Medici cause,' I said quietly. 'There are . . . friends of mine who want to know this sort of information.'

'And what would they do, these "friends" of yours?'

I didn't know the answer to that.

'Will you tell me anything else you find out?' I asked, taking her hand.

It was a rough hand, not like Clarice's, but rough with work like Rosalia's. I respected them both for that. She blushed but did not take her hand away.

'There is no need for you always to go straight home after you have finished posing for Leone of an evening, I suppose?' she said.

It was true that it was always Grazia who guided me to the front door when I had finished my supper. She carried a lantern, saw me out through the postern door and then locked it behind me. It was probably her last duty of the night.

'I can tell you what I have learned in the previous few days if you come to my room before you leave,' she said. 'I have a room to myself.'

That meant she was a favoured and superior servant. But the thought of being alone with her in her bedchamber put me in a new kind of danger. I needed her information to help my chosen companions, but the price I would certainly have to pay for it, though sweet, would cost me dear.

Angelo had nearly finished the statue. We had turned it again so that he could work in more detail on the front.

'I am going to leave the top of his head unfinished,' he said.

I climbed up to have a look. There, at the crest of this David's curls, was a rough patch of unchiselled marble. My hand went unconsciously to my own hair and Angelo laughed his harsh, grating laugh like a key turning in a rusty lock.

'Why?' I asked.

'It marks the extreme limit of the original block,' he said. 'That way the Operai will see that I have used every bit of it and added nothing.'

It was a matter of pride with him that he had looked at the botched slab of marble and found a way of creating a figure in the round that had been buried exactly within its confines.

'You have such genius,' I said. And I meant it. Who but my brother could have pulled off a commission like this? That was why he had accepted, of course. It was the challenge of working within prescribed limits that excited him. He didn't want just to make a passable statue out of a discarded block, but to turn that overlooked and ignored slab of marble into a work of art that would make people gasp.

It made me gasp and I had posed for it and seen it grow out of the stone day by day. Apart from the Sangallo brothers, no one else had had that privilege. I could just imagine how it was going to shock the citizens of Florence once the public were allowed to see it. At least some of them. The *frateschi* were going to love it but not the de' Medici supporters.

It said as clearly as if it were chiselled into a stone scroll in the shepherd boy's hand that here was defiance: the ordinary working man from the fields going out against a giant clad in armour, with only a slingshot and stone. And we all knew the outcome of that story. Angelo didn't have to show it. There would be no head of Goliath in his helmet lying bloodily under this David's foot.

The determination in his eye and the concentration of his frown meant that the stone would land squarely between the brows of the Philistine giant and fell him at a blow. I know that this David looked like me but for the first time I felt like him. Armed only with a little knowledge and a lot of idealistic feelings about the Republic, I was daring to pit myself against the most powerful family the city had ever known.

No wonder Angelo had wanted to show the hero naked; when you were faced with a seemingly impossible task, that's how you did feel. I climbed down from the scaffolding and found him waiting for me, smiling.

'I saw you with another pretty girl the other day,' he said. 'I wonder if you are following my advice, as you said you would?'

I didn't know what to reply. The consequences of going to Grazia's room to talk about the pro-Medici conspiracy had been inevitable. But I had thrust down my guilty feelings about Rosalia – whose very existence Grazia was still unaware of, thanks to my cowardice – by telling myself that what I learned from Grazia was vital in order to foil their plots.

It was some weeks since this arrangement had begun and I had passed on much useful information to the *frateschi*. It appeared that this time the *compagnacci* were taking it much more slowly. Neither Piero nor any other de' Medici prince would appear suddenly at the gates at the head of a hastily assembled army. These conspirators would take every precaution to make sure their own followers were safe before letting the hated tyrants back in.

At the end of February, Altobiondi was again at Visdomini's house, according to Grazia, but this time on his own.

'They were drinking to celebrate the birth of his son,' she told me, as we lay contented in each other's arms.

'His son?' I said stupidly.

'Yes, his new wife – the widow Buonvicini – has given him an heir,' she said.

I was glad she was not looking at my face when she told me. I had a son! A son who would grow up to be a rich man, one of the *compagnacci* probably. He would never know that his true blood father was a commoner who worked with his hands and a republican. I had so many conflicting feelings about this that I could hardly make myself lie still. But I didn't want Grazia to know about my relations with Clarice; she didn't even know about Rosalia.

I know. This makes me a coward as well as a villain. But that was how it was.

'Did they say the boy's name?' I asked as casually as I could.

'Why, yes,' said Grazia, though she sounded surprised that I was interested. 'They were toasting the name Davide.'

Davide! So Clarice hadn't forgotten me! That was her secret code to let me know she would not forget her first son was the child of someone whose portrait she had to keep buried at the bottom of a chest.

CHAPTER EIGHT

Threats and Rumours

I can't remember much about the next few months. It's
odd, when so much is vivid in my memory about the
time before and after, but in those first few months
after the boy was born that the world would call
Davide di Antonello de' Altobiondi I lost all sense of myself.

I was the stonecutter who went to work in the *bottega* every
day. I was the artist's model who posed, first as Hercules and
then as Bacchus for Leone the painter two nights a week. I was a
fratesco spy who met his friends on other evenings. And I was a
lover with two beloveds – and that was without counting Clarice.

But of Gabriele himself I have no memory; I think I stumbled through spring and the beginning of summer as if I were
in a dream or like a man intoxicated by a powerful brew. I was
a figure trapped in an invisible block of marble – without feelings and unable to escape or even to want to escape.

And yet it was a time of great terror in the city; Florence
had some implacable enemies, who had nothing to do with
the de' Medici or Savonarola.

'Cesare Borgia,' said Gandini the baker. 'That's the man
we've got to worry about.'

I scarcely knew the name, but the most important thing about
this Borgia was that he was the son of the Pope. The gossip in
Florence made him seem like a monster and hero rolled into one
– someone no one could defeat or cheat. He was supposed to

have ordered the murder of many victims and gained the love of as many women. And everyone in the city was talking about him.

'He was a cardinal, you know,' Grazia told me. 'And born to a cardinal too – the one who is now Pope – but Cesare gave up his red hat.'

'Why?' I asked listlessly. It didn't seem to matter much to me at the time.

'They do say,' said Grazia, 'that he poisoned his older brother. They were both lovers of a third brother's wife. Can you believe such a thing?'

I didn't feel I could judge anyone else's sexual adventures when I considered my own situation, but I expressed suitable horror at such behaviour in a man of the Church.

'The French king made him a duke and he became a soldier,' said Grazia. 'He leads the Pope's armies with five *condottieri* underneath his command.'

'Why does that matter to us, Grazia?' I asked. 'What has an army in Rome to do with Florence?'

'Don't you listen to any of the rumours in the city?' she scolded me. 'One of those *condottieri* is Vitellozzo Vitelli!'

It meant nothing to me and I could see my ignorance was exasperating her.

'Vitelli fought with Florence against Pisa,' she said.

'So he's an ally?'

She snorted. 'Not any more! His brother Paolo was put to death for treachery a few years ago and Vitellozzo vowed to avenge him. He and Cesare are out roaming the countryside, getting nearer to the city all the time. Heaven help us if their armies combine and march on Florence!'

It wasn't long before Grazia's fears seemed to be coming true. A message reached the city that Vitelli had captured Arezzo, which was much too close for comfort.

There were rumours in Lodovico's house that Florence had sent ambassadors to Rome to get Pope Alexander to intervene. And while the tension in the city grew as Florentines waited for the reply, a new and more alarming rumour began to circulate.

'Pisa has declared for Borgia,' said Sigismondo. They called him Gismondo in the family. He was the one who wanted to be a soldier and always had his ear to the ground about military matters. 'The Pisans are already flying the Duke's banners from their turrets.'

This was seriously worrying. Pisa and Florence had been at odds for a long time and the Florentines were incensed that their rival city had gone over to Cesare Borgia instead of coming back into the fold of their old relations with the city.

'Borgia won't have them, though,' said Gandini the baker, my other source of information. He picked up a lot of gossip in his shop. 'He's gone off to take Camerino.'

My knowledge of geography was no better than of history but it sounded further away than Pisa. But I had heard of Urbino – who hadn't? – and it wasn't long before news came that Cesare Borgia had deposed the legitimate Duke of that fine city, Guidobaldo Montefeltro. This he had done himself, sending just a portion of his army to besiege Camerino.

Soon there came a message to Florence from Cesare Borgia that the city should send an ambassador to him in Urbino.

'They're sending Soderini,' said Gismondo.

'The *gonfaloniere?*' I asked.

'No. His brother, Bishop Francesco. And they're sending Machiavelli with him.'

I didn't recognise the name but not many people had heard of Niccolò Machiavelli at that time. Later, he became famous throughout Italy for his intelligence and diplomatic skills.

Soderini sent back a message that Cesare Borgia was an extraordinary man – magnificent and formidable were just two of the words used – and that if Florence would not declare itself his friend, Cesare would regard the city as his enemy.

Well, no one in Florence wanted such a powerful and seemingly unconquerable enemy. But it was a proud city, which had got rid of one family of tyrants and was in no hurry to replace it with another. There were rumours that a huge French army was on its way, which would be a protection for Florence, so the Signoria played for time.

'Ha,' said Gismondo, hurrying back from the Piazza della Signoria with fresh news. 'It seems that Cesare Borgia has heard about the French army too! He has ordered Vitelli to withdraw from Arezzo.'

While all this was going on outside the city, it was Grazia who told me about the secret information network that operated between Florentine women, the grand ladies and their servants. At first it seemed to me that it was just to help aristocratic ladies find good-looking lovers. But gradually I realised it could be helpful in finding out more about the pro-Medicean conspiracy.

'Antonello de' Altobiondi is their leader,' said Grazia, confirming what Lodovico had told me a year earlier. 'His wife and my lady are friends.'

This was news to me. And as the weather grew warmer, it seemed that Florentine ladies liked to visit one another.

The evenings were getting lighter too and Leone took down the shutters and painted by natural light. I was still posing as Bacchus with a leopard skin – another length of ordinary cloth that the painter would transform – and holding a wine cup which would look far richer on his canvas than the ordinary pewter goblet I held.

I suppose I should have expected what happened one warm July evening but, as I said, I was sleepwalking through my days. There was a knock at the door and I hardly bothered with much dressing since I was sure it was Grazia and she had seen everything many times by then.

And Grazia it was but followed by Monna Visdomini and . . . Clarice. Worse still, my lady was carrying a sturdy curly-haired baby of a few months old. My son. Davide.

'Oh, you were right, Maddalena,' said Clarice. 'Your husband's model is indeed like a Greek god.'

Imagine how I felt! Clarice and my child in the same room as Grazia, and indeed my patron's wife! It would have taken a much older and wiser man than I was then to carry the situation off.

Maddalena Visdomini introduced Leone and myself to her friend, clearly blissfully unaware of the tension in the room, but Grazia was looking daggers at me. Still, I couldn't miss what might be my only chance.

'May we offer you a seat, my ladies?' I said. 'And shall I take the child? He must be heavy.'

Without a word, Clarice handed Davide to me. I could not say anything myself. Brought up as the youngest among a large family of sisters, the only babies I had ever known anything about were my little nieces and nephews. And to be honest, I had never found them very interesting until they could walk and talk.

But this was different – my own firstborn. He looked up at me with a solemn dark blue gaze and in that moment I would have given my life to protect him. Even though I didn't know from what.

Fortunately for me, Leone was keeping up a polite conversation with the ladies, showing them his finished Hercules, which was still in the studio waiting to be framed. They looked with discernment at his work in progress too. I must have held little Davide for about ten minutes, unconsciously rocking him until his eyes closed and his little body relaxed.

Then his mother reached for him and I handed him back. I felt as if a part of my own flesh was being ripped out of my chest, but still could say nothing.

That night in her room Grazia quizzed me about Clarice.

'You know her, don't you?' she asked.

'I knew her,' I admitted. I was not going to lie to this good woman.

'They say you were her lover,' said Grazia in a very small voice.

I did not need to ask who 'they' were. I was surprised only that it had taken so long for this information to travel to Grazia's ears via the women's network.

She took my silence as agreement. 'And the child . . . ?' she asked.

I turned my face away from her. I could not talk about the child.

I had a few days to myself after that because I was not due at Visdomini's house till the following week. The day after my unsettling encounter with Clarice, I was with the *frateschi* and they were in an excitable mood. I hadn't given them all that much information but they had followed up various leads and were now sure that the *compagnacci* were in active contact with Piero de' Medici and planning a restoration of the family as de facto rulers of the city.

'They will have us to contend with if they try it,' said Gianbattista, who was as fiery as he was short.

'How many of "us" are there?' I asked. I hadn't wondered about that before but surely six or seven of us meeting in one house could make no difference?

'More than you'd think,' answered Daniele. 'There are groups like ours meeting in many houses all over Florence. And we can count on public support too. There are many, many people who have not forgiven the Signoria for killing our leader.'

'And how will we come together to halt the *compagnacci*?'

'We have a good network,' said Fra Paolo. I was sure he didn't want me to know the details. He had never trusted me. I thought of the women's network and wondered if the republicans would have such a good system.

'Don't worry, Gabriele,' said Gianbattista. 'Just be ready when the call comes. We will need to make sure the *compagnacci* inside the city can't let Piero and his army in.'

So I would be kidnapping nobles or defending the city gates?

'What are you smiling about, Gabriele?' said Fra Paolo. 'This is not a boys' game.'

I was thinking about kidnapping Antonello de' Altobiondi and administering to him the punishment due to a traitor to the Republic. And yet, as far as he knew, the man had never done me any harm.

'I wish there was some action I could take,' I said honestly.

'It will come soon enough,' said Donato. 'And then you will wish otherwise.'

I walked back a little way with Donato and his brother Giulio that night. It was still light because we were close to the longest day of the year and the moon and sun could be seen at the same time in the sky above Piazza Santa Croce.

'How did you two become followers of the Friar?' I asked. I had never been alone with them before.

'We were among his *fanciulli*,' said Giulio.

I had heard a bit about these groups of boys that roamed unchecked round the city about five years ago. These two would have been just boys then; they were close to me in age.

'What was it like?'

'It was the best two years we ever had,' said Donato and his brother nodded his agreement.

'We went round to the houses of the *compagnacci*,' said Giulio, 'and got them to give us their fripperies.'

'You burned them, I think?' I said.

'We had huge bonfires outside the Palazzo della Signoria,' said Donato, 'piling on combs and masks and wigs and paintings and laces – how they burned!'

'You kept nothing for yourselves?' I asked. 'It must have been a temptation.'

They exchanged uneasy glances.

'Of course not,' said Donato. 'There were thousands of us – the Friar trusted us all.'

I tried to imagine thousands of young boys roaming through the city in their black robes, olive leaves in their hair, cajoling and bullying people into giving up the pretty things that meant so much to them. I somehow didn't believe that every one of those angelic youths put everything he collected on to a bonfire.

And were the women who took pleasure in jewels and combs and laces, like Clarice and Monna Visdomini, terrible sinners compared with the grave and devout Simonetta? I couldn't see the harm in it. Even Rosalia liked pretty things – though she didn't have many of them – and she would not have been allowed to keep my cameo ring in the days of Savonarola. I was beginning to wonder if I was such a follower of his after all.

The next Sunday Angelo took me with him to visit his oldest brother, Lionardo. We walked up to San Marco, a route now familiar to me from my sessions with the *frateschi* in Gianbattista's house. But Angelo didn't know where I went of an evening when not at Visdomini's house.

'This is where I used to work for Lorenzo,' he said unexpectedly.

'At the monastery?' I asked.

'No. In the sculpture garden,' he said. 'It's right opposite.'

'Is it still there?' I hadn't realised that this was where it had been, Angelo's first proper school of art.

'Let's look,' he said and led me over to an iron gate in the road that ran up beside the Piazza San Marco.

It was such a quiet part of the city – hard to believe that only a few years ago it had rung with the sounds of rioting as Savonarola had been besieged in the monastery. After that the monastery's bell had been silenced, as Fra Paolo had told me, taken away from the friars for fifty years.

'Look through there,' said Angelo. 'It used to be full of Roman statues – some complete and some fragments. They were part of Lorenzo's collection.'

'Where are they now?' I asked. The garden was quiet and still. No statues and no young sculptors ringing out with hammers and chisels on blocks of marble from quarries like the ones near my home. It was easy to imagine them, though. In this peaceful setting it was easier than summoning up images of men with torches and muskets.

'I imagine they were taken – or maybe even broken up – when Piero was chased out of Florence,' said Angelo. 'The state took all the statues from the Medici palazzo and put them in the government palace. The bronzes are there now but I don't know what happened to the marble statues that were here.'

So if Piero ever did come back to Florence, he'd find his father's treasures scattered all over the city. I wondered if my brother was thinking about that, but in fact his mind had gone along another track.

'What we make is so fragile,' he said. 'As transitory as human life.'

'But works of art can live on long after the people who made them have gone,' I said. 'Remember those frescoes by Big Tom you showed me? And didn't you say he was long dead?'

'Yes, but take a big hammer to a statue or cast a canvas into the flames and it will not survive, any more than a human being would,' he said. 'That's where I couldn't follow Savonarola. He had no time for things that are beautiful in their own right. You know that even *Il Botticello* threw canvases on to his bonfires, at least so it is said?'

I had met this Botticello, the little barrel, once with my brother. He had been a great painter, according to Angelo, and a favourite of Lorenzo de' Medici, but had fallen under the sway of the fanatical friar and, although he had survived the upheavals and the overthrow of his leader, had lost a lot of his standing as one of Florence's great artists.

I could see that it pained Angelo to think of the destruction of works of art, more perhaps than the fate of the three men who had been executed in the square outside the government building. Of course, he wouldn't have agreed with Savonarola about paintings and sculptures; that's where he would have had to part company with the Friar.

Although so careless about his own appearance and belongings – apart from his tools – Angelo celebrated and revered beauty. He would never have thrown any work of his own on to the flames.

'I was just a boy when I worked in that garden,' said Angelo, turning away from the gate with a sigh. 'I don't think I've ever been happier. It was half my lifetime ago.'

As we walked back towards the monastery, I saw Simonetta on the other side of the street. She was accompanied by her brother, but she was the one that caught my eye. As luck would have it, Angelo crossed the road at that point and we were forced to step back into the road to let them pass. Gianbattista gave me a curt nod and Simonetta acknowledged me with a glance.

I wondered whether to introduce them to Angelo but the encounter was over in a flash and the opportunity passed.

'Do you know that lovely young woman?' my brother asked.

I admitted that I did. He laughed softly.

'Gabriele, what are we to do with you? How many women have succumbed to your charms since you arrived in the city?'

I fought hard not to blush. 'Simonetta has not "succumbed", as you put it,' I defended myself. 'It is her brother who is my friend. They are both *frateschi*.'

'Really? Ah well, never mind. She must be one of the few Florentine women you have not impressed then.'

We walked on and into the monastery.

The atmosphere was cool and refreshing after the hot summer afternoon. The tiled floor rang with our footsteps which sounded loudly in the still quiet of the friars' home. We walked towards the stone staircase to the brothers' cells and as we ascended it I gasped with surprise.

The whole of the wall at the top of the stairs was filled with a huge painting of the Annunciation. The angel, just alighted on the left was delivering his eternal message to the Mother of Our Lord, who was sitting on a humble wooden stool on the right. Each had their arms loosely crossed at the chest, as if unconsciously imitating the other.

'The archangel you were named for,' said Angelo.

I thought again of my mother's story of the night of my conception. My brother and I had both been named after archangels. But my namesake was a messenger of hope and joy, his a forbidding guardian with a flaming sword. I had never been more aware of the differences between us.

'You like it?'

'It's magnificent,' I said, my breath quite taken away.

'Then you are in for a treat,' he said, smiling.

When I had finished gazing at the fresco, he led me down a corridor to the side of it and knocked at the door of the first cell on the left. In fact, the door wasn't fully shut; it was the practice of the friars to leave them ajar except at night. And this was evidently Lionardo's cell. It was tiny and as he came to the door to greet us I caught a glimpse of the painted wall behind him.

'Every cell has a painting by the master we call our brother – Fra Angelico – or one of his followers,' Lionardo told me, seeing the respect I had for art. 'Come in and see this one. It is thought to be one of the best.'

There was scarcely room for three people to crowd into that cell but there was Our Lord, almost floating on the wall. It was the first meeting with Mary Magdalene after the Resurrection and He was putting out a warning hand for her not to touch Him. The thought struck me that Jesus in this painting was like a newly hatched butterfly, still damp and weak, not yet ready to spend His brief remaining lifespan on the earth. I hoped this thought wasn't blasphemy.

'Come down to the Refectory,' said Lionardo. 'There is more room there.'

There was another huge fresco on the wall of the Refectory, a Last Supper with all sorts of miraculous details like a peacock and a cat. I thought it was wonderful but Angelo was a bit dismissive.

'My old master painted that,' he said. 'Ghirlandaio. My father apprenticed me to him but I got out of it.'

'I remember the scenes about that,' said Lionardo. 'You always knew your own mind even as a ten-year-old.'

'My father did not want me to be a sculptor,' said Angelo. 'But once Lorenzo took an interest in me and invited me into his own house, even Father could not object.'

'So you were going to be a painter?' I had not known that.

'Not much of a one,' said Angelo. 'I have always preferred stone.'

We drank a cup of cool wine at the long scrubbed table and then walked in the cloisters with Fra Lionardo. After a while, I plucked up courage to ask him if he knew Fra Paolo. He nodded.

'He was a devoted follower of our martyred leader,' he said. 'How do you know him?'

'Yes, how do you know him, Gabriele?' asked Angelo.

'He is a friend of those people we passed in the street,' I said, as if this explained anything. 'But I don't think he thinks much of me.'

'I will tell him that he underestimates you then,' said Lionardo. 'No one who responds to art as you do should be dismissed.

I felt very warmly towards this oldest of Lodovico's sons all of a sudden. We didn't share the same bond I had with Angelo but he was sort of family all the same.

CHAPTER NINE

Another David

I
t was not long after our visit to San Marco that Angelo
told me he had a new commission. His marble David
was approaching completion, though the finishing
of it moved very slowly, inch by inch, as there was a
danger of damaging what he had already done if he worked
too boldly.

'I am to make another David,' he told me one morning in
August.

'A copy of this one?'

'No. A bronze for a *maréchal* in France,' he said. 'I think he
wants me to copy Donatello's one.'

Even I had heard of the Donatello David, a daring bronze
that showed the hero naked but for his long boots and
garlanded hat, but I had never seen it.

'We'll go and look at it on the next holiday – in a few days
in fact.'

It was two days before Ferragosto – the Feast of Our Lady's
Assumption into Heaven – and we would have two full days
off work. In fact, it was forbidden to work during the festival.

So after the feasting and celebrations for Our Lady, we set
out for the government palace to look at Donatello's statue.

'I didn't want to come before,' said Angelo. 'Though I
remember the bronze well from when it was in Lorenzo's
courtyard, I wanted to do my David differently.'

96

I wouldn't have been allowed into the palace on my own but my brother's name was opening more and more doors in Florence. Word was spreading that he was working on a masterpiece – either in spite of or because of the secrecy in which he worked.

Donatello's David was a much smaller statue than the giant my brother was working on. But it was in its way perfect. So highly polished and gilded it was hard to think that it had never just not been there in the world. Like the Fra Angelico frescoes I saw at San Marco, it filled me with awe at the power that artists like my brother had.

'Well, Gabriele,' said my brother, rubbing his hands together with relish, 'you'd better resign yourself. I'm going to need you to pose for another David!'

So now I was David again in my spare time. It was as well that Leone's Bacchus was finished. His next subject was to be Leda and the swan so I was not needed for a few months. Visdomini was paying me a retainer but I was back on short rations at Lodovico's and seeing very little of Grazia.

It meant I had also lost my best source of information. But I found a substitute in an unlikely place. Angelo's youngest brother, Gismondo, was only a year and a bit older than me and I found him an easy-going, rather lazy but good-hearted companion. He was supposed to work in the cloth business with Buonarroto but he spent little time there because of his fascination with all things military.

Gismondo was the one who had explained to me about Cesare Borgia and now he made it his business to continue my military education. He had friends in the city who kept him up to date with what was going on in the country as a whole and when he found out I was interested in what had happened to Piero de' Medici, he decided to undertake my education. He took to coming and chatting to me while his brother sketched me in the evenings.

This was a new pose with me holding the head of Goliath in my left hand. Since there were, naturally, no severed heads in the Buonarroti household, I actually clutched a mophead. But I was way past being embarrassed by my props or even by posing in the nude now.

So, while one brother sketched, the other told me more about the military situation of Florence than I had known so far in my life. Occasionally Angelo would add or correct something.

'After Piero failed to get back into the city in '97,' said Gismondo, 'he joined up with the French army.'

'Um,' I said, twirling my mophead. 'Can you just assume I know nothing and tell me all the background? What do the French have to do with anything?'

Angelo grunted. 'Keep that mop still! I can't believe you are so ignorant. It was Piero's deal with the French that let them into Florence and that was – what? – only eight years ago.'

'So I was eleven,' I defended myself. 'I didn't know anything about politics.'

'You don't seem to know much about them now,' said Gismondo good-naturedly. 'But you would certainly have known something if King Charles had taken his troops through Settignano. I was only twelve and I remember it vividly.'

'What happened?'

'Well, Charles had an army of thirty thousand men and in September of '94 he marched them across the Alps.'

I could see that Gismondo was settling in for a proper history lesson but I didn't mind – it took my mind off the cramp in my right calf.

'He sent an envoy to Piero – not that Piero had the right to negotiate on behalf on the city – asking him to acknowledge the French claim to the Kingdom of Naples.'

'And Piero said yes?'

'He said nothing at all for five days,' said Angelo.

'And then he decided that Florence would stay neutral,' said Gismondo. 'You can imagine how that went down with the French king. His army just pushed on into Tuscany, murdering as it went. Piero went and met Charles and conceded everything he asked for.'

'And you can imagine how that went down with the city!' said Angelo.

'The Signoria locked him out of the government palace and rang the bell to call the people into the square,' said Gismondo. 'Piero and his family had to flee to Venice and the Signoria passed a law that no de' Medici should ever set foot in Florence again.'

That bit I did know. 'And then the French came?' I asked.

'Not straight away. First Charles went to Pisa and told them they were now "free" of the tyranny of the Florentine Republic.'

'And all the while his envoys were looting the Medici palace,' said Angelo, drawn into the discussion in spite of himself.

'Do you remember how Father tried to keep us all in the house and I escaped to go and see the soldiers?' said Gismondo, clearly relishing the memory.

'I remember you got a good thrashing for it,' said Angelo.

'But it was worth it! The French king, all in gold, had a bodyguard of at least a hundred men. Then there were thousands of cavalrymen, infantry and archers. I'd never seen so many soldiers in the city. The king himself came into the Piazza del Duomo at sunset on a huge black horse.'

'That must have been a sight to behold,' I said, caught up by Gismondo's enthusiasm.

But his face fell. 'The problem was,' he said, 'the king was such an ugly little man. I was glad he stayed only eleven days. He marched on to Rome and Naples and Savonarola encouraged people to put to death any Medici supporter left in the city.'

'What happened to the French king?' I asked.

'He did become king of Naples,' said Gismondo.

'But not for long,' said Angelo. 'He went back to France and killed himself.'

'It was an accident,' Gismondo explained to me. 'King Charles was playing a game of royal tennis. He leapt up to take a shot and hit his head on a door frame. Knocked himself out and died a few hours later.'

Angelo laughed rustily. 'What kind of idiot kills himself like that? Aren't there enough people wanting to assassinate monarchs without doing their work for them?'

'So who's the king now?' I asked.

'Another Louis,' said Gismondo. 'They're always Charles or Louis. This one's the twelfth. You must have heard of him. He took Milan less than three years ago. He's the one bringing a huge army into Italy from France.'

I had heard that Milan had fallen to the French but only that bare fact.

'So that's the king that Piero de' Medici's joined up with?' I asked. 'The one that's going to save us from Cesare Borgia?'

'Piero thinks the French will support him in an attempt to get back into the city,' said Gismondo. 'But I think Giovanni de' Medici is more likely than Piero to get the support of the French.'

'The Cardinal?' I asked, on safer ground here.

'The youngest one ever,' said Gismondo. 'It was a present his father bought for him when he was sixteen – like a horse or a pet dog. But you must ask my brother about Giovanni – they were practically brought up together.'

'We're the same age, it's true,' said Angelo, narrowing his eyes as he tried to capture my awkward pose. 'But neither Piero nor Giovanni was a patch on Lorenzo. They were both lazy, greedy and more interested in football and athletics than in learning anything. And Giovanni at least still lives that life in Rome, hunting and hawking and pawning the family silver to pay for lavish feasts.'

'So how does that make him more likely to take back the family interests in Florence?' I asked.

'Don't ask me,' said Gismondo. 'I'm not a Medici man after all. I'm a republican. But I'd dearly like to be a soldier in whatever army would take me.'

'Even King Louis' army?' asked Angelo.

'What we need is a proper Florentine army,' said his brother, evading the question. 'You can never get the same loyalty from mercenaries.'

And the conversation drifted on to Gismondo's views about military strategy. But he had given me a lot to think about. Neither Piero nor Giovanni seemed at all likely to make good leaders. But there were other de' Medici contenders and I wondered if the *compagnacci* were in contact with them.

It was a hotter than usual August and I spent my free time walking down by the river, trying to get some fresh air. Living in Florence in high summer was like sitting inside a bowl surrounded with boiling water. One Sunday I walked on my own up to Fiesole on the hillside outside the city. It was a long walk and stretched my leg muscles well but once I got there, I could take in great lungfuls of breeze-cooled air. I felt as if I hadn't been able to breathe properly for weeks.

Looking down on the city from up there made all the political factions and intrigues seem as petty as the antics of insects. What difference would it make if one of them carried a leaf or not? It was what I needed and for a long time I just revelled in the view. It was impossible to miss the cathedral with the great dome Brunelleschi made for it; that cupola dominated the skyline.

So down there was the marble statue that looked like me and there would soon be another in bronze. I wondered how much longer than my own lifespan these copies of me would last.

I came back down from the hillside in thoughtful mood, temporarily refreshed but soon sweating again in the damp heat. Thunder rumbled round the hills. On an impulse I set out to walk to Gianbattista's and arrived there tired and famished.

Gianbattista was not at home but his sister was and the servant who answered the door and knew me well showed me into the small parlour where Simonetta was sewing. She jumped up when she saw me and seemed flustered. It was the first time we had been alone together since the day I had seen her leaving flowers for Savonarola.

'Was my brother expecting you?' she asked. 'Do you have information for him? I'm afraid he has gone out.'

'No,' I said. 'I was out walking and just found myself nearby. Don't let me disturb you. I'll go.'

'Don't go,' she said. 'You look tired. Sit down. Where did you walk to?'

'Up to Fiesole,' I said.

'So far? You must be exhausted. And hungry too. Let me send for refreshment.'

I was glad enough to rest. The little parlour was snug and comfortable and if I had to feel warm and confined, where better than in a small space with a beautiful woman?

Simonetta was just going to ring for a servant when there came a mighty clap of thunder that seemed to be right above us. We both jumped and instinctively, I put my arm around her. There was a delicious moment – not more than a second or two – when she seemed to lean into me and relax her whole body into my arms. Then she sprang away as if stung by a bee and rang the bell hard.

I sat down and waited in silence, listening to the heavy rain that had at last fallen. It would feel fresher tomorrow. I knew Angelo had been wrong when he said Simonetta was a woman I hadn't impressed. I knew she liked me. And I liked her too. But my life was so complicated that I dare not make any approach to her.

It seemed to me that if anything happened between us it would be bound to end in unhappiness. And I did not want to face an angry Gianbattista and a gang of *frateschi* as well as a disappointed woman.

It was a relief when the servant came back. Simonetta picked up her sewing and I ate and drank with a good appetite. Anyone watching us would have thought us an old married couple.

'You visited the monastery the other day,' she said at last.

'Yes. I went with the sculptor to see his brother, Fra Lionardo. It was full of the most wonderful paintings,' I said. I was glad we had found a subject of conversation that was quite safe. Even Savonarola must have approved of Fra Angelico's frescoes or he would have had them whitewashed over.

'I wouldn't know,' she said. 'A woman can't go there and visit the friars.'

'That's a pity. You would like them – they are all on religious subjects and beautifully done.'

'Perhaps I should go into a convent,' she said. 'What do you think?'

This was sudden and unexpected and, I thought, a dangerous topic. So I avoided answering and left as soon as I could, even though it was still raining hard. I ran back towards the house in Santa Croce, letting the rain soak through my hair and clothes. I resolved never to call in at Gianbattista's house again without being invited.

CHAPTER TEN

Mars and Venus

R ound about this time, Angelo had a new idea. Apparently he had been impressed by the way I had appreciated all the paintings and sculptures he had shown me in the city and had got it into his head that I should become an artist.

'Do you want to be a stonecutter all your life?' he asked me one day when I was posing for the new David.

We were on our own, as Gismondo was out gathering more information about the French army.

'I wouldn't mind,' I said. 'It's an honest trade.'

'Indeed. But I've seen your skill with a chisel and I've watched the way you respond to works of art,' he said. 'I think I could teach you to make a statue of your own.'

I was astounded. In all the time I had known him, Angelo had been quite determined that he would never take an apprentice.

'I thought you always hated the idea of teaching,' I said.

'I hate the idea of taking on a pupil for money,' he grunted, turning the paper round and starting again on a new version of my arm. 'My old master couldn't teach me anything under that system.'

'Yes, but you have genius and probably knew more than he did,' I said. I was the only person that Angelo ever allowed to tease him.

'Possibly,' he agreed in all seriousness. 'I might not be a good example. But how can you know if a pupil shows any promise till you see him work? I know you can square stone and cut moulded corners, but I also know your *maestro* has had you working on acanthus leaves for capitols and other fancier stonecutting tasks.'

He must have been talking to my *maestro del bottega*.

'Well, yes,' I said. 'I can do that. That's just copying. But I can't do what you do – conceive a design for a commission. I wouldn't know where to begin.'

'Apprentices don't start by planning whole statues,' he said. 'They start by doing tasks very like the ones you work on all day. And they use their eyes. They look at all the statues and friezes and reliefs they can find in their own city and they develop a sense of how sculpture works – in the round, in high and low relief. And they draw. Do you draw?'

I shook my head. It had never occurred to me.

'Is that how you manage to get all the muscles and veins so like those of living people, even though they are carved in stone?' I asked.

He laughed. 'If they are like the living, it is because I have studied the dead,' he said.

I shivered. He had not admitted this before.

'When?' I asked. 'Where?'

'At Santo Spirito, on the other side of the Arno,' he said. 'I had an arrangement with the Prior there, old Bichieli. I drew the corpses that came in. Cut into them so that I came to understand the ways in which bone and flesh and organs and the vessels that carry blood all relate to one another.'

'It must have been difficult.'

'The only difficulty was in getting it right,' he said. 'In finding out what was just the way one man was put together and what was true of us all. If you regard it as another stage in learning your craft, it becomes bearable.'

'Do you still do it?' I asked.

He shook his head. 'No. It was when I was in the city before, after Lorenzo died. I made them a wooden crucifix to thank them.'

I remembered that Clarice had mentioned seeing it in Santo Spirito. My brother was a constant surprise to me; was he suggesting that I should learn by cutting up corpses?

'But perhaps I am wrong to think you might be a sculptor,' he said. 'Perhaps you would feel more comfortable as a sculptor's assistant?'

'Are you offering me a job?' I asked.

'I'm offering to teach you some more skills to add to those you are learning in the *bottega*.'

This was something I would have to think about.

Florence had heaved a huge sigh of relief when the French army reached Milan. According to Gismondo, King Louis had invited all sorts of people with a grievance against Cesare Borgia to meet him at his court there and then – in a clever twist – invited Cesare himself!

'Their faces were a sight to see,' said Gismondo, as if he had been there in person. 'They'd all been griping and complaining about Cesare and then they saw the French king kiss him on both cheeks! They were all there – the Duke of Urbino, Sforza of Pesaro, Gonzaga of Mantua – all people whose cities Cesare had taken or threatened.'

'What happened?' I asked. 'Did they meet him?'

'No, they packed up and left Milan as if the Furies were chasing them!'

Gismondo was highly amused by this tale.

'There's more,' he said. 'It's taken a while for the news to reach the Signoria here, but Cesare has now changed course and is aiming at taking Bologna! His *condottieri* are furious with him, because he has his eyes on their cities too. Florence is safe for the time being.'

I wondered how long it would be before this fearsome young prince turned his attention back to our city. It seemed as if he wanted to make all Italy his kingdom.

'Do you think Cesare Borgia wanted Florence for himself?' I asked. 'Or is he friendly to Piero?'

'Who can say?' said Gismondo. 'When your father is Pope, you can ask for almost anything. But no, not even Cesare Borgia can be everywhere. I think he would make his base at Urbino – he would like to show off in its magnificent ducal palace – and he would have probably installed a de' Medici here.'

I shuddered. 'Then it's good news he has turned his attention to Bologna.'

Leone had finished his Leda and the Swan. I saw it when I was called back to the studio to start posing for his new subject: Mars and Venus. It was a good painting. But while I was admiring it, I saw that Leda's ecstatic face had something about it that looked like Grazia.

I hadn't seen her as often over the summer because of posing for Angelo instead of Leone, though I was admitted to the house as an accepted 'follower' of hers. Lords and ladies turned a blind eye to such liaisons.

That first night back after posing as the God of War, I asked her point blank if she had modelled for the painter.

'I did,' she said. 'My master told me to and we do what our masters tell us, don't we?'

'But did you pose like that – with no clothes on?' I asked. 'And with that expression?'

'Do you dare ask me that?' she said. 'You who lay with a grand lady and got a baby on her and God knows who else? Do you dare to be jealous?'

'I can't help what I feel,' I said, sounding sulky even to my own ears. 'And there was no one else.'

'Oh, really?' said Grazia. 'Does that mean you are true to me now? Are you offering to marry me?'

I was silent.

'I thought not,' she said. 'Well, until you do, you have no right to ask who sees me – with or without my clothes.'

I gathered up my things and left immediately. At that moment I really thought I would follow my brother's advice and give up women for good.

But my body betrayed me as it had done before.

I was walking to work next morning, wondering what would happen when I next went to Visdomini's house when someone I hadn't seen for over a year hissed my name from the street corner.

It was Clarice's pert maid, Vanna.

'Psst,' she whispered. 'Come here.'

I went; I was always being told what to do, usually by women, and it was instinctive to obey.

'What do you want?' I asked her.

'It's not me that wants anything,' she said contemptuously. She was taller than before and her figure had rounded out but I did not find her attractive. I never had.

'My lady sends for you to the Via Tornabuoni.'

'I am on my way to work,' I said. 'I can't just go visiting when my *maestro* is expecting me. I might lose my job.'

'She said you'd say that,' said Vanna. 'She said, "Tell him to come after work." My lord is away.'

That made me think. Dangerous as it was to go back to Clarice's house, I could see my son. Surely that was why she had asked me? And I suddenly considered that maybe I could find out more about Altobiondi and the pro-Mediceans. That would be useful if my relationship with Grazia was to end.

'So,' said Vanna, 'shall I tell my lady you will come?'

'Tell her I might.'

I thought about it all day and spoiled the latticework for a stone window frame. My *maestro* shouted at me for the first time. Perhaps Angelo was wrong to think he could make an artist of me. But gradually I took control of my emotions and by the end of my day's work I had won back the *maestro*'s good opinion.

'Everyone has the occasional bad day,' he said. 'We all make mistakes. No one can learn anything without making mistakes.'

That was kinder than I deserved but I'd worked for him long enough to show that I wasn't usually unreliable.

I went to the Via Tornabuoni. Of course I did. And I went just as I was, with all my stone dust on me. Clarice knew what I did and what I was and if, before, she had dressed me up and pretended I was something other, at this meeting she had to be reminded of the gulf between us.

It was another house but that was the only difference in my reception. I was brought warm water to wash in and good wine to drink and all the time I said nothing. Clarice never took her eyes off me. But when the servant withdrew, she seemed shy and embarrassed.

'How are you?' she asked. 'I mean how has your life been since . . .'

'Since you threw me out?'

'That's not fair! You left my house to live with the sculptor.'

'You know what I mean. I couldn't come to your palazzo any more once you were to marry Altobiondi.'

I think I spat out his name. I wasn't usually envious of the lives of rich men; I didn't crave what they had and they always seemed so anxious about losing it. But I suddenly wondered, looking at Clarice, why it was that some men lived in big comfortable homes with their small families while poorer men struggled to house their larger broods.

But to be honest I wasn't really thinking revolutionary thoughts; I was just sore that Antonello de' Altobiondi was bringing up my son.

As if I had conjured him up, a nursemaid brought Davide in. I felt a surge of pride that I had helped to make this strong and sturdy boy. He was over six months old and could sit up straight on his mother's lap. He put his hands up to her face and they looked together like a Madonna and Child painted by one of the past masters.

The impression lasted an instant; Clarice was no saint.

'He's a fine boy, your son,' I said.

'Isn't he?' she said proudly.

'Do your daughters treat him well?' I asked. I could not bring myself to ask about his supposed father.

'The girls love having a little brother,' she said. 'I want you to know,' she said very carefully, 'that he is very much loved. He will have a good life.'

I nodded. She was right.

'But I didn't ask you here to see Davide,' she went on. 'Though you may hold him if you wish.'

She held the boy out to me and I took him as before, full of wonder at this beautiful creature who had a year ago simply not existed in the world. He was like a work of art, only one conceived without intention.

'Why did you want to see me then?' I asked as I let the boy bury his little hands in my curls.

If she thought we could just resume our life together as lovers whenever her husband left town, she was playing a very dangerous game.

'I felt I owed you something,' she said.

If she had offered me money, I would have given her back the child and walked out of that house never to see her again. But it was not that.

'My . . . Altobiondi is involved in something I think you want to know about,' said Clarice. 'He is at this moment in Rome, meeting Giovanni and Giulio de' Medici.'

'The Cardinal and his cousin? Are you telling me that your husband is conspiring to bring back the de' Medici?'

'It is well known, I think,' said Clarice.

I was still holding Davide and must have squeezed him too hard because he started to cry and turned to reach out for his mother.

'Sorry,' I said, smoothing the boy's curls as I handed him back to Clarice, who quieted him by jogging him up and down on her lap.

'Antonello doesn't tell me everything,' she said. 'But he and his friends have frequent meetings here – your patron Visdomini is one of their number – and I overhear things.'

'Why are you telling me this?' I asked.

'Because, although it might surprise you, I don't want the Republic overthrown any more than you do. I'd like to help you.'

So Clarice was no more pro-Medici than Grazia was!

'I believe that Lorenzo did some good things,' Clarice said. 'But I am just old enough to remember what it was like under his son, Piero. The de' Medici name is no guarantee of a good ruler.'

'You sound like my brother,' I said.

'Will you let me help you?' she asked.

So my life as a spy and my romantic life continued to be entangled. The room where Altobiondi met his fellow conspirators had an alcove covered by a tapestry of a hunting scene and sometimes, before a meeting, Clarice would send me a message and I would get there early, let in by the maid, Vanna, and hide behind it.

This was incredibly dangerous and I had to stay for the whole evening. Often they were dull with no real new information for me to pass on. But one night there were some new men I didn't know and their presence seemed to excite the other pro-Medici conspirators.

One was called Ridolfi and the other Bellatesta – that much I managed to pick up. I didn't know them but the *frateschi* might.

The one called Ridolfi had been in Rome and come back with de' Altobiondi. They were reporting on their meeting with the de' Medici.

'Giovanni says the Pope is ill,' said Ridolfi. 'It could mean the end of Borgia rule in Rome.'

'And of Cesare Borgia's rise, then,' said Altobiondi. He sounded quite pleased.

I tried not to sigh but I was confused. It seemed that the pro-Mediceans were not in league with Cesare Borgia. But then the Bellatesta one made me think again.

'I am not so sure. Giulio de' Medici told us Cardinal Piccolomini will be the next Pope,' he said. 'And he is certain that Piccolomini will support Cesare. Giulio and Giovanni are both courting the Cardinal's favour. It will be a long time before Cesare stops rising.'

'And Giovanni will vote for Piccolomini in conclave when the Pope dies. The one they don't want is della Rovere. He hates Cesare and all the Borgias.'

There was a lot more talk after that but it was so uninteresting that I fell asleep. It's fortunate that I don't snore – or rather that I didn't as a young man – or my hiding place would have been revealed.

When I woke, the room was dark and I was curled into an awkward position behind the tapestry. Vanna was shaking my shoulder. I came stiffly out of my hiding place and was soon on my way home. But I was still half asleep and not taking notice of my surroundings.

Otherwise I would have seen my attackers. A group of masked men jumped out from behind a pillar in the Via Tornabuoni and started laying into me. I felt for the knife that Angelo had given me but one of the men held my arms behind my back while the others punched and kicked me. At least they used no weapons.

When they had finished and I slumped to the ground, their leader, who had taken no part in the attack but looked on with satisfaction, bent down and hissed in my ear, 'Stay away from de' Altobiondi! Death to the de' Medici!'

They left me and I rolled on to my knees and hands, spitting blood. *At least I haven't lost any teeth*, I was vain enough to think. But I was a total mess, my eyes swollen and my lips bloody. My entire body ached from the beating but I knew things would be a lot worse by the next morning.

I limped home to Lodovico's and I smiled, although it hurt the split in my lip. I had been beaten up for being a Medici supporter! And probably by another cell of the *frateschi*! The irony wasn't lost on me but I had no idea how I was going to explain the attack to my brother and his family. Or to my *maestro* and my patron.

My life was getting so complicated I hardly knew how to explain it to myself!

CHAPTER ELEVEN

A Telling Blow

'*Dio mio*,' said Gismondo, who was the first member of the household to see me next morning. 'What have you done to yourself?'

'It was done to me rather,' I said, scarcely able to speak for the pain in my jaw. My eyes were closed up and I could tell I would not be able to work for some days. I would not know where to make my chisel blows.

'Who did this then?' he asked, looking as if he would like to take a weapon and go and deal out summary justice to them.

'Fellow republicans,' I said. I would have smiled wryly if I could.

'*Frateschi*?' he asked. 'But why? Did they think you had betrayed them?'

'I am not sure. It was no one I knew. They saw me coming out of de' Altobiondi's palazzo. Maybe that was why they jumped to the wrong conclusion.'

'And what would have been the right conclusion?' Gismondo asked.

I had no desire for anyone else to know about my past liaison with Clarice so I said, 'I was spying on him and his friends.'

I groaned. I had so much to tell my own cell of *frateschi*, but that too would have to wait. My ribs were aching and it would take a long time for my bruises to subside. Another thought struck me: I could hardly pose for Leone's Mars looking like this. Even though the God of War must have been in a fair few scraps, I'd wager he was never shown as having come off worse.

Angelo came in while we were talking.

'Who has ruined your beauty?' he asked, pouring me a cup of wine. He sent to the cook to make me a bowl of gruel since there was no way I could chew crusty bread.

I told my story again and the two brothers were both sympathetic. Angelo promised to call in at the *bottega* on his way to the Duomo and tell my *maestro* that I had been set upon by robbers and beaten and would not be able to work for the rest of the week.

Gismondo undertook to take a message to Ser Visdomini and also to get in touch with my cell of *frateschi*. Perhaps one of them would come and visit me and I could tell him my news? Being well-off young men they had no work to employ their hands during the day, unlike Gismondo, who was supposed to go to the wool shop but much preferred to think of pretexts that kept him busy around the city.

The cook herself brought me the bowl of slop and tut-tutted over my appearance.

'You must rest,' she said when I had eaten what I could. 'I will bring you a cold compress for your poor eyes.'

I went back to bed, very sorry for myself, but wondering – true Florentine that I had become – how to turn this attack to my advantage. I must have slept heavily and long, because a servant came to tell me I had visitors.

There was a little cry, which I recognised as Grazia's voice, as they were shown into the room.

'Oh, poor Gabriele!' she said and immediately took over nursing duties from the cook.

As she bathed my eyes in an infusion of herbs in cold water, I gathered that my other visitor was Gianbattista. He clasped my hand.

'Who did this?' he asked. 'Ser Buonarroti told me it was *piagnoni*.'

His use of that term showed me that he disapproved and, as I thought, had nothing to do with the attack.

'They shouted "Death to the de' Medici" as they ran away,' I said. 'And I was coming out of de' Altobiondi's palazzo.'

I heard the sharp intake of breath, though my eyes were being soothed by Grazia's attentions.

'Who is this young woman?' asked Gianbattista. 'Is it safe to speak in front of her?'

'I work for Ser Visdomini,' said Grazia, putting a finger to my wounded mouth. 'He is a *compagnaccio*, like many of his class. But I am as republican as Gabriele is, or yourself, sir, if you are indeed a *fratesco*.'

'I am indeed,' he said and I could hear he had decided to trust her. 'Visdomini's is where you go to pose for the painter, isn't it?'

I nodded. It was still hard to speak.

'I will put word out across the city to all the *frateschi* that you are on our side,' said Gianbattista. 'You will not be set upon again.'

'I was thinking that I might be able to use the misunderstanding to my advantage,' I said as best I could.

'Yes?' said Gianbattista.

Grazia, quick to grasp the possibilities in any situation, said, 'I could tell my lord that you had been set upon for your support of the de' Medici. He need not know where you had been or how the mistake arose.'

'You would do that for us?' said Gianbattista.

'I can do it for Gabriele,' said Grazia and though I couldn't see him I knew that the *fratesco* must see how it stood with us.

And it appeared that Grazia had forgiven me my jealous outburst the last time we had been alone together. I had not been back to her room since. She was tending me so gently and had not even questioned why I had been at de' Altobiondi's palazzo. After Gianbattista had left, I launched into an account of what I had learned while hiding there.

Not one but two artists wanted to draw my battered face. First Angelo, after his day's work. And later, Leone himself came to see me. The two men got on surprisingly well. Leone had a deep respect for my brother's work and showed himself well informed and intelligent in his appreciation. Angelo was not one for flattery but he liked a fellow artist who could speak knowledgeably about techniques and themes in painting and sculpture.

'Do I mind if I draw you, Gabriele?' Leone asked at last. 'I see Ser Buonarroti has been sketching.'

'No,' I muttered. 'Will it count? Will you tell Visdomini I still posed for you?'

'Always thinking of the money,' said Leone, which was a bit harsh, but that was what I had meant. 'Don't worry. I'm sure that I will be able to make use of a battered face in a painting one day. It is really interesting the way the bruises round your eyes have so many colours too. I will make a note of them.'

So the two men drew and I think I must have nodded off again because when I was next aware of my surroundings, they had gone. Leone had left a bag of money which he said his master had sent for me. I was glad to add it to my savings but struck again by how much largesse Visdomini could afford to dispense.

My next visitor in the evening was old Lodovico. Gismondo had told him what had happened and he came to bring me soup and a little pasta. It was painful to eat but I was very hungry, in spite of not having worked all day.

'My poor boy,' said Lodovico. 'How distressed your poor mother would be if she could see you!'

And Rosalia, I thought.

'This is a wicked city,' the old man said, shaking his head. 'But my sons tell me you did nothing to provoke the attack? They say you were just set upon in the street when walking home?'

They obviously had kept the de' Medici connection from him.

'That's right, sir,' I said. 'But I'll be all right. There is nothing broken – only bruised.'

'Well, that's something, I suppose,' he said. He lowered himself into an armchair. 'Eat, boy, eat,' he said. 'I've promised the cook to see you get it all down you. My word, but those eyes of yours will be all the colours of the rainbow in a few days.'

'Thank you, sir, I will eat,' I said.

'And to think the Republic can do nothing to stop such violence,' he went on, talking to himself as much as to me. 'We should be able to make the streets safe for citizens or what's the point of having rule by elected representatives? We might as well go back to the bad old days under Piero. But don't tell anyone I said so, heh, Gabriele? Walls have ears and I must not be denounced as a traitor to the Republic. That would not be fair.'

Any more than it was fair for me to get beaten up as a de' Medici supporter, I thought. But I promised not to tell anyone.

Next day, when I felt rested, I got up and sat for a while in the courtyard garden. It was good to feel the warmth of the late September sunshine on my skin.

There was a slight commotion and Lodovico came bustling out into the courtyard looking very flustered (I could open my eyes a bit better by then).

'Come indoors into the *salone*,' he said. 'Your master is here.'

'From my *bottega*?' I asked. It seemed most unlikely.

'No, no,' said Lodovico testily. 'Your patron – Andrea Visdomini. He wants to speak to you. Get inside while I order up some decent wine from the cellar.'

When I arrived in the *salone*, Visdomini jumped to his feet and turned so pale I thought he was going to faint.

'My poor Gabriele!' he said. 'They told me it was bad but this is awful! Your beautiful face.'

'It looks worse than it is,' I said.

'Leone showed me his sketches,' he said. 'But it's so much worse seeing it in reality.'

'I'm sorry I can't come and pose for him just yet but later in the week I could still come and model for Mars's body. He doesn't have to paint the bruises.'

'Your body too!' said Visdomini, his hand to his mouth. He held a scented handkerchief, as if he was trying not to be sick.

It was quite clear to me that he knew nothing about street fights; he had never been in one or witnessed one. And he seemed such a milksop I couldn't help hoping he never did.

'Show me,' he said.

I was reluctant but he was looking at me very intensely and he was the man who gave me the money.

So it was that when Lodovico came back in with a couple of dusty bottles of wine followed by a servant with a tray of glasses, he found me with my shirt off and Visdomini looking at the array of colours around my ribs.

'Ah, Ser Lodovico,' he said easily. 'I was examining the damage to my poor model. That was a bad beating he got.'

I had the curious feeling this was not the first time he had smoothed over the discovery of himself with a half-naked young man.

'Indeed, indeed,' said Lodovico, fussing round with the bottles. 'It has come to something when a boy can't walk home from his work unmolested.'

'The time is coming,' said Visdomini, 'when Florence will again know peace in her streets.'

'Again?' said Lodovico. 'When did she last know peace like that? Not in my lifetime.'

'Well, under the de' Medici, of course,' said Visdomini stiffly. 'Only with a rich and powerful family at the helm will we know such times again.'

I was willing Lodovico not to say anything more but he pulled himself together, remembering the allegiance of his guest.

'Well, this wine is from Lorenzo's time,' he said, pouring a large glass for Visdomini and a smaller amount for me. 'We can drink to his memory.'

That we could all do. Even Angelo would have joined in that toast. But I saw Visdomini eyeing me up as I scrambled back into my shirt and I wondered if Grazia had already told him I had been set upon as a de' Medici supporter.

After another day spent idling in the sun, I was so bored that I took my hooded winter cloak and headed up to San

Marco. The *frateschi* were pleased to see me and crowded round to examine my face. It had gone from purple to yellow and I still looked a fright but the swelling was going down. Still, Simonetta gave a little cry when she saw me, which was gratifying.

Her brother and his friends were more interested in what I had heard at Altobiondi's than in the attack.

'Pope Alexander sick?' said Gianbattista. 'That is good news. With him out of the way, Cesare Borgia's plans will be held in check.'

'Not if the cardinal they want – Piccolomini – gets elected,' I said. 'He's another Borgia supporter.'

'And that's what the de' Medici Cardinal will connive for,' said Daniele. 'You can be sure he thinks his choice will help get Piero or one of his other relatives back into Florence.'

'But wait,' said Fra Paolo. 'You said you were beaten as a follower of the de' Medici?'

'Yes, because I was leaving Altobiondi's house after spying on the *compagnacci*,' I said.

'It's all right,' said Gianbattista. 'I have put word out through the brotherhood that you are one of us. I can promise it won't happen again.'

'But this is just what we have been waiting for,' said Fra Paolo.

I, for one, certainly had not.

'Now that Gabriele has been attacked as a de' Medici supporter, the *compagnacci* will accept him as one of them, even though he isn't of noble birth. We can go back to our plan of infiltrating him into Altobiondi's house as a conspirator.'

'I have already planted the idea in Ser Visdomini's head that I am of their persuasion,' I said.

Fra Paolo looked at me approvingly for the first time in our association.

'That's perfect then,' he said. 'You can spy for us from inside the movement. So much better than skulking behind curtains.'

I bit my lip and the pain stopped me from retorting that I had brought them useful information from my hidden alcove.

'But won't it be very dangerous?' said Simonetta. 'Look at him now. Won't it be much worse if the *compagnacci* discover he's a spy? Surely they will kill him?'

The men looked at her as if they had forgotten she was there.

'You're right,' said Daniele. 'We can't just assume he is willing to take this role on for us.'

'Gabriele,' said Gianbattista, 'it must be your decision. We won't think any less of you if you say you are not willing to take up this dangerous burden.'

They were all looking at me. I was a stupid, vain child, I see, looking back now. These men were my friends and I wanted them to like me. I wanted Fra Paolo to approve of me. And most of all I wanted to impress Simonetta; I wanted her to fear for my safety and care about me. I wondered if her brother had told her about my relations with Grazia.

'I'll do it,' I said.

But the moment of backslapping and cheers was rather ruined by the entry of Donato, flushed and excited.

'Have you heard what's happened?' he asked, downing a goblet of wine in almost one gulp. 'They've made Soderini a permanent gonfaloniere.'

'What?' asked Gianbattista. 'A permanent *gonfaloniere*?'

'*The* permanent *gonfaloniere*,' said Donato. 'Ruler of the city for life.'

'They can't do that!' protested his brother Giulio. 'Florence has always had a new gonfaloniere every two months.'

'Not since the de' Medici was driven out,' said Daniele.

'But a permanent one! What does that mean?' asked Giulio.

'It means that Piero Soderini is ruler for the rest of his life,' said Daniele. 'It doesn't mean he will have a long life.' He touched the dagger at his belt.

My heart sank; just when I was beginning to understand Florentine politics, here was a republican threatening to kill the head of the Republic.

And I had just volunteered to pretend to be a de' Medici supporter! It seemed to me that I would have to steer a very careful path to get through the coming months. I would either get caught up in an assassination attempt on the city's ruler or be unmasked as a *fratesco* spy in the de' Medici camp.

There was only the slimmest of chances that I would survive unscathed.

But my companions were discussing this development in great detail.

'It certainly means the end of any chance of de' Medici rule,' said Fra Paolo, rubbing his hands.

'But a permanent gonfaloniere, even if a republican, might be no better that a de' Medici tyrant,' said Daniele. 'Soderini's not a bad man but power will go to his head – it always does.'

'Perhaps we should give him a chance?' said Giulio.

'Yes, and he has a brother who was a follower of our leader,' said Donato.

'But there was another candidate closer to us,' said Fra Paolo. 'Giocchino Guasconi was a true Savonarolan.'

'You knew about this plan?' asked Gianbattista. He was clearly shocked that Fra Paolo had withheld such a piece of information.

The Dominican shrugged. 'Our leader himself said he approved of one elected ruler for life – provided he had no sons,' he said.

'Does Soderini have any sons?' I asked.

'Let us hope not,' said Daniele.

But whether he meant because they would become claimants to their father's title or because their lives would now be in danger, I did not then know.

CHAPTER TWELVE

The Mouth of Truth

My bruises faded and my ribs healed and I was soon back at work. I was Mars again in the evenings and Grazia was my Venus, in the studio and elsewhere. Angelo was making the model for his bronze David and the marble one was being a bit neglected. It was so near to completion but he still had most of a year left on his contract to finish it and the bronze commission had been sanctioned by the Operai del Duomo, so there was no problem in working on two Davids at the same time.

And now I had a new role: spy in the Medici camp.

It happened so easily I didn't have to do anything about it. The first night that I went back to pose for Leone, still with a multi-coloured face but no longer a swollen one, Visdomini made a point of coming to see me.

'I'm glad to see you looking better,' he said. 'Your eyes have not been damaged?'

'Not at all, my lord. I am quite well, thank you. It will take a while for the discoloration to go but your painter does not need to portray that.'

'No, indeed. Gabriele, will you come to see me after your supper? I have something I wish to discuss with you.'

So after my modelling session, Grazia led me, not to her own chamber, but to the master's small office. More wine was brought and he invited me to sit in a comfortable chair. I must have winced a bit as I settled down.

'You are still in pain?' he asked, full of concern.

'Only a little,' I said. 'It will pass.'

'I'm so sorry about what happened,' he said. 'But Grazia told me why they did it.'

I kept quiet, drinking my wine.

'I didn't know you were a supporter of the de' Medici,' he said. 'You must have guessed that I and my family are of the same opinion?'

I nodded, though I was agreeing only with the second half.

'Would you like to join us?' he asked. 'I mean, be a more active member of the *compagnacci*? We don't meet regularly, only as needed. Antonello de' Altobiondi is our leader so when we do gather it is usually at his palazzo, though sometimes here. You may remember that he and our companions came down to see you in Leone's studio once.'

He was gabbling a bit, as if nervous of what I might say. In all my relations with him, he had never behaved as a lord to his dependent; he always seemed to be asking me for a favour.

'I do remember, my lord,' I said. 'They were very gracious.'

I could feel a pulse beating in my neck; what he was offering was very dangerous but it was what my real friends had been hoping for.

'I would like to give you some more suitable clothes,' said Visdomini. 'I would not want you to feel awkward among the nobles.'

'But do they not know what I am and what I do?' I asked. 'I should not want to deceive them.'

It's a wonder I didn't blush, since that was exactly what I was planning to do.

'Of course,' said Visdomini. 'There is no shame in being a working man – especially when, if I may say so, you are such a magnificent example of one, but when you are in their *saloni*, amid men richly dressed, I should not want you to feel uncomfortable.'

He rang the bell and a servant brought in a bundle. I saw the colours purple and green; he wanted me to wear de' Altobiondi's livery, to be seen as one of de' Altobiondi's men. It made my gorge rise.

'I took the liberty of hoping you would say yes,' said Visdomini. 'Will you try them on?'

I knew he had seen me naked, and I had no need to strip right off to try these clothes on, so I did as he asked.

'Wonderful!' he said, walking round me to see me from all sides. 'At last I see you dressed in a manner that is in keeping with your looks.'

He stroked the purple velvet of the jerkin and patted my arm. It was clear he liked me even better as a Medici man than as a painter's model.

'Thank you, my lord,' I said. 'I will . . . do my best to merit your good opinion.'

I extricated myself and bade him goodnight.

Gandini the baker kept me up to date with what was going on in the world at large.

'You'll never guess what's happened,' he said one day in October. 'Cesare Borgia's *condottieri* all rose up in rebellion against him!'

I wondered what Gismondo would make of this – the supreme war leader overthrown by ordinary generals.

'But he had them all thrown into prison and murdered!' said the baker.

This was bloodcurdling news; the man was even more ruthless than I had guessed. He would kill all his military chiefs to show his strength and the terrible consequences of crossing him.

'He's worse than the de' Medici,' said the baker, lowering his voice.

Well, at least none of my regular contacts thought I'd be on the side of the city's old rulers.

At my first meeting with the pro-Medici plotters, I wore my purple and green velvet, which came with a very fancy hat, and I did feel rather self-conscious as I set out. If I were set on and attacked now, it would have been my own fault but I had to trust Gianbattista that all the *frateschi* in the city now knew that I was playing a double game.

It felt very peculiar to pull the bell at the palazzo on Via Tornabuoni and for the first time be admitted as de' Altobiondi's guest. On their marriage, Clarice's household had combined with her husband's and it was just my luck that, as well as her maid, Vanna, they had retained that sour-faced manservant who clearly remembered me from a year and a half ago. He saw right through my new clothes to the stonecutter beneath and looked pointedly at my hands.

I was relieved to see Visdomini there. He introduced me again to Altobiondi and for the first time to the others.

'You should have seen him after the beating he got for being one of us,' said Visdomini. 'His poor face was just a mass of bruises.'

There were sympathetic murmurs and I saw that I recognised some of the people there. Two of them were plotters I had overheard that night behind the tapestry: Arnolfo Ridolfi

130

and Alessandro Bellatesta. They were older men, who could have known Lorenzo il Magnifico.

I suddenly had an inspiration. 'How can you be sure you are not being spied on?' I asked. 'Do you check the room for listening places? What about that tapestry?'

I strode across the room and pulled the hunting-scene back. With a tiny part of my mind I almost expected to see Gabriele the stonecutter concealed there in his rough working man's clothes. I did see some old crumbs on the floor from a pastry Clarice had given me to eat but I crushed them to dust under one of the new soft leather boots Visdomini had added to his gift.

'Nothing there,' I said with satisfaction. 'But we should leave the curtain drawn back.'

The others seemed impressed and were soon looking behind other drapes and opening doors to check for eavesdroppers.

'You are quite right, Gabriele,' said Altobiondi. 'We have become lax. We must be more alert to the possibility of spies.'

I smiled with secret satisfaction. He was right to be wary, as I knew better than anyone else.

'Have you heard who's back?' said Lodovico. 'The Painter.' He said it like that, as if it had a great letter at the beginning.

And Angelo clearly knew who was meant, because his head snapped up and an expression I had never seen before crossed his face, a mixture of curiosity and distaste.

'The dandy?' he asked.

Lodovico nodded. 'Leonardo from Vinci,' he explained to me, adding in a whisper, 'Now we shall see the sparks fly.'

It was six months since I had become a Medici spy and I had been better fed than at any time since my arrival in the city. I still posed for Leone, and for Angelo when he needed me, still spent some satisfying hours with Grazia, and still managed to find time to meet the *frateschi* at San Marco.

I never had any time to myself and I did not in all that time visit Settignano. My head was too full of plots and intrigues to spare any room for my first home and my first love.

The city had been in an uproar since Soderini's permanent appointment as Gonfaloniere. My new Medici friends had been incensed by it and muttered all sorts of dire threats against him but nothing had happened. In fact, although I was privy now to both main factions in the city, the prospect of a revolution in government seemed further away than ever.

But the arrival in Florence of Leonardo caused trouble of another kind.

He came to visit Angelo in the workshop. I happened to be there, eating my lunch when the man and his companions arrived. I might have said 'retinue' since that was the air he had – a supremely important man and his courtiers. I smelt him before he arrived: a good smell, I should add, one of an expensive perfume. I had to admit it was a preferable fragrance to my brother's.

And after the perfume, the man, clad in rose-coloured velvet with a short purple cloak. At his elbow was a good-looking young man with luxuriant blonde curls and behind them a cluster of youths. What on earth would Angelo say to such an invasion of his private working space?

As it happens, he said nothing. He just roared. And descended from where he was working on the marble David, shrouded in sheets, in a shower of marble dust and colourful curses.

'Ah, I had forgotten what a bear you are!' said the man who had to be Leonardo da Vinci. 'Wait outside, boys. No, hold on.' He threw them a purse. 'Go and find some lunch. Gandini the baker on Via Larga will feed you. I'll meet you there later.'

Angelo looked as if he would like to throw the rose-coloured vision out of his workshop after his troop of boys but he restrained himself.

'How are you?' said Leonardo, looking at me till Angelo had to introduce us.

'Well enough,' he grunted. 'This is my friend and model, Gabriele.'

'Friend and model, Buonarroti?' said Leonardo. 'You sound like me. And such a handsome one. Be careful or tongues will wag.'

After the briefest of handclasps, he looked round the workshop with keen interest. His languid manner didn't deceive either of us. Here was a man as intelligent as any I had met in Florence. His dark eyes were full of life and, though he was as old as the Sangallo brothers, he was still lithe and vigorous. He walked round the workshop like a fastidious cat while Angelo stood with his arms folded, his expression revealing nothing.

'I heard you were working on that old marble block that Rossellino couldn't finish,' said the painter.

Angelo grunted.

'Oh, come on, don't be so cantankerous!' Leonardo said in a wheedling tone. 'You know I'm only curious. I thought they might give it to me, you know.'

'Ha!' said Angelo, stung at last into speech. 'Why would they give a commission for a statue to a painter?'

'Ah, dear boy, you make it sound as if I apply tints to the stucco of rich men's palaces,' said Leonardo. He hadn't dropped his lazy, teasing tone since he came in, but I could see that his eyes were still darting everywhere.

'You are working on a bronze too,' he said, looking at the model, which was nearly ready for casting. 'And I see it is also of your "friend" as David.'

He caressed the model's smooth back, stopping just short of the buttocks.

'You have caught his appearance well,' he said. 'You are right, too. I shall never be able to achieve anything like that that in the round. Though my portraiture is coming along.'

Coming along! Can you believe he said that? He was the most famous artist who had ever lived in the city – though I didn't know then that one day my brother's reputation would eclipse even his.

It served to mollify Angelo a bit, because he said, 'Each to his own mystery then, Ser Leonardo. I prefer to sculpt. Painting bores me.'

'I remember how you ran away from Ghirlandaio's *bottega*,' said Leonardo. 'Does your father still live – is he well?'

'He is in good health, though he grumbles all the time,' said Angelo. 'I am living with him in the old San Procolo house. You should pay him a visit. Gabriele can show you the way.'

He was clearly trying to get rid of both of us.

'Gabriele knows the way?' said Leonardo.

'I live there too, sir,' I said. 'It is not far from Gandini's.'

His arched eyebrows shot up into his dark and immaculately combed hair. 'You live there?' but he soon recovered his poise. 'And you know dear old Gandini? He's always asking me to paint his wife, you know.'

'Maybe you should,' said Angelo. 'I hear she's very pretty.'

'It takes more than a pretty face to interest me in painting a woman,' said Leonardo. 'But I mustn't keep you from your work any longer. I must collect my boys. And young Gabriele here can then show us to your father's house.'

I would be late back to work but it would be worth it to spend more time in the company of this man who had become a legend in the city. And I dearly wished I could stay to see how old Lodovico would greet him. There was obviously a whole history here.

Leonardo's arrival was a real feast day for the city gossips. Rumours flowed from his circle like wine from a jug. I came to believe he encouraged it. He had once been officially denounced for sodomy, old Lodovico told me.

'It was all hushed up but he left the city till the scandal died down,' he said. 'That was years ago, when Michelangelo was a baby, but he has always had a reputation for scandal.'

I could believe it. I had seen with my own eyes how Leonardo had provoked Angelo in his own workshop. And I had walked with him and his 'boys' back to Santa Croce.

First among them was the golden-haired young man. He said his name was Gianni but everyone called him 'Salai' – meaning 'little devil'. And I could soon see why. He was casting jealous looks at me all the time I was talking to his master but I wasn't afraid. I was much taller and stronger than him.

He was about halfway between Angelo and me in age and I could see he must have been a very pretty boy ten years earlier. Now his looks were fading but he still behaved like a charming if petulant youth. And Leonardo encouraged him.

But they gave me the strongest feeling that it was all just a game to them. Leonardo liked being looked at and so did Salai. They liked the way that, as they walked along a street, heads turned and whispers began rippling outward. The Painter walked through the city as if he owned it – just like one of the de' Medici family.

Even I had seen his big drawing in the church of Santissima Annunziata – the Virgin and Child with Saint Anne and Saint John. It had attracted a lot of attention and I fear had made my brother a bit jealous, even though he admired it.

'He never waits until he has finished to show his work,' he grumbled. 'Leonardo is an exhibitionist, always needing to soak up praise while he works.'

'I will kill him,' growled Angelo. 'I will personally strangle him with my own hands or stab him with my chisel.'

'What are you babbling about?' asked Lodovico.

We were sitting at dinner when Angelo stormed in late from his day at work.

'Who is going to be strangled?' asked Gismondo.

'Leonardo da Vinci,' Angelo spat.

'Sit down and eat. Have some wine,' said Lodovico. 'What has he done to annoy you now?'

'He has had me arrested!' said Angelo.

That got our attention.

'He denounced me,' said Angelo, collapsing into a chair and drinking thirstily. He waved away all food. 'I had the Devil's own job to convince them to let me go.'

I think we all shouted 'What for?' at the same time.

Then the strangest thing happened. He looked straight at me and his face just closed up. 'It doesn't matter,' he muttered, and then, 'but I will truly kill him and then they can arrest me for murder.'

'Tell me what he said,' insisted Lodovico.

'Not in front of Gabriele,' he said.

It was like being slapped in the face. I got up and left but looked at Gismondo to signal that I expected him to tell me everything later.

But it took days to get it out of him.

'Someone put an anonymous denunciation in the Mouth of Truth at the Palazzo della Signoria,' he eventually said.

'Saying what?' I demanded.

'That . . . that my brother was having . . . unnatural relations with you.'

'With me?' I asked, staggered. 'It gave my name?'

'With "Gabriele, the model", it said, according to Michelangelo,' said Gismondo.

'But that's ridiculous! That's . . . that's slander.'

'I know it and so do you but you know what they say – where you see smoke there's sure to be something roasting. Some people will believe it. Especially if my brother is prosecuted.'

'And he's sure it was Leonardo?' I asked, feeling as bruised as I had been after the beating.

'The same thing happened to Leonardo years ago and Angelo thinks he did it out of spite because it is his star on the rise now, while Leonardo's is on the wane.'

But I felt sure that whatever else he was Leonardo was not a spiteful person. Capable of envy, yes, but not of something so – petty. I remembered the way he had admired Angelo's work.

'I think I know who did this,' I said. 'And I'm going to make sure he pays for it.'

CHAPTER THIRTEEN

The Beast in the Labyrinth

A nyone could put an accusation in the Mouth of Truth. They didn't even have to sign it. So there was as much gossip as genuine discovery of crime. Neighbours' tittle-tattle about adultery or suspect business practices, like bribes, formed the majority of the denunciations.

Though common, sex between men was officially a crime in Florence and had to be investigated. And, although I hadn't known it, 'artist's model' was at the time almost synonymous with 'prostitute' of either sex.

I had posed only for Angelo and Leone; the one my milk-brother and the other, as I had swiftly found out, not interested in my nakedness except where it served his work. I felt hot to realise that I had told Angelo I would be willing to work in the city as a model for unknown painters. What had he thought I was saying? But surely he knew me better than that.

It also made me very uncomfortable to realise that anyone – like Vanna or the haughty manservant – could put a note about my relations with Clarice into the Mouth of Truth. And there would be the unfortunate complication that those accusations would be true.

But I wrenched my mind away from these worrying thoughts. I would have to cope with that if it happened. What mattered now was the false denunciation of my brother.

I was absolutely sure who had made the denunciation; it had devilry written all over it. It wasn't hard to find out where Leonardo was lodging; the difficulty would be in getting Salai on his own, and in getting to either of them before Angelo had carried out his threat. It had taken too long to persuade Gismondo to tell me what had happened.

I went to Angelo and told him I knew. He was gruff with embarrassment.

'Can I go to the magistrates and tell them that it is all lies?' I asked him.

'No, it would make it worse,' he said.

'Why?'

'Because then they would see how beautiful you are,' he said simply.

I was now more embarrassed than Angelo. I knew he didn't think of me in that way and yet he had warned me on my very first day of unwanted attentions from rich men who preferred their own sex to women. I knew that Visdomini had lustful thoughts towards me. I didn't mind that, as long as he never acted on them. And as far as I was concerned, what two men did together in private, although it wouldn't be my preference, was their own business.

'You're not really going to confront Leonardo, are you?' I asked, to cover my confusion.

'Well, I haven't yet,' he conceded, 'but he'd better watch out the next time he crosses my path. I think I convinced the Officers of the Night that it was a malicious and untrue accusation.'

'I don't think it was him,' I said.

'Who else in the city has reason to hate me? You heard what he said when he came here – he wanted the David block himself. Though he would have made an awful mess of it.'

'It might have been someone acting on his behalf – without his knowledge,' I said.

'He could never have cast that bronze horse that he tried to make for Sforza in Milan,' said Angelo, still musing on motives for Leonardo's malice towards him. 'He's just not a sculptor.'

I could see I wasn't going to convince him of the Painter's innocence but I was glad that his eruption of anger towards the older artist had subsided to a low rumble.

I couldn't get away till the next Sunday but I went to seek Leonardo out then. The door was answered by one of his acolytes – not Salai – who said his master was resting after coming back from church. He eyed me curiously as if trying to remember where he had seen me before. Then light dawned.

'Ah, you are the model for Michelangelo!' he said.

At that point, Salai came out. He had the face of a ruined angel, framed by those amazing golden curls. But I was taller than him and could see that his hair was beginning to thin on top. If he lost that distinguishing feature of his, he would look very like a devil, I thought.

'Well, look who's here,' he drawled. 'The sculptor's boy.'

'If one is still a boy at twenty,' I said. It was not my plan to rile him.

'Some of us are boys for ever,' he said and I felt a flash of sympathy for him.

He had nothing but his looks and his youth, which were both rapidly receding. He might be Leonardo's apprentice but he had none of his genius. I hoped that his master would continue to love him for the beauty he had seen in him as a boy; the man was certainly not attractive.

'Were you looking for the *maestro*?' he asked.

'It was you I hoped to talk to,' I said.

'Then let us take a walk,' he said.

We strolled through the Piazza Santa Croce, attracting plenty of attention as we walked. Salai seemed to relish this. He positively preened. I was rather amused by his vanity and wondered if he would have lorded it over me quite as much if I had been dressed in my Medici finery.

'Let's go down to the river,' he said. 'It's such a warm day maybe we will see the boys swimming.'

'A bit cold for that yet I fear,' I said but turned my steps to follow his.

'I can guess why you came,' he said abruptly.

'Really?'

'Yes. It's about the denunciation,' he said.

'It's not true, you know,' I said. 'I like girls.'

'Pity,' he said straight-faced. 'What about the sculptor?'

'His preferences are his own business,' I said. 'But let us be clear that they have nothing to do with me. You have missed the mark there.'

'I have?' He looked at me with exaggerated innocence. 'What does it have to do with me?'

'We are milk-brothers,' I said. 'I live in his father's house because he entrusted his son to my mother as a baby.'

Salai's face fell but he was soon blustering confidently again.

'My master is a bit short of money,' he said unexpectedly. 'He needs a new commission.'

'What has that to do with the sculptor?'

'Nothing. I just hope the next big commission doesn't go to him.'

It was as close as he was ever going to come to admitting his guilt.

'Michelangelo has quite enough work,' I said. 'He is not seeking more. But even if he were, this city is big enough to house two great artists, don't you agree?'

He tried his most flirtatious smile on me but it didn't reach his heavy-lidded eyes. He understood what I was saying.

After the Mouth of Truth incident, I took up Angelo's offer to teach me to sculpt. He even let me do some work on my own toenails – at least the toenails of his giant David! Once I had got over my fear of chiselling one of the statue's toes off, it was enjoyable. And it was a great honour to work on the statue that was going to cause a sensation in the city.

I don't know how I knew then that it would – but I was right.

'You can help me polish the legs too,' he said, handing me a piece of very fine emery stone.

I approached the task as cautiously as if I were sandpapering my own bare legs. Angelo looked on approvingly.

'It's good to be slow and careful at this stage. So much can go wrong.'

The idea of damaging this magnificent statue made me sweat with fear.

He laughed. 'Don't be afraid. It has to be done – all of it.'

Yet he seemed to be working more on the bronze than on the marble David.

I was musing as I worked that I had now been David (twice), Hercules, Bacchus and Mars. And now Leone was designing an ambitious new scheme for Theseus and the Minotaur. Visdomini never seemed to tire of subjects which could depict me as a muscular hero or god, preferably naked or at least wearing minimal covering.

While I was working, the younger Sangallo brother came to visit.

'Guess what,' he said. 'The Signoria are going to give Leonardo a commission!'

'Soderini will, you mean, I suppose,' said Angelo. 'What is it?'

'To paint a mural in the Palazzo,' said Sangallo. 'In the Sala del Gran Consiglio, to be precise. But it's only a rumour so far – nothing's been signed.'

I smiled to myself. I didn't know if Salai's malicious ruse had been the cause, but his master had got his commission and the fee would keep the little devil in rose-coloured stockings a while longer. But would Angelo have been given this commission if he hadn't been slandered? I wasn't to find that out yet.

It was enough for me that he wasn't troubled by Sangallo's news.

The next time I saw Gandini the baker, he was so cross he was practically foaming at the mouth.

'Have you heard the news?' he asked.

I was so used to his telling me all the gossip about Cesare Borgia and the other threats to the city that I expected some new nugget of military news but I was quite wrong.

'He's only taken another commission!' he fumed.

'Who?'

'The Painter, Leonardo from Vinci!'

'Oh, yes,' I said carelessly. 'The mural for the Palazzo.'

'Mural? What mural? No, he has agreed to paint Giocondo's wife! And haven't I been asking him for years to make my wife's portrait.'

'Giocondo? The silk merchant?'

I knew him slightly; Clarice had ordered the material for dresses from him and Buonarroto, Angelo's brother, sometimes did business with him. I seemed to recall he had married a much younger woman, after losing two earlier wives in childbirth.

'That's him,' said Gandini. 'Is my money not as good as his? People need bread more than they need silk, don't they? You try eating silk in a famine and see how it agrees with you!'

I suspected that Francesco di Bartolomeo del Giocondo might have offered Leonardo more money than the baker had and that his 'little devil' would have encouraged him to take the richer commission. With that and the possibility of the Signoria's mural, the court around the painter would be safe for quite a time. But I could see that Gandini was genuinely upset.

'I'm sorry,' I said. 'It's probably political.' It was the first thing that came into my head.

'Political?' he asked, stopped at last in his tirade.

'Yes, you know, she's probably distantly related to a de' Medici or a Tornabuoni or something,' I said, making it up as I went along. 'And Leonardo used to work for Lorenzo, just like the sculptor. Perhaps that's the reason.'

Gandini, though he was republican through and through, liked the reason, because it cast no bad reflection on him or his beautiful wife. He was so mollified he gave me a sweet pastry for free.

As I walked away from his shop, I mused on this new work of Leonardo's. I had made up the explanation to soothe a friend's hurt but maybe it was true. He had said it would take more than just beauty in a woman to make him want to paint her. What did Giocondo's wife have that Gandini's didn't?

At this time, Angelo seemed to abandon both Davids and was working on something very different – a relief in the shape of a tondo. It was a Madonna and Child, the first he had attempted since that marble he had shown me of the Virgin sitting on the stairs, nursing her baby like a common working woman.

I like to think that had been a sort of portrait of my mother, just as the face of the Virgin in the Rome Pietà had been – so he told me – a tribute to his own birth mother.

This new one was nothing like either. He was working so fast on it that you could see the figures emerging from the stone, the Madonna with her head turned to look over her right shoulder and the Child standing beside her lap, leaning on his arm and an open book. Another child was beginning to peep out from behind the Holy Mother's back and the whole had a quiet, domestic quality, unlike anything of his I had seen before.

'It's beautiful,' I said, feeling the word was inadequate. It reminded me of Clarice and our boy, Davide, whom I had not seen once since I started visiting their palazzo as a spy. He was more than a year old now and must be able to stand like that sturdy little Christ, if supported by his mother's arm.

'You like it?' Angelo asked. 'It is for Bartolommeo Pitti.'

I couldn't do more than nod.

'Is that John the Baptist peeping out from behind?' I asked when I could say more.

'Yes, but he is a minor figure in the composition,' said Angelo. 'Not like that one of Leonardo's.'

Still thinking of his rival!

'Do you see how I'm working the relief?' he asked. 'It's quite different from carving something in the round.'

I saw what he meant. He had to keep a part of the figures standing out proud from their background so that you believed in their solidity but he was not cutting away so much that there was any danger of their breaking away from the marble that held them.

It gave me the strangest feeling – as if I had moved from being a figure in the round, to one bound by his background never to be free. I suppose it was the thought of Davide that made me so pensive. I was sure in a way that I would never be free of him and his mother.

And then I noticed something even stranger; it was not the Child that had a face like mine – which would have made me think that my brother practised witchcraft and could see into my heart. It was the Virgin herself that had my features, at least she had features like a softened version of the face of the marble David and that had been based on mine.

I wondered whether to mention it. Then decided against it. It was bad enough what had happened with the Mouth of Truth, without wondering if the man I saw as my brother really did admire my appearance so much he would recreate it even without realising it. I just hoped Leonardo and his Salai would not see it and make something of it.

I posed for Leone that night, though I was so unsettled I would have made a better Minotaur than Theseus. Half man, half beast and no part of me a god.

'You can't stand still tonight, Gabriele,' said the painter. 'Do you need to go and relieve yourself?'

'No. I'm sorry. I am agitated in my mind, not my body,' I said.

'Well, the one has influence on the other,' he said, very reasonably, considering I was spoiling his work.

'Leone,' I asked, 'are you married?'

'No,' he said. 'Can't afford it. But if I continue in my lord's service, I should save enough money to marry in a year or so. There's a girl I have my eye on.'

'Me too,' I said without thinking. He looked at me oddly.

'You don't mean Grazia, I take it?'

That was not likely to make me feel any more tranquil!

'Look, why don't you sit for five minutes and tell me what's on your mind?' he said. 'You're no good to me like this.'

He sent the little apprentice away and I sat on the stool, wrapped in a cloth that was going to be transformed into Theseus's cloak and tunic.

'You know what this hero did?' Leone asked, gesturing at the canvas.

'Killed the beast in the Labyrinth,' I said.

'And afterwards?'

I shrugged. I had never thought about 'afterwards'; I never did. That was part of my problem.

'He abandoned Ariadne, who was the one who helped him kill the Minotaur,' said the painter. 'He accepted her ideas and her help . . .'

'The string?' I remembered.

'The string and everything else. Took her to an island and then left her. Sailed away without her.'

'Is Grazia posing for your Ariadne, as she did for Venus and Leda?' I asked.

'Are you planning to abandon her?' he said in return. 'I think she has given you help with your spying.'

147

'What happened to Ariadne?' I asked.

'She was rescued by Bacchus,' said Leone. 'He married her and took her to live on Mount Olympus.'

'Well, I was Bacchus too,' I said. 'So she ends up with me anyway.'

'I think all of us are part Theseus, part Bacchus,' he said.

'And part Minotaur?' I asked. 'That's what I've been thinking.'

'You are very young, Gabriele,' he said. 'Don't be too hard on yourself. We all make some mistakes as we are growing up.'

'I wonder when I shall be a grown man,' I said. 'I can't imagine I am going to get much bigger but I still need to be a lot wiser.'

He laughed but not unkindly.

'I don't think wisdom comes with height,' he said. 'But it will with a few more years. I don't think you should agonise over what can't be changed. Just try to do better in future.'

He was absolutely right. I resolved there and then to tell Grazia about Rosalia that night. What happened after that was up to her.

CHAPTER FOURTEEN

A Glimpse of the Moon

T he next time I saw Angelo, he was rubbing his hands in glee.

'A new commission!' he said. 'All twelve apostles!'

'Wonderful!' I said, since he was expecting enthusiasm. But secretly I thought, *How can he manage that, together with the two Davids and the tondo? Not to mention the statues for Siena.*

'We are going to choose the marble,' he said.

'We?'

'You're coming with me, I hope,' said Angelo. 'I've spoken to your *maestro*. The Operai will pay for me and an assistant to go to Carrara and choose twelve blocks.'

I was thrilled. I hadn't been in a quarry since I left Settignano two years before. I hadn't realised till then just how much I had been missing them.

'And even better,' said Angelo, more animated than I had seen him for ages, 'the Operai are going to build me a house and a studio in the city!'

'They must be very pleased with what you are doing here,' I said. But I was thinking, *Will Lodovico want me to stay at his house if Angelo moves out?*

'You must come and live there with me,' said Angelo. 'It's going to be on the corner of Borgo Pinti and Via della Colonna.'

It was as if he read my mind! I suppose he was thinking that it would be good for him to get away from his father and brothers and strike out on his own in the world. In spite of having lived in Rome for five years, he was still treated very much as a son of the house in his father's home. And to think he was to be given this honour just because of his great skill!

'Of course, it will take a while to build,' he said, his face falling a bit.

I suppose mine did too because I had a vision like his of us two bachelors living on the Borgo Pinti, with perhaps a middle-aged woman to look after us. We could be like a pair of hermits, keeping what hours we pleased and maybe working together in his new studio without distraction. After my last meeting with Grazia, it really appealed to me.

We didn't know then that neither of us would live in this house or that the Apostles would not be made.

'When do we go to Carrara?' I asked.

'At the beginning of next month, if you're willing,' he said.

So, on the first day of May, we set out in some style. That is to say, we travelled by cart all the way to the marble mountains of Carrara. I had never been so far from home and was in high spirits.

Grazia hadn't exactly finished with me but she had wept when I told her about Rosalia.

'So you have a *fidanzata* in the country already?' she said. 'As well as a grand lady in the city. How many others are there?'

'None,' I had promised her. 'I told you before.' But I must have looked uneasy because she pounced on me and pursued her questions.

'Are you sure?' she asked. 'No other women in Florence you have looked on with desire – or who have looked on you in that way?'

She was without mercy or pity.

'There is another woman I find attractive,' I admitted. 'But I would never do anything about it. Her brother is a friend of mine and he would be horrified if she attached herself to a humble stonecutter.'

'So – another grand lady,' Grazia said.

'And you said yourself that you thought your lady cast amorous looks at me,' I said, determined to excavate every last piece of incriminating evidence against myself so that there should be no more misunderstanding between us.

'Well, it's not your fault if women look at you with lust, I suppose,' she conceded. 'As long as you do nothing to encourage them.'

I honestly didn't think that I did but was just wise enough not to say anything about it.

'And you don't see the lady Altobiondi any more?' she asked in a small voice.

'Only sometimes in passing,' I said. 'When I go to her house, it is to spy for the *frateschi*.'

'So it is just between me and your first love?' she asked.

'Don't say it like that,' I said. 'I haven't seen Rosalia for a year and a half. I don't even know if she will wait for me.' (You see, I had grown up a little.)

'But you definitely will leave the city and go back to Settignano to marry her?'

'If she'll have me,' I said.

'But what is there about her that is better than me? Is she prettier? Younger? More . . . adept in the bedchamber?'

What can a man say when a woman asks him these things?

151

I had made a very bad fist of answering Grazia. So much so that when I left her I had more or less admitted that the only advantage Rosalia had over her was that I had met her first.

'You are quiet today,' said Angelo. 'What are you thinking?'

'I'm sorry,' I said, pulling myself together. 'I am glad to be leaving the city.'

'Is it love or politics this time?' he asked.

'Am I so transparent? Well then, love I suppose. There is nothing much happening on the political front – at least not to me.'

'And all too much happening with your complicated romantic life?' he guessed.

'I don't see how I can follow your advice when women keep throwing themselves at me,' I grumbled.

He laughed. 'Some men would be very grateful to have your problems!' he said. 'It has never been an issue for me. I suppose I should be grateful to Torrigiani for that.'

'It would almost be worth getting my nose broken,' I said. 'But I'm sorry – I don't want to think about women at all. Let's concentrate on stone for the next few days.'

Stone! I was born to it, my father, my uncles, every male I knew back home worked in the quarries. My childhood and youth passed in a haze of stone dust. Even Angelo used to boast that he got his calling from imbibing chisels and mallets with my mother's milk!

Mind you, Lodovico didn't like that. He was always opposed to Angelo's work, and so was his uncle Francesco – until my brother's reputation and fortune started to grow. Because Lionardo was a friar, Angelo was in effect the oldest brother and there were already signs that his father and younger brothers saw him as their own personal bank.

The love of stone was something he had in common with me and my family that his birth family could not understand. We both hated feeling anything sticky or greasy on our hands but the dry certainty of stone was what we were used to and never minded, no matter how dredged with white powder we were. There was something clean about it.

Those who work with stone must be strong and prepared to hard work; cutting marble out of a mountainside is no occupation for a weakling. And then it all has to be squared and transported before it can be turned into whatever its ultimate fate is. Statues are only a part of it – the high pinnacle of destiny for a block of marble. It might end up as table-tops or bathtubs or the facing for pillars. Some of it is used for grand schemes like the cathedral in Florence, other bits end up as marble chips in mosaics or some kinds of floor, while even the dust is valued and used, mixed with glue and lime to make a kind of artificial stone that was becoming popular as a cheap alternative to real marble.

I marvelled at how the earth seemed to have an inexhaustible supply of stone for us. The quarries at Carrara had been worked since the time of the Romans and were famous for the whiteness and purity of their marble. The ones at Settignano were almost as old – certainly for hundreds of years men like me had crawled over the face of the mountains hacking stone out and carting it miles away.

It was a dangerous craft too. I'd seen men fall to their deaths and others crushed by blocks of stone. Some had lost fingers but kept working when they had recovered. There were not many other ways of earning a living in my village; you either farmed or cut stone.

And families did one thing or the other; I suppose farming gets in your blood the way that marble does. I could imagine what it might be like struggling to raise food out of the ground but for me it would never match the sheer physical triumph of wresting workable stone out of a mountainside.

We took three days to reach Carrara, taking our time and staying the night in inns along the way. Angelo had been before – all the way from Rome when he was commissioned to carve the Pietà. How I wish I could have seen it!

That old block that was now David – or me – came originally from the same quarries. But Angelo was as excited as I was when our cart neared Carrara. As we wound slowly up the hillside, I spotted something I had never seen before or expected ever to see – the sea! I jumped up and nearly tipped the cart over.

'When our business is done, we will go down to the shore,' said Angelo. 'Every man should see the sea at least once in his life.'

And then we saw them. Angelo was watching me, his lips curled in a rare smile; he had known how it would strike me.

'They call this place "Luna" – the moon – because of the vivid whiteness of the marble it produces,' he said.

Even I, with all my experience of cutting stone, had never seen anything quite like these mountains.

We went to lodgings Angelo had taken in the town, in a place where he had stayed before. It was in a road behind the cathedral but there was no time to explore it; Angelo had us leave at dawn the next day for the quarries. The cart took us up some very dangerous tracks in the mountainside and then we got to a point where wheels would not take us and we had to walk the last bit.

It was no problem for either of us to climb the white mountain following the newly risen sun. The day was fresh and the sky an intense blue above the white of the cliffside. I hadn't felt this full of vitality since the day I had walked out of the city up to Fiesole in the sweltering heat of the summer before.

We stopped for a short rest and I took deep breaths of the good clean air.

'This is good for you,' said Angelo. 'It will clear your head.'

'I hope so,' I said. Suddenly, it was not just my romantic adventures that felt sordid but the whole sorry business of spying, of pretending to be what I wasn't – the deceit and lies.

And it was being back close to the stone that made me feel this way. Here was something you could rely on, something you could not disguise. If there was a flaw in the marble, it revealed itself. It wasn't like the flaws in a man, which could be covered up and only later bring ruin on everyone around him.

'You know what you said about being a sculptor's assistant?' I asked Angelo.

He grunted an assent.

'I think I'd like it – if you were the sculptor,' I said.

He clasped my hand in a rare gesture of affection.

'I wouldn't let you go to anyone else,' he said.

And so our pact was made there and then, in the best place possible, surrounded by stone hacked out of the mountains. It made it more solemnly sealed than if we had been in the presence of priests or judges. I would leave the stonecutters' *bottega* and go to work with my brother, first at the Opera del Duomo, where two images of me were already lying and later, as we both thought then, in his new studio.

We moved on and down into the heart of the quarry,

where our work lay before us. Men were already busy cutting or hauling stone.

Angelo obviously knew the quarry overseer well. They clasped arms and were soon involved in a deep conversation about the merits of different strata of marble. When they had finished, Angelo brought the man over to meet me.

'This is my assistant, Gabriele,' he said. It was quite true that he had brought me on this trip to assist him, but the title had a new meaning for me now and I stood straight and proud to bear it.

The overseer looked me up and down.

'My word, Ser Buonarotti,' he said. 'You have chosen well. Your Gabriele looks a strong lad.'

'He is,' said Angelo. 'There is an old family connection. Gabriele is from Settignano, from a stonecutting dynasty.'

We all laughed at that and I thought I could see the overseer displaying just a touch of condescension – Carrara was the king of marble quarries, as I could see with my own eyes now, and Settignano a mere courtier in comparison.

'What do you think of our mountains of the moon?' he asked.

'Like nothing I could ever have imagined,' I replied sincerely.

'Well, we have to do our best for Buonarroti the famous sculptor,' he said. 'Twelve matched blocks of the highest quality, I gather?'

'For twelve apostles,' said Angelo. 'Nothing but the best. But you have already given me marble for Our Lord and His Lady so I don't doubt you can supply me.'

'You don't want one with a flaw in it for Judas?' I said without thinking.

The overseer's mouth dropped open.

'I would never sell Ser Buonarroti a flawed block,' he said.

'Take no notice of him,' said Angelo. 'Gabriele has some fanciful ideas. I shan't be carving a Judas. I shall make a Matthias, the man who took the traitor's place.'

The man seemed mollified.

'But talking of flawed blocks,' Angelo went on, 'did you know I was working on that old slab that was quarried for Agostino?'

'The one that neither he nor Rossellino could finish?'

This was no reflection on the quarryman's work, since the block had been cut out of mountain before he was born.

'It's nearly finished now,' said Angelo. 'You must come and see it in Florence. It's a good deal closer than Rome. I'm sorry you never saw my Pietà.'

Then we got down to serious business. All the separate quarries had different names and this one was called La Tacca Bianca, the white blow, because the first workman who ever struck his mallet into the rock found a pure white strain of marble. It was from here that the marble for Angelo's Pietà had come.

'You need a road here, Matteo,' said my brother.

'Yes, how do you get the blocks out?' I asked.

'You put them on a heavy sledge made of tree trunks,' said Angelo, 'and float them down the river.'

I looked at the riverbed, at present a dry scramble of scree and boulders.

'You have to wait for the rains to come,' said Matteo.

I suppose I looked disappointed.

'You thought we would be taking the blocks back to Florence with us?' asked Angelo.

I had. Both the older men laughed.

'You know the secret to working with marble?' asked Matteo and then answered his own question. 'Patience.'

I nodded as I remembered how slowly the marble David was nearing completion after the intoxicating activity of the first few months that broke him free from the block.

They led me inside the mountain, along the sloping floor. The deposits of marble towered on either side of us, like cliffs. Or like the walls of a vast natural cathedral. Walls veined with grey, red and green where minerals had stained the rock. If you half-closed your eyes you could imagine it as a church interior with worked marble columns and floors.

The stone was cut from the roof of the quarries downwards; we could see men swarming over ladders and on wooden ledges, as sure-footed as any whose safety depended on being so. Their cries to one another echoed through the cavernous space.

'I think this is where we will find your apostles, Ser Buonarroti,' said Matteo, pointing upwards to a vivid slash of white rock that cut through the grey. 'You have to have the purest of white – the marble of the moon – for statues,' he explained to me. 'The coloured veins are beautiful and much prized for pillars or for memorial slabs but it must be purest white for statuary.'

All three of us stood gazing up at the pure vein at the top of the quarry wall. I know I was thinking about the work that lay ahead to convert sheer rock into art and I was sure that Angelo was thinking something similar. But it seemed as if Matteo was thinking of more urgent practical matters.

'Come to my shack,' he said. 'And I'll write down the measurements for the blocks you need.'

After two more days of bargaining for prices, selecting areas of stone and the actual quarrymen he wanted to work on them, my brother was ready for the return journey home. But he had not forgotten his promise.

The carter, who had been having a welcome holiday, sitting and drinking in the town square, was surprised to be asked to take the coast road. It would add another half day at least to our journey. But he was not complaining. As long as he was paid, he would do whatever we asked.

I started to shiver as we approached the shore. One more bend and then there was the most frightening sight I had ever seen. Of course, I knew what the sea looked like – I had seen it in paintings. And I knew it could be different colours like marble or glass and that it might be calm or stormy.

But I didn't know that it would smell as it did, pungent with salt, or be so noisy. Most of all I did not know – how could I? – that it would be so big. Before us stretched a whole bay, light sparkling on the water and the waves coming in, one after another, like the years of our lives.

We jumped down from the cart and walked down to the water's edge. I was entranced by the sound of the waves coming in and withdrawing over the small pebbles. The shore was dotted with clumps of seaweed in strange and marvellous shapes. When Angelo picked up one that was like a complicated arrangement of bladders and showed it to me, I smelt the salty, fishy odour of it and felt its rubbery surface.

'Do you want to go in?' Angelo asked.

'In the water?'

'Why not? It's cool and refreshing on a hot day.'

He proceeded to strip off his boots and leggings. I was full of fear. I couldn't swim and I didn't know if he could either.

Would I soon be having to rescue him from drowning? Surely that would end in the deaths of both of us?

'Don't be such a baby, Gabriele,' he said. 'The water is shallow near the edge – see!'

He waded into it, showing me how the sea reached only to his knees. I could see his white feet and legs distorted by the water.

I tore off my own shoes and hose and stepped in beside him. It was like walking in ice at first and then it seemed to warm as my feet got used to it. We splashed about like children in a bath, until Angelo said it was time to leave.

We walked back up to the cart, sand clinging to our wet legs, as we carried our shoes and stockings. The carter looked at us as if we were mad.

And then we were on the road again, heading back to the city and all its warring factions. It was the last happy day I ever remember having with my brother before my life changed out of all recognition.

CHAPTER FIFTEEN

The Best-known
Face in Florence

I came back to Florence refreshed and feeling ready to take on the world.

Angelo teased me for having thought we'd be bringing the marble for the Apostles back to the city with us; goodness knows what effect twelve such heavy blocks would have had on our cart! It would be months before the marble reached Angelo's studio. The cutting out of the blocks would take a time and then the transporting would have to wait till the river filled up. It would still mean a procession of a dozen carts to take them from the main road to Florence.

He was frustrated by the prospect of waiting so long and had already started to sketch ideas for a Saint Matthew. For once I was not his model. Matthew was a mixture of the younger Sangallo brother and Angelo's imagination. But it was to be over a year before he had the chance to carve him.

And then there came a message from the Operai that they wanted a public viewing of the marble David as soon as possible.

'You'll have to help me, Gabriele,' he said wildly, running his hands through his hair. 'I'll go to your *maestro* and get you released from your work there straight away.'

I was a bit startled but not worried; it was only what we had agreed in Carrara – just a bit sooner than I expected.

'Why do they want a public viewing so soon?' I asked. 'You had two years to make it and those aren't up yet.'

'I know. I've got two months left but they want it on display next month! They told me last year I could have a bit longer – next spring in fact, so I didn't think they would want me to show it yet. But it is nearly finished.'

These were the days when my brother took the terms of his contracts a lot more seriously than he did in later years. I've heard he often left work unfinished altogether, as was to be the fate of all those Apostles we had chosen the marble for. Only the Matthew got partly made.

But neither of us knew that then – or that it would be more than another year before David was on full public show.

'The viewing is set for the twenty-third of June,' Angelo said. 'I think the Operai want to make it as close as possible to Saint John's day.'

That was fair enough, since John the Baptist was a patron saint of the city but it didn't give us long. From that day on, Angelo and I were working all the hours of all the days to get the statue ready for viewing. It couldn't be moved, of course; it was much too big for that. The people who were coming to see it would have to invade the private studio that Angelo had constructed around the David. How he was going to hate that!

I had to tell Ser Visdomini and Leone that I would not be available for modelling until after the date set for the public viewing. They didn't protest; Leone had enough sketches to work on his painting without me and he was putting Grazia in as Ariadne. As for her, I expect she was glad to put some distance between us.

So I was living like a monk and crawling round in awkward spaces, carefully chipping and polishing, taking few breaks, constantly thirsty from the dust and not even going out in the evenings to either the *frateschi* or the *compagnacci*. I had told Altobiondi that I was having to work extra long hours. He had no idea of what went on in a *bottega*, so raised no objections. But he promised to send me word if there were any developments.

Surprisingly, I didn't really mind being so occupied all the time. It took my mind off so many things and I was proud to be the official assistant to the man I believed, with many others, to be the greatest sculptor in Italy.

One late afternoon, a week before the showing, when I had slipped out for a breath of fresh air, though there was little enough of that to be had in the city in June, I saw the rosy vision of Salai, lounging in the cathedral square. Starved of company, I raised my hand in greeting and he joined me.

'Salutations,' he said listlessly.

I wasn't used to this version of the little devil. He didn't look capable of causing any mischief today.

'What's the matter?' I asked. 'And where is Ser Leonardo?'

'Hah!' he said, animated at last. 'You may well ask! Gone to Pisa and left us all behind.'

This was unusual; Leonardo went nowhere without his little court and Salai was clearly very put out about it.

'Pisa? What is he doing there?'

'Moving the river, apparently,' grumbled Salai but then looked guilty. 'Forget I said that. It's a military secret. Soderini has sent him there to investigate moving the Arno.'

This seemed beyond fantastic to me but I knew that his master had skills as an engineer as well as a painter. He had advised Lodovico Sforza in Milan on his defences against the

French, for all the good it had done either of them. But who could move a river from its course?

Still, I did agree that Salai shouldn't be telling me; he was far too indiscreet for Leonardo to place any faith in him.

'He has gone on his own?' I asked.

'No,' said Salai, frowning, and I then understood more of his bad humour. 'He has taken some of the men he worked with on military matters in Milan. But he didn't want his "artistic assistants" with him.'

He sneered at the words. Clearly his nose was severely out of joint.

'Perhaps he thought you would be bored?' I said.

Either he liked that explanation or it was just one of his mercurial shifts of mood but Salai suddenly became more animated.

'Enough of my grumbles,' he said. 'What is happening with you?'

I told him about the public viewing and he was very interested.

'I'll come and take a look myself,' he said. 'And bring the boys. My master would like me to give him a full report when he gets back.'

It wasn't quite what I wanted to hear but if the little devil and his gang wanted to come there was nothing I could do to stop them.

The day of the viewing was a Friday and the city was preparing for a huge celebration in honour of Saint John the next day. But lots of people escaped from their workplaces to come and see the statue that the whole city now talked about as 'The Giant'.

Angelo was as nervous as I had ever seen him. Not because he had any doubts about the sculpture; he never seemed to suffer from false modesty about his work. I think it was more that he just didn't like having strangers in his work space. He'd had to open the doors of his private studio in the Opera del Duomo for the first time for nearly two years.

Two days before, the Sangallo brothers had helped Angelo and me to bring the statue to the upright position. It wasn't 'finished' in the sense that it was ready to go on display in a public place but it was certainly impressive, even half supported by scaffolding as it was – since its plinth had not yet been made.

There was also the model for the bronze David and the Pitti Tondo in the workshop. And even though the wax figure of me as David had long been melted down, the gesso model was also there, showing how the conception had changed on its way into the marble statue.

There was a sort of grand opening first, to which Gonfaloniere Soderini came in his robes of office. His brother the Bishop had just been made a cardinal and he was puffed up with self-importance.

We had rigged up a kind of viewing platform on one side of the studio – just a rough wooden stage with steps on each side so that the viewer could look at David from closer to eye level.

'Otherwise they'll just look straight up into his crotch,' Antonio da Sangallo had said.

So the Gonfaloniere had the first view of the statue that was to cause so much dissent in the city and he pronounced himself well satisfied.

'It is well done, Maestro Buonarroti,' he said graciously. 'I can't wait to see it set up and finished in its proper place.'

'Wherever that is,' muttered my brother.

I think everyone I knew in Florence came through Angelo's workshop that day – from wealthy noblemen to merchants to working people. Among the first was a little knot of *frateschi*, Gianbattista to the fore. It was his name day on the morrow so he was in holiday mood; 'seeing the Giant' was just a part of the festivities.

But he was impressed – I could tell. I had told the cell of Savonarola followers about my brother but they had been more interested in his politics than his artistic skills. Now their eyes were opened.

'It is magnificent,' said Gianbattista when he climbed down from the platform. 'It is you and yet not you – a faithful copy of the outward form but with some inner fire we haven't seen in you, at least not yet.'

I wasn't sure if this was a compliment but I was proud that he praised Angelo's work. My eye was on Simonetta, who had come to the viewing with her brother. She seemed pale and as if overwhelmed by what she saw. She didn't speak to me but passed quickly out of the door.

It was just my bad luck that the next person coming in was Grazia, with Leone. She looked at Simonetta's colourless face in passing and looked straight at me, as if I had been responsible for upsetting another young woman. It was so unfair.

But then Leone led Grazia up on to the platform and it was her turn to be impressed. I was amused to see just how disconcerted this huge representation of me with no clothes on made her. It was left to Leone to go and congratulate the sculptor, while Grazia exchanged a few words with me.

'Was that the woman you told me about? The one leaving just now?' she asked.

'What do you think of the statue?' I asked. I didn't think I had to answer her question.

'I think it's . . . it's . . . terrifying,' she admitted. 'So . . . huge and naked . . . it's almost obscene. Well, indecent anyway. How does it make you feel to see yourself on display like that?'

'I'm used to it,' I said. 'I've been either posing for Angelo or helping him with the fine details of the statue for about two years. I have to see it through others' eyes today.'

'It's a fine piece of work,' she said. 'But I can't see it as a piece of art. I see it as you. And I think a lot of other people in the city will see it that way too. You won't be an unknown person any more.'

Wolf whistles from the platform alerted me to the presence of Salai and a little gaggle of his friends. I excused myself from Grazia and mounted the steps in a hurry to stop them from causing trouble.

Salai looked me up and down appreciatively. 'Here he is, boys,' he said. 'About to be the most famous . . . face . . . in Florence!'

'Stop it,' I said, trying hard not to blush. 'You are absolutely not to make a scene here. Your master would be most annoyed to hear that you had behaved badly and shamed him in front of so many citizens and his fellow artist.'

'Really? And what about how he shamed my master in the Piazza Santa Trinita, criticising him for his work in Milan?'

'I know nothing about that,' I said truthfully. 'But Leonardo is a man of courtesy. I am sure he would not want you to let him down in your manners today.'

Salai paused for a long time, then shrugged and said loudly, 'It is a very superior piece of statuary. You must be proud of your master – as I am of mine.'

Then he led his little gang off the platform and one dangerous moment had passed.

Next came Gandini the baker and his beautiful young wife, Alessa. I really was beginning to feel self-conscious at the number of Florentine women who were gazing at such a large-scale representation of my nakedness. True, some had seen me naked in the flesh, but not Simonetta or the baker's wife! I wondered if I'd ever dare go into their shop for a pastry again.

The day was as much of an ordeal for Angelo as for me. He had to listen to a lot of praise and even some criticisms from people who knew nothing about sculpture or any other of the arts. It was my body and face on display but it was his work, his art being scrutinised and assessed.

A few of the visitors were fellow artists, like Leone, the Sangallo brothers, even the 'little barrel' Sandro Botticelli limped in on two sticks. Angelo himself helped the older man up the stairs and brought him a stool to sit on.

But most were ordinary citizens, the ones who would walk past the biggest statue in their city every day for – well, who knew how many years? They were the ones whose opinions would carry the day. Would David the Giant meet with their approval or their disdain?

Florentines took their art seriously and were not backward in expressing their views. Would they cast their flowers at David's feet or throw stones at his head?

I recognised the silk merchant Giocondo, who had also brought his wife. I looked at her with interest because this was the woman Leonardo was going to paint when he returned from his military adventure trying to shift the river Arno. The portrait that had so annoyed the baker, because he really wanted Leonardo to paint his wife.

Francesco di Bartolomeo di Zanobi del Giocondo was clearly very proud of his young wife and introduced her to Angelo, who summoned me over.

'Gabriele,' he said, 'I think you have met Ser Giocondo? And let me introduce you to his wife, Monna Lisa del Giocondo. This is my assistant and an old friend of the family, Gabriele del Lauro.'

I clasped hands with them both but it was the wife who glanced from me up to the Giant and said, 'And your model too, I think, Ser Buonarroti!'

'Quite right,' said Angelo. 'You are observant, Monna Lisa. Let me escort you up to the platform so that you may see the work more clearly.'

I followed with del Giocondo, who was a pleasant man. They both seemed to me intelligent and cultured people, at ease with each other in spite of the great difference in age between them.

'Your master has done a great thing,' del Giocondo said to me. 'Of course, I can see that this statue is in some ways based on you – its youth and strength and fine physique. But he has also made a man for all time, a man whom others will look upon in the future and see not Gabriele the Tuscan, but David the Israelite king-to-be and saviour of his people.'

'It is a great responsibility,' I said.

'More so for the sculptor,' said del Giocondo, moving forward to congratulate Angelo.

I saw him yield Monna Lisa's hand to her husband and was struck by the thought that maybe this very composed and charming young woman could have been the cause of his early disappointment in love.

But I dismissed the thought as ridiculous. Even though the accusation in the Mouth of Truth had been a vicious lie, it would not have been made if Angelo's reputation in the city had been one of a lover of women.

I had not long to think about my brother's love life for Altobiondi was leading his wife up the other side of the platform. They stopped to speak to del Giocondo, who was obviously an old acquaintance and the two women made deep curtsies to each other, as if they were of the same social degree.

The de' Altobiondi were followed by many men that I knew well from my meetings in their palazzo. Indeed I had dressed myself for this important viewing in my best quasi-Altobiondi livery of purple and green. Visdomini was among his pro-Medici friends, with his pretty wife, and I was very glad that Gianbattista and the other *frateschi* had come earlier; it would have been uncomfortable for me to have both groups in the same room at the same time.

'A fine thing, a very fine thing,' Altobiondi was saying to my brother. 'I congratulate you. People will come to Florence from far and wide to see this statue you have made.'

I was in an agony of tension. Altobiondi was behaving as if Angelo was one of his circle and indeed he must have known that the sculptor's first great patron had been Lorenzo de' Medici – everyone in Florence knew that. But everyone also knew that Angelo had left the city nearly ten years ago to escape that connection.

Visdomini was frowning and pointing out something to the other *compagnacci* about the statue. I wasn't paying much attention because of the way that Clarice and Maddalena Visdomini were both looking at it. I knew that Clarice was thinking of the pose in sketch I had given her and was comparing the naked Giant with his original. And I wondered if Maddalena was remembering the night she had surprised me in Leone's studio. My face felt hot.

'Ah,' said Altobiondi's commanding voice. 'I see what you mean, Ser Buonarroti. You have shown our young friend as

170

a defiant champion about to slay the attacker of his people. It is a republican symbol, is it not? And yet your model is no republican, I think?'

There was laughter among his friends and Angelo looked furious. Giuliano da Sangallo, who had also been a de' Medici protégé, stepped forward to smooth the situation over.

'You know well, Ser Altobiondi, how we artists must work to please our patrons,' he said, putting a restraining hand on Angelo's arm. 'The statue was commissioned by the Operai del Duomo and encouraged by the Signoria. The artist is not at liberty to change the subject or the manner of its depiction.'

In fact, this was exactly what Angelo had done, as Sangallo well knew, but Altobiondi was satisfied by the explanation.

Still, as he and his friends left, he beckoned to me.

'It is a great work of art,' he said, not bothering to lower his voice, 'but it pains me to see such a stout supporter of the de' Medici and our exiled princes posing like a republican firebrand.'

Then he and his entourage swept out.

'That's it,' said my brother, shooing out the last visitors and closing the doors. 'The show is over for today. I need a drink.'

CHAPTER SIXTEEN

White Smoke

Leonardo was back in Florence. Whether he had changed the course of the Arno or not, nobody knew. What we did know was that he had begun his portrait of del Giocondo's wife, Lisa. I even saw him working on it.

It turned out that old Lodovico was on quite friendly terms with the silk merchant and had known his wife's family, the Gherardini, when they lived in the Santa Croce district. He knew Leonardo's family too. His father, at any rate.

'Not that Piero da Vinci was too ready to acknowledge his son,' Lodovico told me. 'At least not until he became famous.'

He saw no irony in this statement.

'Piero could get no legitimate heirs till he'd been through several wives,' said Lodovico, with all the pride of a father of five sons born in wedlock. 'And young Leonardo was a by-blow from his youth. But he put him out to apprentice with di Cione, the painter, and he turned out all right.'

'Di Cione?' I asked. I had never heard the name.

'Oh, they called him Verrocchio,' explained Lodovico. Of course I knew him! He had made his own David. His nickname meant 'true eye' – a wonderful name for an artist.

'Is Piero still living?' I asked.

'What? Oh, yes. Though he's very old. Nearly eighty, I believe.'

I couldn't imagine the sophisticated dandy I had met having an old father and wondered what Piero thought of his celebrated son now. But it opened up a new world to imagine Piero da Vinci, Lodovico Buonarroti and Lisa Gherardini's family all living in Santa Croce and knowing each other at least by sight.

It had taken me a while but I was at last beginning to realise that life hadn't begun with my own birth. Anyway, two of Angelo's brothers, Buonarroto and GiovanSimone, were in the wool trade and one day they asked me if I would go round to del Giocondo's house in the Via della Stufa, with a package of samples.

I accepted willingly because I'd been intrigued by the couple when I met them at the viewing of the Giant, and I had no objection to seeing the striking Lisa again.

I was on the way to their house when I first heard someone shout out 'David!' to me in the street. It was no one I knew – a complete stranger – but the snub-nosed youth shouted and waved and grinned at me from across the street and I realised he had recognised me from the statue. I waved back and went on my way.

That was the day I found Leonardo painting Monna Lisa's portrait. When I had delivered my samples, del Giocondo asked me if I'd like to go and see the progress of the picture.

Leonardo wasn't a bit like Angelo; he positively welcomed visitors while he worked. There was already another young man in the room, playing softly on a recorder.

'Ah, Gabriele!' Leonardo greeted me, recognising me straight away.

'Forgive me if I do not rise,' said Lisa del Giocondo, smiling but not moving. 'I dare not change my position while Ser Leonardo is at work.'

'I hear that Buonarroti's statue is a – huge – success,' said Leonardo, laughing at his own joke.

'Salai told you, I suppose.'

'He was very impressed.'

'As we all were,' said del Giocondo.

'May I look at your painting?' I asked.

Leonardo made a graceful gesture that meant, 'Be my guest'.

I moved closer, feeling self-conscious and a bit intrusive. But when I saw the painting I forgot everything else. I think I might have gasped.

The portrait was not very far advanced but two things struck me straight away: the first was that it was just like the sitter. The second that it had the face of Salai.

I went back to Ser Visdomini's. He had a fine collection of paintings on classical subjects now but he was still eager for more. Theseus and Ariadne was finished but his new idea was for a painted version of *Lo Spinario*, the boy of the Roman statue, who sits peering at the thorn in his foot.

'Am I not a little old to be the boy, my lord?' I asked.

'Leone can soften your features,' said Visdomini, 'and reduce those muscles a bit.'

He took the opportunity to squeeze my upper arm.

'Anyway, I'm glad to have you back,' he said, giving me a little pinch. 'I hope to see you back in your old place at Altobiondi's too. He was shocked to see you as David, you know. We all were.'

I said nothing; merely bowed.

That night was the first I had spent with Grazia for months but it was as if neither of us could help it; we were just drawn back to each other even though we both knew our love affair wouldn't last. I no longer needed to go to her private room for secret information about the *compagnacci* now that I was freely admitted to their houses, but I went with her all the same and we fell upon each other like starving people offered a feast.

Later, as I was stroking her hair, I said, 'I'm glad we are friends again.'

'Friends!' she snorted, then smiled. 'Yes. Better to be friends than nothing.'

'We were never nothing,' I said.

The next night I went to Altobiondi's palazzo for the first time for weeks.

'Ah,' he greeted me. 'Here comes our David!'

There was a fair bit of ribbing, which I was expecting. And there were new people there since our last meeting – more aristocrats, but much younger. One of them who was smiling at me looked vaguely familiar.

'Gherardini,' he introduced himself. 'Gherardo Maffei de' Gherardini.'

'Gherardini!' I said. 'You are related to Monna Lisa del Giocondo? You were playing the recorder yesterday when I came to see her portrait.'

'Ser Leonardo likes her to stay entertained while he paints,' said the young man. 'I am her cousin.' He looked at me curiously and I could tell he was wondering why I appeared so well dressed now when I had come to the house on the Via della Stufa dressed as a working man. But he was too well bred to mention it.

Instead he introduced me to his young friends, Vincenzo, Filippo and Raffaello. It turned out that they had all been to see the statue at the public viewing so they joined in the good-natured mockery.

'That is all very well, boys,' said Altobiondi. 'But which of *you* has ever been asked to model for a hero?'

'Perhaps the day is coming when we can *be* heroes, not imitate them,' answered Vincenzo, who was a Martelli and had a warlike air.

I pricked up my ears. I was beginning to think that this bunch were all words and no action; their 'plot' to return the de' Medici didn't seem to have advanced at all since I had last been in their midst.

'Perhaps it is,' said Altobiondi. 'We have heard from Cardinal Giovanni and from Giulio. They want to know more about the loyalty of their followers in the city before they come back. After Piero's last effort . . . well.'

'What do we have to do to prove ourselves to them?' demanded Filippo. It was clear that these new recruits were hotheads, desperate to be put to the test. I thought that it would not be long before their enthusiasm boiled over into action.

It was strange to be working alongside Angelo every day now. He had finished the tondo for Bartolommeo Pitti, who had been appointed one of the Operai of the Duomo, but it was still in the workshop. But he had not finished the bronze David. He seemed to be in a kind of limbo. We still worked at refining the marble giant but Angelo seemed more interested in teaching me skills.

We worked side by side on small blocks and he tried to teach me to see what might be inside them. And, while we worked, sometimes we talked.

'Are you being careful?' he asked me suddenly one day in August.

'In what way?' I answered cautiously, not sure if we were talking about Grazia or something else.

'Those are dangerous friends you are seeing now,' he said.

But I still didn't know if he meant the *frateschi* or the *compagnacci*.

'Which ones?' I asked.

'The fancily dressed ones,' he said. 'The ones with the long names and high pedigrees. The ones who didn't like your posing for a symbol of the Republic.'

'Altobiondi and his friends,' I said.

'And Visdomini,' Angelo said.

'He is one of the friends,' I agreed.

'But *why* are you friends with them?' he asked. 'I would have thought they would repel you.'

'They do,' I said. 'You would find no new Lorenzo among them. I am there in their midst only as a spy.'

He sat back on his heels. 'I thought so. That's why I said you should be careful. It is a dangerous game you are playing. In fact, it isn't a game at all, although you seem to think it is.'

'What makes you say so?'

'You dress up in their fancy silks and velvets and plumed hats and doubtless drink their wine and eat their rich food. But if they find out you are really a republican, you will find that those daggers they carry at their belts are not worn as ornaments.'

'I *am* careful,' I said. 'Really. I don't care about the life they lead. I just want the *frateschi* to be ready when they try to let another de' Medici into the city.'

Angelo looked at me in some horror. 'Another de' Medici?'

'Yes. If not Piero then the Cardinal or his cousin.'

'You forget – I know these people. At least I knew them. You had better be very sure that the *frateschi* will win before you are identified as a traitor.'

'Guess what!' said Gismondo. 'The Pope has died!'

After last year, when the rumours had us all expecting it, it came as a surprise.

'So Cesare Borgia has lost the protection of his papa?' I said.

'Who was also the Papa of us all,' said Gismondo. He seemed very cheerful about it. 'But everyone expects the new Pope to be Cardinal Piccolomini and he is favourable to Cesare too.'

I remembered that I had heard that at Altobiondi's.

'He has been levying troops in Rome, you know,' said Gismondo.

'The Cardinal?'

'No, idiot, Cesare Borgia! He has given them a livery of red and yellow with 'CESARE' lettered back and front.'

'His own private army?'

'He will be invincible,' said Gismondo. 'He was supposed to be going to take his men to fight for the King of France in Naples but then his father got sick.'

'What did he die of?' I asked.

Gismondo shrugged. 'A fever. Rome is full of the pestilence this summer.'

'So he wasn't poisoned?' I asked. One never knew with the people around the Borgias. It was rumoured that at least one cardinal had been poisoned by Cesare.

'No, it seems it really was a fever. Cesare had it too.'

'Why didn't he die as well?' I asked.

'Well, he's much younger, of course,' said Gismondo. 'But I heard he had himself put into a jar of ice-cold water up to the neck to bring the fever down.'

'And it worked?'

'It worked,' he said, 'but all Cesare's skin sloughed off like a snake's.'

I thought about this newborn pink hero with his fresh skin hearing that his father and protector had died. It made him seem vulnerable for the first time.

'It's the bad air in Rome,' said Gismondo. 'It seems Cardinal Soderini had the fever too but he is expected to recover. But they say the Pope never once asked to see his children when he was dying.'

I wondered if Cesare Borgia knew that; truly his father had abandoned him at the last and thought only of his own end.

'There are all kinds of rumours flying around that the Devil himself came to collect Pope Alexander, so great were his sins in this life,' said Gismondo.

'There are always wild rumours when a Pope dies, I suppose,' I said.

'But they say he was in the room, in the shape of a baboon, and flew out of the window with Alexander's soul.'

I marvelled at the man's credulity.

'Do you believe that?' I asked.

'Well, no, probably not,' he said. 'But there are other stories that both Alexander and Cesare really were poisoned – by wine they had put the deadly powder in themselves, to poison a cardinal. Then there was a mix-up about the jugs.'

'Well, there have been so many stories about Borgia poison, it's hardly surprising. Still, if Cardinal Soderini is also ill with fever – they can't all have been poisoned.'

'True,' said Gismondo. 'And some of the rumours really are incredible. Some people are saying it wasn't a jar of water that Cesare had himself plunged into but the body of a freshly slain bull. I ask you!'

'That's because his family symbol is a bull, surely? That's how legends begin.'

It was a few weeks later that we heard we had a new Pope – Pius the Third, who had been Cardinal Piccolomini. So the de' Medici had been right and Cesare Borgia's rise would continue. But gradually further rumours filtered through – that Cesare was a man ruined in body and strength and might never live to see another victory.

And the Pope was over eighty years old! I couldn't imagine then that such an ancient being could even walk and talk, let alone be the most powerful man in the Church and in the country. I'm older now than Pope Pius was then and I suppose all the young bloods think of me as a doddery old fool teetering on the edge of the grave.

But about Pope Pius, they would have been right. Hardly had we heard of his election in the city, before new messages came to say that he too had died; he had been Pope for less than a month. Poor man! He never got more than four of his fifteen statues from my wayward brother.

'Now they will elect della Rovere – you mark my words,' said Gandini the baker. 'It was a close thing last time but they need a strong man on Saint Peter's Chair in Rome and Piccolomini was never going to be that.'

I had got over my shyness about buying pastries from Gandini's after his wife had seen the Giant in his nakedness

180

at the public viewing. But ever after the viewing I was known just as 'David' at the baker's. It was getting late into October now and I could breathe again now the days were cooler but I craved crumbly *pasticcerie* still warm from his oven.

Angelo was not particularly interested in the news when I bore it to him along with one of Gandini's pastries. He had news of his own.

'Da Vinci has got that commission he was boasting of,' he said, eating his pastry in three bites, too fast to taste it.

'Monna Lisa's portrait?'

'No, the fresco in the Palazzo della Signoria.'

'Oh.' I didn't really know what to say to that. And I didn't see why Angelo should be so agitated about it.

'I'd wager he won't complete it,' said the sculptor. 'He's a great one for accepting commissions he doesn't complete.'

I tried very hard not to look at the model for the bronze David that the Maréchal de Rohan was still waiting for.

'He's still painting del Giocondo's wife, I believe,' I said. Her cousin sometimes mentioned it when I saw him at Altobiondi's and in fact the portrait was beginning to be well known in the city.

'If del Giocondo ever gets that, I'll eat my boots,' said Angelo. He was thoroughly out of sorts that day.

It was not long before white smoke again billowed from the Vatican chimney to indicate the selection of a new Pope. And Gandini was right; it was della Rovere who carried the vote in conclave and took the name of Julius the Second. Neither I nor Angelo had any idea at this time of how significant this election was to prove. But Gismondo was on fire with excitement.

By the time the news reached Florence, it was clear that Julius and Cesare Borgia were already in conflict.

'The Pope said he'd give Cesare a safe conduct through Tuscany,' Gismondo told me. 'So he could recover his territories in Romagna. But then he didn't. Florence is sending an army to stop Borgia – I want my father to let me serve.'

He was unable to keep still, he was so agitated.

'Do you need his permission?' I asked. 'You are older than me.'

'You're right,' he said. 'I'll go and see if I can enlist.' And he ran off to the Palazzo della Signoria.

I wondered if Lodovico would blame me if Gismondo went rushing off to stop Cesare Borgia marching through Tuscany.

He was accepted into the force that the city quickly mustered and even Lodovico raised no objections. 'Let him get it out of his system,' he said. 'It seems this is not the most dangerous commission he could undertake.'

And he was right. Within weeks Gismondo was back, his face shining.

'Did you take Cesare then?' I asked him.

His face fell. 'He wasn't with his troops,' he said. 'The rumour is that Pope Julius won't let him leave Rome. But there was a force of seven hundred horsemen, led by del Corella and della Volpe.'

'What happened?'

'We cut them to pieces!' he said. 'Our general Gianpaolo Baglioni gave the order and it was a complete rout. They say Cesare is furious but the Pope has written to the Signoria thanking them for their help.'

That didn't seem like the act of a Christian to me, let alone the head of the Church. First to promise safe conduct and then to thank the forces that had slaughtered Borgia's army. It seemed clear that the new Pope was more of a politician than a holy man.

I had never thought much about Popes in the past but now, with the *compagnacci* dealing with Cardinal Giovanni de' Medici in Rome, I had begun to wonder if it was the same issue as with the difference between the rule of a single despot or a republic. What mattered was the man and not the office. But this was probably blasphemy.

'Cesare's followers are deserting him one by one,' said Gismondo. 'The cardinals who supported him have fled from Rome to seek the protection of the Spanish army in Naples. And Florence is demanding two hundred thousand ducats from Cesare's confiscated properties. The Borgia's ruin is assured.'

He sounded as triumphant and knowledgeable as if he had knocked Cesare off his horse himself and trampled him into the dirt.

Lodovico was very glad to have his youngest son back unscathed but from then on Gismondo was even keener to enter the army full time and showed less and less inclination to help his brothers in their cloth business.

But now I had to go and see the conspirators at Palazzo Altobiondi and find out what the news from Rome meant for them.

CHAPTER SEVENTEEN

Death of a Prince

'Well, I think it's more or less done,' said Angelo.

He was gazing at the giant replica of me in his workshop. I was surprised because I had never witnessed him working on a sculpture before and I couldn't see that it looked any different on this day from how it had any day since the public viewing six months earlier, even though I knew we had both spent time on it since then.

'How can you tell when a piece is finished?' I asked.

'You can't,' he said flatly. 'All you can tell is when you can't do any more to it. And then you need to stop because if you don't, you will spoil it.'

'Well, it's certainly magnificent,' I said. Though I felt strange saying it, in case it sounded as if I were praising my own form and face.

'And you have contributed to it with your new skills,' he said.

'Hardly,' I protested. 'Just a little bit of refining in places that no one will ever see.'

'And there'll have to be a bit more of that once we've moved it,' he said, flicking imaginary specks of marble dust from the statue's toes.

'When do you think that will be?' I asked.

'I don't know. I don't even know where it will be placed. They say there's going to be a special inquiry next month to decide.'

'You don't have any say in the matter?'

'Oh my voice will be heard,' he said. 'But indirectly – through others. I am not invited to be part of the meeting.'

'It's going to be quite a job to move it anywhere,' I said. It had suddenly struck me just what a monumental task this was going to be, even if David had been going to go on the cathedral buttress for which the original block had been ordered.

'I've been thinking about that,' he said blinking his horn-coloured eyes. 'I think the Sangallos are the men to help with that.'

Another Christmas came and went and I had not gone back to Settignano. I don't know why; it was such a short distance away. I sent a basket of Gandini's best pastries to my parents and the same carter took a pair of gloves of the softest leather for Rosalia. She sent me a fine cambric shirt, which she had embroidered with her own tiny stitches. I gave Grazia a bottle of jasmine cologne from the friars at Santa Maria Novella – she was delighted with it.

A few days before Epiphany, I walked to Altobiondi's palazzo hugging my velvet cloak tight against the cold. I wasn't wearing Rosalia's shirt. Though it was finer than anything I had owned in Settignano, it wasn't of the same quality as the linen Visdomini had given me.

The usual gaggle of young men on the street corners recognised me and greeted me as David. I was used to it by now.

As soon as I got to the Via Tornabuoni, I knew something had happened. There was an air of excitement and hushed voices; I couldn't tell if it was good news or bad. And when Altobiondi made the announcement, I still didn't know; nor, I suspected, did he.

'Some of you have already heard the news,' he said solemnly. 'Word has come from the south that Piero de' Medici is dead.'

Well, even if most people did know, there was still a shocked murmur in response.

'He was killed at the Battle of Garigliano, fighting for the French against the Spaniards.'

I had no idea where that was and only a very vague notion of what they were fighting about. But I did remember Gismondo telling me ages ago that Piero was trying to join the French king's army – Louis, I seemed to remember.

'He was drowned in the Garigliano river,' Altobiondi was continuing, 'and aged only thirty-one. He would have been thirty-two next month.'

So Piero had been really young when his father died and he became head of the de' Medici family. I reckoned he must have been no more than twenty. And I was now twenty-one!

'Let us drink to the memory of Piero di Lorenzo de' Medici,' said Altobiondi, who had ordered one of the best vintages from his cellar. 'He could not live up to the achievements of his father but they would have been hard for any man to match. Today we will remember not his failings but his strengths – his physical strength and beauty engulfed by the waters of the Garigliano. And his pure blood as a de' Medici and an Orsini on his mother's side. He was a true prince.'

We all drank deeply and called the dead man's name till 'Piero de' Medici' rang round the room. If what my brother had told me was true, poor Piero had never been so popular in his lifetime.

'And now,' said Altobiondi, 'we must talk about what this

means for our future plans. We have suffered setback after setback – Soderini's permanent election and Piero's untimely death are just two of them. We must now strengthen our ties with Cardinal Giovanni, for he is the new head of the family now that his brother has gone.'

'Did Piero not have a son?' someone asked.

'Yes, he has a boy, another Lorenzo,' said Altobiondi. 'But he is a mere child of only eleven.'

So Piero had been married and already a father when his own father died. It made me feel very immature. And then I remembered Davide, who was nearly two years old.

'The time may well come when little Lorenzino inherits his father's position in the family,' said Altobiondi, 'especially since Giovanni is a cardinal and, unlike Borgia, not so ungodly a one as to sow a crop of bastards.'

Bastards. Like Altobiondi's own 'son' if he had but known it.

'But for the time being,' he went on, 'Giovanni de' Medici together with his cousin Giulio are the men we must continue to work with to restore the family's fortunes in the city.'

'What about the other brother?' asked one of the younger men. 'There were three, weren't there? Piero, Giovanni and . . . ?'

'Giuliano,' said Altobiondi. 'He is still in Venice, as far as our information tells us. We are in contact with him too.'

I told Angelo next morning about Piero and he stopped what he was doing and made the sign of the cross.

'For a year or so,' he said, 'he was like an older brother to me. We ate at the same table, played with the dogs, went riding together – and now he's gone. Drowned, you say?'

'In the course of a battle,' I said.

'An ignoble death,' he said but whether he meant because Piero died while fighting in the French army or because Angelo regarded all death by water as demeaning, I didn't know. I wondered if he was remembering that Piero had set him to carve a man out of snow that had melted into ice-water.

'We will close the workshop today, Gabriele,' he said, 'and go to the cathedral to light candles and pray for his soul. There's bound to be a Mass said now the news has reached the city.'

That was not going to do my credibility with the *frateschi* any good but it would be useful for my disguise as a de' Medici supporter.

I put on my fine clothes again and set out with my brother to pay respects to a man I had never met and now never would.

The cathedral was packed but the atmosphere was tense. Luxuriously dressed de' Medici supporters, many of whom I knew, were flaunting black velvet cloaks and sooty plumes along with their tears and laments. Piero Soderini was there, resplendent in purple, as a halfway house of mourning. He could hardly absent himself from a service to honour a predecessor as ruler of Florence but nor could he be seen to show much genuine grief.

Gianbattista was in the middle of a bunch of *frateschi*. Perversely they had left off their usual black clothes and were dressed in a variety of gay colours I had never seen them wear before. Gianbattista was in bright scarlet. To me, in the mood I was in, brought on by Angelo's sadness, it seemed an act of tasteless triumphalism.

The *compagnacci* saw it as the lack of respect it was and hands rested on daggers all through the service. But surely there would not be outright violence in such a sacred space? I whispered as much to my brother. He looked at me oddly.

'Do you not know that Lorenzo and his brother were both stabbed in this very cathedral during High Mass?' he whispered back. 'Giuliano died and Lorenzo survived to take a terrible revenge on the Pazzi who were the assassins.'

I looked at him in horror and around me at the tense rivals listening to the words of the Mass.

'It was before you were born,' said Angelo. 'I was only a baby. Perhaps Florentines have become more civilised since then.'

But I could see he didn't believe this.

People were now going up to the altar to receive the Host. As they shuffled slowly forwards, I could see some jostling. And the *frateschi* were ostentatiously keeping their seats. They would not join in a Mass to commemorate a man they despised as an unelected tyrant; they just wanted to be there to crow over his disappointed supporters.

But Angelo and I went up. As we came down and stopped to light candles, Gianbattista hissed at me, 'You are prepared to go to some lengths to keep up your pretence as a Medicean, I see.'

I looked at him coldly, feeling the eyes of the *compagnacci* on us and threw back my cloak just enough to rest my hand on my own dagger. Yes, it was a pretence, since I was a spy for his group but during the Mass I had felt no hate for the de' Medici – just sadness at the passing of someone who had not been able to live up to his city's expectations of him.

I felt a hand on my arm; it was Angelo.

'No weapons,' he said. 'We are not Pazzi, to shed blood in God's house. Let the dead rest in peace. If you have arguments to settle, do it somewhere else. This is hallowed ground.'

Gianbattista continued to glare at both of us but the moment passed.

On the cathedral steps, Altobiondi came up to us and put his arm around my shoulder, though he had to stand on tiptoe to do it.

'Good fellow, Gabriele,' he said. 'We must get you some black clothes – Visdomini will organise it.'

'Thank you,' I said, trying not to flinch from his touch.

'I saw the way you faced down that fellow in red. I was proud of you.'

When Epiphany came and went, Christmas was truly over and I returned to work.

'I didn't tell you,' said Angelo. 'I have a new commission.'

'Another one?'

I was beginning to worry. Of all the works that had been commissioned since I came to Florence, he had completed only the Pitti Tondo and – almost – the marble David. The bronze for the French *maréchal* had not been cast; of the fifteen statues for Siena, only a handful had been made; and there were the twelve apostles whose marble blocks would be arriving soon.

'It is a Madonna and Child in marble,' said Angelo. He had a dreamy expression on his face, the way I remember him looking when he was sketching me for the Davids. I suppose it signalled the beginning of a new conception.

'For the Signoria?' I asked.

'No, this one is for Bruges,' he said. 'Two wool merchants came to see my father and one of them – Alexandre – asked for me to sculpt this piece.'

'Well, you have carved Our Lady before,' I said, wondering if this one would also be a memory of his mother or might, as the one for Pitti had, bear my face.

'I think it will be a sort of companion to the Rome Pietà,' he said. 'With the child not in her lap but standing in front of her – about to take his first steps into the world and his terrible future. It will be a vertical composition, just as the Rome one was horizontal.'

I loved to hear him talk about his work. I knew he was imagining the new statue in his mind's eye, even as he described it, and the next stage would be feverish sketching. It was a good thing the marble David was finished.

I wondered when it would be moved out of the workshop; life was going to get a bit cramped there until the house and studio on Borgo Pinti were finished, if we had to accommodate a new full-sized marble too.

'They've set the date of the inquiry for the twenty-fifth of this month,' said Angelo, as if he had read my mind. 'Then we will know where David is going and when we can get him there.'

'The Signoria will not mind that you are starting something else?' I asked.

'Not when they see the reaction to my David,' he said.

He was like that: not boastful but well aware of his powers. And though he didn't like being observed while he was working, he accepted his due when the sculptures were on public view. He was at that stage when he wanted to put the marble giant behind him and reclassify it as one of the things he had already made and could feel proud of, like the Rome Pietà. But his heart was with the new work.

I worked that day on my own small marble piece: a sleeping child. I had sketched it from memory of my nephews but given it the face of little Davide. Angelo had corrected the drawings to make a shape easier for me to carve and gave me my first block of marble, on which I had drawn the lines of the child's body.

'I made a cupid like that once,' he had said, showing me how to get the curving lines to flow to make the statue more lifelike.

I would dearly have loved to sketch my own son or at least see him but all that had stopped when I had become a false Medicean. Antonello de' Altobiondi regarded me as his friend now but I never saw Davide, who would be two next month.

I started my first tentative blows with the chisel. I knew that Clarice had become pregnant with another child that she had lost: Altobiondi had worn a black rosette for a few months at that time. And now I knew, through Grazia and the women's network, that she was about to have another. Davide would have a little sister or brother in time for his birthday. I hoped it would be another boy for him to grow up with and that it would look just like his father so that Altobiondi would transfer his affections to the new child and not caress my son so much, but I knew that was wicked of me.

The first time I went back to the *frateschi* after Piero's Mass in the cathedral, Gianbattista came up and shook my hand.

'I am sorry for what I said,' he began. 'I realise that you were doing what you had to, to deceive the pro-Mediceans. Daniele tells me that I was mistaken not to trust you.'

I bowed stiffly. I didn't have to tell him that I had found all his behaviour objectionable, especially his scarlet clothes at what had been almost like a funeral.

'Say that you forgive me and we can be friends again,' he said.

'We have never stopped being friends as far as I am concerned,' I said.

'Good,' he said. 'Simonetta would never forgive me if I drove you away from our house.'

I hid my surprise; the lovely Simonetta had spoken to her brother about me?

'But tell us what the *compagnacci* are saying about Piero's death,' he went on. 'They must be putting their faith in the family members in Rome now.'

'Yes,' I said. 'They were already in contact with the Cardinal and Giulio. And I think in a strange way the death of Piero frees them to deal with his brother and cousin. They know how unpopular Piero was in the city and can make a fresh start with their new candidates for ruler.'

'The Cardinal will never be ruler in Florence,' said Daniele. 'Not now we have a permanent gonfaloniere. The Republic wouldn't stand for it.'

'You and I know that,' I said, 'but the Medicean party will never believe it. Not until all the family are in their graves.'

'Maybe we should make that the case,' said Daniele.

He had always seemed the most bloodthirsty among us but I couldn't believe he meant that.

'Piero left a young son and daughter,' I said quietly.

'Sometimes the only way to secure peace is to get rid of the causes of war,' he said.

I didn't want to think of two little children as a 'cause of war'. And it still left the Cardinal, his brother in Venice, his cousin Giulio and a whole other second branch of the family descended from Lorenzo's great-uncle, for whom he was named. (I had become a bit of an expert on the de' Medici family tree through my connection with de' Altobiondi.)

'Well, we don't have to think about assassinating the whole family,' said Gianbattista. 'It will be sufficient to stop any plot to bring the Cardinal or any other de' Medici back into the city. And Gabriele's our man for that. This time we'll know well in advance and our men will be in place. No one is ever going to open a gate to that family again.'

At that moment I just wished that someone would and that the coming battle would be over. I was tired of waiting for it to happen and weary of my life as a spy. But until that moment I had never wondered what would happen to me afterwards. For the first time, I realised that the danger I was in now would be much worse when my disguise was revealed – whether the de' Medici won or not.

CHAPTER EIGHTEEN

The City Decides

T he flower of Florentine artists was assembled in the Opera del Duomo – and a fair few weeds in my opinion. As Angelo had told me, he wasn't invited to be part of this grand *practica* to decide where his statue would be placed in the city and, of course, I couldn't be expected to be one of the people who decided its location, as a lowly artist's model, even though it was my face and figure that would soon be displayed for every citizen to see.

But we were not without friends to be part of the discussion. The Sangallo brothers were there and Angelo's old friend the painter, Francesco Granacci, and since it was a public hearing we could be present in the chamber. Very little work was done in the workshop coming up to that chilly grey day, as the fate of the statue which had been part of our lives for two and a half years was to be decided.

'And why should da Vinci have any say in the matter?' Angelo fretted, unnecessarily polishing David's toes for the umpteenth time. 'Or Ghirlandaio's brother for that matter?'

It was true that both Leonardo da Vinci and Davide Ghirlandaio, the brother of Angelo's first master, had been invited to take part in the deliberations.

January 25th, a whole month after Christmas Day, dawned at last and Angelo was up even earlier than usual. There was time for no more than a quick splash under the water pump and for me a crust of bread grabbed from the kitchen. But I knew we would be much too early and made my brother stop at Gandini's, where I got a much tastier pastry.

I tucked another in reserve inside my finest Medicean jerkin of black velvet.

'How can you think of food on a day like this?' demanded Angelo, looking at me with distaste.

'Because I know I will be hungry if I don't,' I said.

He barked with laughter. 'You do me good, Gabriele,' he said. 'You remind me of my younger, better, self.'

Though I knew he had never had an appetite like mine – not for anything. He was abstemious about everything except work, for which he was a glutton.

It was strange to go to the Opera del Duomo and not into our workshop but into a large formal room where I had never been. Early as the hour was, there were some people already present, but we were in good enough time to get front row seats.

The Herald led the others in – nearly thirty of them – and, when everyone had settled down, two of the Operai read out a list of rules for making contributions to the debate.

At last the Herald – Francesco Filareti – set out what he saw as the two options. ('As if it was up to him,' whispered Angelo. 'Pompous ass.')

'As I see it,' said Francesco, 'we can put the David either where the Judith is now, outside the Palazzo della Signoria, or we can put it in the courtyard where Donatello's David stands. The backward-thrusting leg of that bronze is faulty and the new David is better but myself I favour Judith's position.'

So, either way, the statue that looked like me would usurp a bronze by Donatello. I could feel Angelo tensing when the bronze David was criticised. But the Herald had gone on to complain about the other one now, in which Judith was cutting off the head of Holofernes. I didn't know the details but it was a story from the Bible. Still, old Francesco thought it an ill-omened piece.

'It was placed there under an evil star,' he said. 'Ever since we took it from the palace of the de' Medici, that emblem of unnatural death – the man killed by the woman – has brought us ill luck. We lost Pisa after all.'

('Is it more "natural" for men to kill women then?' asked Angelo in a low voice. 'The man knows less about art than the baker Gandini!')

After a wood-carver had blethered on a bit, the painter Cosimo Rosselli got up and said he thought it should go on the steps of the cathedral! I thought Angelo would explode but then old Botticelli put in a word for the Duomo steps too – and placing Judith at the other corner. We had to take more seriously something proposed by Botticelli because he was still held in respect for his past achievements, and, although no one expected him to do much now he had painted a wonderful picture of the Nativity, which my brother had told me about.

But almost as soon as he'd mentioned the steps, he proposed the Loggia in the piazza instead!

This gave the older Sangallo brother his opportunity to jump in. He was polite about the Duomo suggestion but said he thought the Loggia would be far better, taking into account the survival of a marble statue standing exposed to the elements.

'It would be better under the central arch of the Loggia,' he said. 'It should be under cover.'

Angelo grunted with satisfaction. So this was what he wanted.

After gaining Giuliano da Sangallo's support, the Loggia option had a lot of voices in favour of it, but there was dispute about whether it should go in the central arch or closer to the Palazzo, which was what the Second Herald preferred.

And then Leonardo got up. There was a respectful hush.

'I favour the position in the Loggia,' he said. 'But with this addition. The statue itself needs an addition – some decent ornament to befit the decorum of the solemn ceremonies the Signoria holds in the Loggia.'

My face burned and I could feel Angelo seething beside me.

('He wants to have you emasculated,' he growled to me. 'Or at least covered up and rendered harmless in the eyes of simpering young girls.')

I didn't like the thought of either and I especially didn't like this suggestion coming from Leonardo! It made me feel dirty.

Then Salvestro, who was a worker in precious stones, said very sensibly that the sculptor's own opinions should be listened to. For himself he favoured the position outside the Palazzo but 'He who made it surely knows better than anyone the place best suited to the appearance and character of the figure.'

Filippino Lippi said virtually the same. I was fascinated to see him for Angelo had showed me some of his paintings. His father had been a great painter too and a monk but one who couldn't keep the vow of chastity. It seemed as if the artists in the inquiry were shifting the balance in favour of the sculptor's own views, which they knew very well were expressed in this formal setting by Sangallo.

But then Davide Ghirlandaio had to say his piece and he latched on to the idea put forward by an embroiderer. ('An embroiderer, I ask you!' said Angelo. 'Maybe he wants to make

you a pretty skirt to hide your nakedness with "decent ornament" – fool of a man.')

The foolish embroiderer had suggested taking down
Donatello's marble lion, known as the Marzocco, and putting
David in its place in front of the Palazzo. Ghirlandaio called it
'the most worthy place of all'.

('He doesn't think that for a moment,' said Angelo. 'He
just knows it isn't the place I want. The Ghirlandaio brothers
haven't forgiven me for leaving Domenico's workshop when I
was thirteen! He's just saying that to spite me.')

The meeting droned on with no one having anything new
to add. Antonio da Sangallo said, with great tact, that he would
have favoured the Palazzo position if it had not been for the
delicate nature of the marble. One of the Signoria musicians
said it would be easier to attack the statue with a stave if it
were in the Loggia and that made me very uneasy. I wasn't the
only person in the room dressed as a de' Medici supporter;
our black clothes marked us out as still in mourning for Piero
and I didn't want any of the conspirators to be given ideas
about damaging the statue. I knew that they already regarded
it as a hateful symbol of the Republic.

Piero di Cosimo, another painter, had the last word, agreeing with the Sangallos and saying again that the sculptor's
own opinion was the most important one to be consulted.

As the meeting broke up, I asked Angelo if he thought it
had gone well.

'As well as can be expected,' he grunted, 'when they consult
people who know nothing of marble or chisels. They should
have got a group of *scalpellini* like you to come from the quarry
in Settignano and give their opinion.'

'But the Sangallos did well,' I said. 'They were backing your
ideas, weren't they?'

'Yes,' he said. 'I'd like to see my David in the central arch of the Loggia, gleaming out white against the darkness.'

'And that's what most people at the meeting thought,' I said. 'Even Leonardo.'

'Leonardo!' he said. 'He wants him to wear a modesty garment!'

He seemed more annoyed by that than by anything else that had been said. And I agreed with him.

'Mark my words, Gabriele,' he said. 'Just because it seems to have been decided, that doesn't mean a thing. The real decision will be made behind closed doors. But the Sangallos did their best. Let's find them and buy them a drink.'

Next day after work I made my way to del Giocondo's house in the Via della Stufa. It was a few months since I had seen the portrait of his wife and I had a strong urge to know how it was progressing. This time I had no commission from the Buonarroti brothers; I was just curious to see the painting, which had caused quite a stir in the city already.

Giocondo himself welcomed me warmly enough and even said, 'I think you know my wife's cousin?'

The recorder-playing Gherardo was there again, entertaining Lisa as before. I had struck lucky to find Leonardo at work so late in the evening and without Salai or any other of his hangers-on.

'Welcome, Gabriele,' he said pleasantly. 'Come to see the picture of Monna Lisa?'

It was glorious. He had captured a quality in the sitter that would have been easy to overlook. Truthfully, she wasn't as lovely as Gandini the baker's wife but she had a restful presence – I can't explain it any other way – that had nothing to do with any of her features nor yet her figure.

She was past her first youth and had borne several children but was not yet quite matronly. Yet she radiated tranquillity, sitting still as one of Angelo's marbles while the painter corrected something he felt he had not got quite right about her face. She acknowledged my presence with the slightest possible widening of her eyes and intensifying of her smile. I was spellbound.

She inspired no desire in my admittedly lustful younger self – just a deep sense of peace in her presence, which had been given by her to the portrait but was now given back to her a hundred-fold by Leonardo's art for anyone who had been fortunate enough to see his depiction of her. He had enabled me to see that within her which he saw himself. Her husband would be delighted with the portrait.

'It is wonderful,' I said to the painter who had been watching, amused, while my eyes had travelled again and again from the canvas to the sitter and back again. 'I don't know how to express myself, *maestro*, in words that would mean anything to someone with your genius. But you have made me see not Monna Lisa herself, although that itself is a gift, but – how may I say it without seeming to presume? – something of the quality of womanhood itself.'

I stopped, feeling that I had made a poor job of expressing my admiration for all three – the woman, the portrait and the artist.

And in my confusion, I did feel desire – something more overwhelming than I had ever experienced before, even in the presence of Angelo's great works. I wanted to own something so beautiful for myself – though whether it was the woman or her picture I couldn't have said – to clasp this vision of the eternal in my own mortal grasp. In fact, I think that was the first time I saw myself as mortal, like other men, in the presence of something as enduring as a great work of art.

Then Gherardo made a bad note on his recorder because, I'm sure, he was so amused by my awkwardness, and the moment passed. Monna Lisa's smile turned to laughter and she looked like an ordinary woman again.

'We shall take a break,' said Leonardo and the hospitable housewife bustled off to organise some refreshment for us all.

But I had learned something that day that I never forgot – that a true artist can see the spark of the divine in each human soul and not just see it but render it in such a way that others can see it too.

Leonardo sensed my mood – he was a very sensitive man, for all that he had companions like the coarse-natured Salai – and he waited till I had recovered my composure before speaking to me. Gherardo had gone with Monna Lisa.

'You were at the *practica* with your master,' he said eventually.

I nodded. 'It will be a great day when the statue is revealed,' he said. 'I can't wait to see it in all its glory. All Florence has been speaking of it since the day of the public viewing.'

'As they have of your portrait,' I said. 'The city is blessed to have two such great works created in it at the same time.'

I no longer thought that the painting looked like Salai's face but there was still something underlying the features that suggested the beautiful young man. Was it something the painter had seen in del Giocondo's wife reminding him of that beloved young man that had made him accept the commission? Or had he superimposed the admired features on another because of his infatuation?

I remembered the Madonna with my face and felt uneasy. I would look closely at Monna Lisa when she came back to scrutinise her for any signs of a resemblance to the little devil.

'If I owned such a painting,' I said, 'I would keep it close to me till I died and even then I would hope to see it again in heaven.'

Leonardo laughed. 'You are a poet, Gabriele! Truly you have a mind as fair and open as your face. I should love to draw you.'

But then he looked thoughtful to the point of sadness. 'I am close to this painting myself. It will be hard to part with it when the time comes.'

I remembered Angelo's words then: 'If del Giocondo ever gets that, I'll eat my boots.'

But Leonardo had changed mood again and now looked at me intently.

'You are in some danger, I think.'

Was he a seer or soothsayer?

'There was a lot of talk after the *practica*,' he said. 'Not all of it very discreet. Soderini has been boasting of how the David will be seen for what it is – a symbol of the Republic – and the de' Medici supporters don't like it.'

That I knew already.

'I know you move in their circles,' he said. 'And are for the moment their blue-eyed boy. But let them once guess that you are not what you seem and you will see that they will take their revenge – not just on you but on the statue.'

And after what had passed between us in the last hour I knew that we both understood which would be the greater tragedy.

At my next meeting with the *compagnacci*, the atmosphere was charged.

'We have heard from Giovanni,' whispered Gherardo, who now seemed to consider me a friend.

'Have we?' I said, a little mockingly; it had been only a matter of weeks that this young cousin of Monna Lisa had been in the conspirators' confidence.

It was lost on him. 'The Cardinal is going to have a secret meeting with Altobiondi and Visdomini,' said Gherardo.

This was some progress at last.

'Gabriele,' said Altobiondi, coming to greet me, 'I see you have heard our news. We are to ride out and meet the new head of the de' Medici family.'

I wondered that he couldn't see how puffed up he was with pride at his connection to the great family and his closeness to a cardinal.

'I shall need a band of strong supporters to accompany me,' Altobiondi went on. 'Would you be one of them?'

'I am no soldier,' I said, wondering if I should do this thing or try to get out of it. 'That is to say I am not experienced with weapons.'

'I hope we shan't need them,' he said. 'Sharp eyes and strong muscle – that's what is required. We leave the day after tomorrow.'

So it was an order, not a request.

When I told Angelo, he was willing enough to release me from a few days' service, but worried about my safety.

'You must let your *frateschi* friends know what you are doing,' he said. 'If they find out any other way, they might suspect you have really gone over to the other side. In fact, take today off too and go and see them straight away.'

His nervousness had infected me and I set off immediately for the house near San Marco, forgetting my resolve never to call uninvited. But, luckily, Gianbattista was there and I didn't have to face Simonetta alone.

'This is a wonderful opportunity, Gabriele,' he said. 'Of course you must go. And you must get as close to the Cardinal as you can.'

'I think I am to be part of Altobiondi's bodyguard,' I said, 'so that should not be difficult.'

'Excellent,' said Daniele, who seemed to spend most of his time at Gianbattista's house. 'I think you should assassinate Cardinal de' Medici! We can make all the arrangements for you. All you'd have to do is the actual killing.'

CHAPTER NINETEEN

The Giant Walks

I had never ridden a thoroughbred horse before. You can't live in the countryside surrounded by farms and not have some experience with horses but the brown mare they gave me to ride out on as one of de' Altobiondi's band of followers was nothing like the placid great beasts I had sat astride at haymaking.

She was called Brunella and was as skittish as a flirtatious woman, seeing dangers in every pebble by the wayside and every little bird that flew across our path. I tried gently rubbing the spot between her ears and she eventually calmed down enough to walk in a straight line. But I could see she was going to cause me problems on a day when I already had enough to think about.

Kill the Cardinal! That's what the *frateschi* wanted me to do. And if I did, amidst all his supporters out at the old de' Medici hunting lodge where the meeting was to take place, what would be the outcome for me? Instant reprisal and death if I was lucky. Long slow torture to reveal the names of my fellow conspirators if I was not.

I thought of Savonarola and shuddered.

'You have a lively mount,' said Gherardo, who had been thrilled to be picked as one of the bodyguard.

Brunella had spotted a particularly menacing twig on the path and was dancing sideways away from it.

'I'm not used to riding a gentleman's horse,' I admitted. 'She is a handful.'

'Do you think we'll really be needed on this expedition?' Gherardo asked.

'No,' I said, and truthfully. Because the *frateschi* were expecting me to do their dirty work there was no likelihood of their attacking the riders, even though they knew all about our meeting with the Cardinal.

Gherardo didn't question my reasons – just nodded. I wasn't sure if he was relieved or disappointed. For all that he was a cousin of the tranquil Lisa del Giocondo, he was a hotheaded young man and I would have thought he would relish a fight.

We neared the lodge after a few hours' riding and I could see that the Cardinal was already there. He had travelled in a carriage, with two hunters being led behind. Perhaps he really did intend to hunt when the meeting was over?

It was a grand building for such a practical purpose, more like one of the villas the de' Medici had had built for themselves all around Florence and only a little smaller. Cardinal de' Medici had evidently sent a small army of servants ahead of him, because they were swarming everywhere, laying out food and drink.

I thought of the packet of white powder in my jerkin.

'Poison would be best,' Daniele had said. 'Because it could not be so easily traced to you. But if you can't get close enough to put it in Giovanni's drink, then just stab him.'

I had the dagger they had given me too, not knowing that I already had a blade in my boot – the one Angelo had given me soon after my arrival in Florence. Altobiondi had furnished me with a weapon too. There would be no shortage of means to kill the Cardinal, only the will to do it.

207

And here he was – my first de' Medici!

I was a bit disappointed. The Cardinal was fat and heavily jowled like a much older man, though he was in fact less than a year older than Angelo. And when I saw the feast laid out for us Florentines I could guess how he had become that way. He spared no expense on the luxuries of his table and set to with a will as soon as the delegation was seated, after a quite perfunctory grace.

One other thing delayed him and that was that he had a taster! So much for Daniele's poison; it was ludicrous to suppose I could administer my packet of powder to such a well-defended man. One servant stood at his right, to sample every dish of food and every goblet of wine, while another, burly and well armed, guarded his other side.

Giovanni de' Medici grew impatient with his taster, scarcely giving time to see if he had any ill effects from the food and drink before plunging into it himself. But after a long and indulgent meal, he leaned back in his chair, satisfied – at least for now.

Those of us who were there to protect the Florentines had been seated much further down the table but had still made a good meal. Now that the preliminaries were over, the Cardinal withdrew, with his bodyguard, to a private room, to talk to de' Altobiondi, Visdomini and the rest, while we younger ones took up a position outside the doors.

It was a long afternoon and we had eaten and drunk well. If there had been any attack, we would have been easily over-come but our most serious problem was boredom. I'm sure I wasn't the only one who slid to the floor and dozed.

At last the double doors were flung open and the Florentine delegation came out. We were all smartly on our feet then, looking alert and ready to do whatever was asked of us. The Cardinal passed us and then stopped, looking up at my face.

'Who is this young man?' he asked in his rather surprising deep voice.

'It is Gabriele, a loyal supporter of Your Eminence's family,' said Visdomini.

'Really?' said Giovanni, looking at me as if he too would like to draw me. 'Nice-looking boy.'

He gave me a gold coin. I was as near to him as if we were about to perform a dance. This was the moment in which, if I had wanted, I could have drawn out any of my weapons and stabbed the head of the de' Medici family to death.

But I didn't.

It wasn't fear that stayed my hand. It was just that I didn't want to kill him. It was clear that he would not be a leader like his father, that he was a worldly and self-indulgent man, who thought more of his bodily pleasures than he did of God.

But was that a reason to kill a man? I bowed my thanks for the coin, which would join my hoard under the mattress, and he had passed on out of the doorway.

Later, as the delegation was mounted up, I saw the Cardinal himself, now in hunting clothes, on his own fine grey mare. Brunella, no calmer than she had been in the morning, went mincing up to Giovanni's mount and I was too poor a horseman to guide her away.

The Cardinal laughed at my inexperience and reined in beside me. He took my chin in his pudgy hand.

'Sweet boy,' he said, as our horses nuzzled each other, giving me another assassin's gift of a chance. 'Come to me in Rome if you ever need help.'

Everyone was looking at me and I was embarrassed but Brunella saved me from bloodshed or something else by shying away. I showed all the regret I could manage in my face as she took me out of harm's way and the Cardinal laughed.

'Gabriele is a great favourite,' said Altobiondi. 'But not the world's best horseman.'

And then the parties separated, the Florentines headed for home and the Roman delegation for the chase. I hadn't wanted to kill the de' Medici myself but I wouldn't have grieved if he had been gored by a wild boar.

Back in Florence, we went with the *compagnacci* back to their houses and I handed Brunella to Altobiondi's stableman with some relief. As the horses were led away, a servant ran out from the house to give his master an urgent message. Clarice was in labour. Altobiondi rushed indoors.

He had already invited us in to dine so we hung around uncertainly, wondering whether we should leave. But a message soon came that we should all stay.

'I hope to have another son before we have finished dining,' he said, greeting us in his *salone*. 'You must all join me in drinking his and my wife's health. The child is rather early but Clarice is strong and in good hands. We shall drink to a happy outcome.'

I would have made some excuse but then he sent for little Davide. He was brought in by his nurse, bemused by suddenly arriving in the midst of so much male company. Everyone made much of him and I could see that Altobiondi was fond of the boy. When he put Davide on to his lap and told him, ruffling the boy's curls, that he would soon be a big brother, my heart lurched.

I knew it was best for Davide to have a father, and a wealthy and loving one at that, but I felt a much greater desire to plunge a dagger into Antonello de' Altobiondi's chest than I had earlier towards the Cardinal.

The little boy clambered down, his shyness gone, and toddled about the room, accepting caresses and sweetmeats from his father's friends. He came to me in turn and I wondered if he recognised me. I hadn't seen him for nearly a year. He put his arms up to me and I picked him up. Altobiondi laughed.

'You should marry and get a son yourself, Gabriele,' he said. 'Fatherhood would suit you.'

I felt a fraud in so many ways. But I let the child snuggle into me and I stroked his hair tenderly.

'They still don't know where they want to put it,' said Angelo. 'But it won't be anywhere on the Duomo. So we've got to work out how to get the thing to the Piazza della Signoria.'

He had invited the Sangallo brothers, with their engineering skills, to come and help solve the problem.

The 'thing' was the seventeen feet of heavy marble that stood in the workshop, towering over us behind its scaffolding. We all looked at it and I certainly felt daunted as to how it could possibly be moved to anywhere else. The Piazza della Signoria was only about five hundred yards away but at the moment it would have been impossible even to get the Giant out of the workshop; we'd have to break down the wall above the doors. I myself had to duck my head to get through them.

But I was no engineer.

'Take heart, Gabriele,' said Angelo. 'The block came down from the mountains in Fanti Scritti, didn't it? And was transported all the way from Carrara to Florence. All we have to do is get the carved block from here to the piazza.'

It was no longer a block that could be heaved around on slings and chains by strong men, was it? It was a statue – with all the dangers to its limbs that a real man would face, but magnified many times.

'If only we could ask him to bend down and go through the door and walk to the Signoria!' I said.

'It may be lifelike,' said Angelo, 'but I don't think we can hope for that.'

Now that the statue was virtually finished I noticed he had stopped referring to it as 'him' or 'David'. I supposed it was his way of detaching himself from the work, of moving it in his mind from something he was perfecting, to something in his past, a separate object that could and would be judged as a work of art, one to compare with Donatello's or Verrocchio's interpretation of the shepherd boy that killed Goliath.

Giuliano and Antonio da Sangallo were not thinking of art; they were taking measurements and sketching a contraption to transport the Giant those few hundred yards that I could stride in less than ten minutes.

Over the next few months I saw the wooden cage grow. David was going to travel suspended by ropes within his protective house of wood and the whole structure would be pulled by more ropes passing through winches. How many men it would take to pull it through the streets was eventually settled at forty and the Operai started searching out the strongest and fittest men in Florence to do the job.

I always thought I would be one of them, right up till the night we moved David. But things worked out differently from what I expected.

Clarice had indeed had a second son and Altobiondi was delighted. He was taken to the Baptistery two days after his birth and given the names Cipriano Francesco di Antonello di Niccolò de' Altobiondi.

Was it the birth of little Cipriano that first planted the suspicion in Antonello's mind that Davide was not his real son? The new baby was said to look very like his father, with a mop of straight black hair and strong features. While his two-year-old brother had fair curls and was already tall for his age.

In fact, the night of Cipriano's birth, when Davide had been brought out to be caressed and admired by the *compagnacci*, one of them had commented on his resemblance to me.

It was only a throwaway remark – something like 'That little boy could be your baby brother, Gabriele.' But had that been enough, followed by the birth of a son that was his exact image, to start Antonello wondering? Even though I had hoped for a boy, I now realised the dangers of comparing son with 'son'.

I don't know, but I believe that night saw the beginning of a chain of circumstances that led to the worst moments of my life.

I began to sense a coolness towards me when I went to the Altobiondi palazzo. And Gherardo was no longer as friendly towards me as he had been at del Giocondo's. He and his three friends often seemed to be whispering together and to stop if I came near.

But it was Grazia who really alerted me to the new danger I was in. The women's network had brought alarming news.

'Altobiondi has been questioning his wife about her life before they married,' Grazia told me. 'And doing his sums about Davide's arrival.'

It seemed at first as though the premature birth of Cipriano had confirmed Clarice's original story that Davide had come before his time. She was just a woman whose babies came early and Altobiondi was reassured that he was the boy's real father.

'But the new baby is so much more like him,' said Grazia, 'that no matter how much she assures him that the first boy takes after her late mother, who was tall and fair, he has begun to suspect that he was gulled.'

I was now seriously alarmed. All Antonello had to do was question the servants and he would find out that I had been a regular visitor to the house before Clarice accepted his proposal – indeed that I had even lived there for a few weeks when I first came to the city. I wouldn't put it past Vanna or the snooty manservant to betray their mistress.

So I was thoroughly uncomfortable on the Via Tornabuoni.

And hardly less so at San Marco. Daniele had been disgusted with my failure to kill the Cardinal. I could hardly think about it. I wasn't an assassin! I was a stonecutter or, at most, a stone-carver, learning a few techniques of sculpture from his master and milk-brother.

Gianbattista and the others were more understanding.

'He had a taster.' 'The horse pulled me away from the Cardinal.' 'Giovanni's bodyguard stayed too close to him.'

They accepted my excuses. But I knew I could have done it if I had been prepared to die in the attempt.

I had almost stopped going to pose for Leone too; my visits to Visdomini's were the occasional ones as Grazia's accepted follower – a below stairs existence, cut off from the aristocrats. I still saw Visdomini sometimes at Altobiondi's and he was civil –warm even – but I was uneasy.

My life had contracted to the workshop near the cathedral and the problems of transporting my colossal image to the Piazza della Signoria. The Sangallo brothers practically lived with Angelo and me in those days in the workshop. And by the month of May we were ready to move the marble statue.

On the night of the fourteenth, we had our team of forty strong men primed with wine. Angelo had told me he didn't want me to be one of them; he wanted me to help supervise the operation, with him and Giuliano and Antonio da Sangallo.

We started by breaking down the brickwork above the door of the workshop and then slowly, slowly the Giant moved out into the Piazza del Duomo.

It was midnight. The square was alight with torches and full of people watching David emerge from his prison. The workmen had to lay fourteen greased wooden planks in front of the wheeled cage, then pull the structure forwards and run back to retrieve the planks from behind and lay them in front again.

It was painstakingly slow. It reminded me of the *lizzatura* – the method whereby blocks of marble were slid down the mountainside from the quarries in the Apuan Alps. Only there they had the slope to help them move. Had the original block that David had been hewn from made its stately progress down the mountain in that way? Probably. But this finished figure gave nothing away. He stood staring sternly over his left shoulder at the crowds in the square, who seemed stunned by his presence.

I was busy running back and forth, checking the placement of the planks and did not at first notice the tensions building up around us. The men were all sweating, even though we had chosen the coolest time of day to start the movement off.

And we had travelled only about twenty yards when the attack came.

Stones hurtled through the air, landing on the workmen and me and a few falling inside the wooden cage.

There were shouts of 'Palle! Palle!' – the cry of Medici supporters for over a century. But this was one occasion on which I could not pretend to be one of them.

I saw Angelo leap awkwardly up on to the structure and slip between the bars so that he was inside with his David.

Stopping only to tell Antonio da Sangallo to summon the City Watch, I followed him, squeezing between the bars with a lot more difficulty. It was eerie inside the crate with the noise from the piazza dampened down and no one but me, my brother and the silent marble giant.

He had one arm round the statue's right leg, its massive right hand brushing the top of his head, and he was sobbing.

I thought at first it was from rage and fear for his masterpiece but then I saw that his other arm was dangling down uselessly at an angle. It was pain that caused the tears to stream down his face.

'It's broken, Gabriele,' he moaned. 'One of the stones hit me. I won't be able to finish the David now.'

CHAPTER TWENTY

A Man of Marble

My mind was working faster than it ever had before. I understood straight away that if Angelo were to be seen injured in public it would represent a great victory for the pro-Medici party. But he could not be left to suffer like that.

'Stay here,' I said, squeezing out through the bars again. 'I'll fetch help to you.'

Outside in the square there was total chaos. Men were shouting and jostling, the Watch were making their slow way through the crowds, some people were running away, others chasing them. Torches were snatched from brackets on walls and carried through the streets above heads. Whooping cries disappeared in the distance up alleys and byways.

I ran back to the workshop. It took only seconds, even though men had toiled for ages to get the statue the few feet it had travelled. There were lots of pieces of wood lying about the floor and I quickly chose two without too many splinters and dashed back to the stranded cart.

The pullers had broken off from their work to fight with the stone-throwers or at least the men they took for stone-throwers. The Watch were having trouble separating and restraining them. I dodged between them, worried in case they'd think my bits of wood were weapons.

'Quick!' I hissed at Antonio da Sangallo. 'Come in with me.'

He squeezed in more easily than I did, being a good deal slighter. Angelo was as I had left him, but his eyes were tightly closed as he grappled with the pain.

I had seen a lot of men with broken limbs in the quarry. And Angelo was lucky: his arm was broken but not crushed by a heavy weight of marble. But it was going to hurt a lot more while we set it and there was no chance of getting a surgeon to him in all that mayhem. And we needed to keep his injury secret.

Sangallo saw immediately how it was. Miraculously, he had a small flask of spirits in his jerkin and he offered it to Angelo, who gulped at it eagerly. Then I tore the bottom of my canvas shirt into strips and we gently laid his forearm on the first piece of wood. Any movement was agony for him, and it was a hard thing to do.

I was glad that Sangallo knew what he was doing. I left it to him to pull the arm straight and align the bones, while I gripped my poor brother by the shoulders. After one stifled scream, he fainted, which was a great relief to both of us. We bound the arm firmly between the two splints and, by the time he came round, it was all over and we poured more spirits down his throat.

There wasn't much left of my shirt by the time we made him a sling to carry the arm in. Then Sangallo took off his cloak and put it round Angelo's shoulders. Apart from his extreme pallor, he now looked normal and no one would see his complexion by torchlight.

'Get him home, Gabriele,' said Sangallo. 'When the madness has died down outside, Giuliano and I will continue to supervise the movement of the statue. We know what has to be done, after all.'

Angelo was too weak to protest. Getting him out through the bars was tricky, with his arm in a sling. But no one in the crowd was looking at us. Slowly, I helped him away from the noise and fighting by the cathedral and led him back to the house in Santa Croce.

It was a slow progress, with many halts. And a cold breeze was chilling my middle where the bottom of my shirt used to be.

'You and Antonio have fixed my arm,' Angelo said, his voice slurring with pain and drink. 'But who will fix my David?'

'We will worry about that in the morning,' I said. 'For now you must rest and we must keep your injury a secret.'

Next morning I left him sleeping, told the housekeeper not to disturb him and ran back to the city's centre. The statue had progressed as far as one block along the Via del Proconsolo but that was more than I had expected. The wooden crate was now surrounded by armed guards. There was no sign of the pullers, but Antonio and Giuliano were sitting on the winches eating what looked like a breakfast of Gandini's finest pastries, while David glared off into the distance.

'How is he?' asked Antonio, quickly finishing his mouthful and brushing crumbs from his jerkin.

'Asleep,' I said. 'What happened after we left?'

'It was a long time before we could get moving again,' said Giuliano. 'But the men worked well, till after dawn. We sent them home for a few hours' sleep and the promise of a bonus for risking injury.'

'Who set the guard?' I asked.

'We told the Operai they had to, or there was a risk of the Master's work being destroyed,' said Antonio.

'And you've both been here all night? You must be exhausted.'

'You don't look very fresh yourself,' said Giuliano. 'Go to the baker's and get yourself some breakfast. Then you can take over from us while we have a few hours' rest.'

I didn't need much urging. Gandini's was full of people and gossip, as it always was in the early morning. And today there was only one topic.

'They've arrested three of the vandals,' said Gandini, who was a staunch republican.

'Who?' I asked, but the answer surprised me.

'Vincenzo di Cosimo Martelli,' said the baker, counting off on his fingers. 'Filippo di Francesco de' Spini and Gherardo Maffei de' Gherardini.'

Monna Lisa's cousin and two of his friends!

'They would have flung Raffaello Panciatichi in the Stinche too,' someone added, 'but he escaped by climbing a water-pipe and running away across the rooftops.'

Raffaello was another of Gherardo's close friends so I easily believed it. These were the younger members of the Altobiondi set, who had only recently joined the *compagnacci*, but they were all from families with a long record of support for the de' Medici.

But was this just something they had cooked up together as no more than a prank? Or was it the first skirmish in a war against the marble Giant?

'And even the three who are in the Stinche will be out soon,' said Gandini. I had walked within feet of the prison on my way from Lodovico's house to the cathedral. 'Their fathers will pay their fines – that sort never serve much time behind bars.'

Gandini was right: a few hours to cool their heads and the young conspirators would be free again.

'Was anyone hurt?' asked one of the customers.

'Not seriously,' said the baker. 'There will be a few sore heads this morning, though, and the odd black eye.'

Thank goodness no one knew about the injury done to my brother.

I was soon back with the marble giant and relieved to see that the pullers were back from their break and were laying the greased planks in front of the cage again. It was a huge responsibility overseeing their labours, but the men knew me and were willing to let me direct them.

We worked all day and were nearly at the Bargello when we stopped. I set the guards to watch and let the pullers go home for a good night's sleep. The day had passed without incident but I had been anxious the whole time, wondering if there would be another attack.

By the time I got back to Lodovico's house, I was worn out and starving hungry; I hadn't stopped for any food since breakfast. But I had to go and see Angelo first of all.

He was sitting up in bed looking very pale. He had a gash on his forehead that I hadn't noticed by torchlight the night before. He held his arm stiffly across his chest.

'What has happened?' he asked, gripping my arm with his left hand. 'Tell me the statue is unharmed!'

'Unharmed and guarded day and night,' I said.

He relaxed his grasp. 'And did they come back?'

'Not today. Three of them were caught and put in the Stinche but a fourth escaped.'

'Who were they? *Arrabbiati*?'

'*Compagnacci*, rather,' I said. 'All from old families – I've met them at Altobiondi's. Just young hotheads.'

Angelo laughed, looking relaxed for the first time since the attack.

'You sound like a disapproving greybeard,' he said.

'Well, I do disapprove,' I said. 'Whatever they think of David as a republican symbol, can't they see what a great work it is?'

'What are we going to do, Gabriele?' said Angelo. 'There is still quite a lot of finishing to do on the statue and all the gilding. And the men need me there to supervise the hoist when we lift it on to the plinth – that's if it even reaches the piazza in one piece.'

'Let me get something to eat and then I'll think about it,' I said. 'You know my mind's no good when I'm hungry.'

'I'll come with you,' he said. 'I think I could eat something now I know the statue is well guarded.'

We went down to the kitchen and roused the housekeeper, who had cleared away supper hours before. Somehow she found enough bread and cheese and meat and olives to satisfy the worst of our hunger. Though her eyes widened to see Angelo's arm in a sling. He put his fingers to his lips.

'No one is to know I've been injured, Marta,' he said and he gave her a gold coin. She then found some stewed pears and cream for us.

After we had eaten and retired to his room with a couple of cups and a second bottle of wine, he looked at me quizzically.

'Well?' he asked. 'Have you had enough food and drink to get your mind working on our problem?'

'There's only one thing to do,' I said. 'I'll finish the statue for you.'

He looked horrified.

'I mean under your supervision,' I added hastily. 'It will only be what I've done before, polishing and refining. And I can do the gilding if you show me exactly what to do. No one need ever know.'

'But they'll know I'm not there,' he objected.

'You can be there,' I said. 'I've thought it all out. I'll go on supervising the move, with the Sangallos and you can come down – with a cloak to hide your arm – from time to time and make a noise about how things are to be done.'

'I can do that,' he said drily.

'Then, as soon as the statue is in place, you and I can put the word about that we are more or less living inside the wooden frame with the statue. All you have to do is poke your head over the scaffolding from time to time and no one will know it's not you working on the final stages. Except the Sangallos, and they can be relied on.'

'You are an extraordinary fellow, Gabriele,' said Angelo, after a pause. 'I think you have it. How long do you think it will take for my arm to heal?'

I shrugged. 'At least six weeks, I should think. But you will soon be able to do a few things with it. Does it still hurt?'

'Like hell,' he said cheerfully, 'but the wine is helping. And so is your idea.'

It took nearly four days to get the statue to the piazza. At midday on the 18th of May, we had it in front of the Palazzo and the crowds in the square had to be seen to be believed.

Angelo was there, a long loose cloak covering his injury, shouting orders as if he were in the best of health. In all the confusion, no one would have noticed that his right arm was useless.

The Signoria had decided that the Judith bronze had to come down and it had already been moved to the Loggia;

223

David was to be set up in front of the doorway after all. With all his other worries, Angelo no longer seemed to care much that the statue would not be in his preferred position. Now the task was to hoist the Giant up on to his plinth without breaking him.

For the next three weeks, Angelo and I carried out my plan and virtually lived with the Giant. He was at last hoisted into his final place on the eighth day of June. He was still surrounded by a wooden castle, remade from the frame he was carried in, and all you could see of him was the top of his head.

In the midst of it all, a message came from the Signoria that they wanted Angelo to paint a fresco in the same room as Leonardo's Battle of Anghiari. It was to be a study of another Florentine victory, the Battle of Cascina.

'I know why they're asking me,' he grunted. 'They want to put some ginger up Leonardo's backside. They think if he knows he has some competition he'll get on faster with his own painting.'

I couldn't see how my brother could possibly take this on in addition to all his other work but I kept silent. For the time being, we had enough to keep us busy with David.

The 'castle' was roomy enough for two men to walk around inside on the scaffolding platforms at several levels and there we ate and slept. I even emptied my brother's slop bucket; the whole enterprise was designed to keep it secret that the Medici supporters had injured the city's greatest sculptor.

His arm was mending well and, under his supervision I began to gild the sling that travelled behind the statue's back – from his left shoulder down to his massive right hand. I also had to gild the tree stump that acted as a prop to the right leg.

Not large areas, I know, but I had never done it before and worked slowly, so as not to make any mistakes.

Maybe it was cowardly, but I knew I was burying myself in the work, trying to avoid seeing anyone – Grazia, the *compagnacci* or the *frateschi*. And as I worked, I thought about going home.

But in the end Grazia came and found me.

I hadn't seen her for some time and it felt to me as if our passionate affair had nearly run its course. Not that I didn't feel affection for her – I did. But I had so much to think about and involve me lately that romance was far from my mind.

And she was an unwanted distraction now. I felt my brow knit into a frown much like the larger one on the statue behind me.

'What is it?' I asked, probably rather abruptly.

She looked hurt. 'I came to warn you,' she said. 'Your secret is discovered. Altobiondi has found drawings of you naked in his wife's chest.'

The women's network! I was glad of the warning but now I dared not go back to the Medici supporters' meetings. I had always feared that I might be revealed as a *fratesco* spy but I hadn't given enough thought to the possibility of being found to be Clarice's former lover.

I was immediately penitent about my treatment of Grazia; it must have cost her something to tell me what she knew.

'Thank you,' I said, clasping her hand. 'It was good of you to tell me. Do you know any more? How . . . how is the boy?'

'I don't know. Altobiondi is very angry with his wife and with you. I don't know how he feels about the little boy but the child is innocent. Surely he wouldn't do anything to hurt him?'

I wished I could believe that. I had seen Altobiondi when his temper was aroused. I wondered which servant had betrayed my secret. It was another unwanted complication now, when there was still so much to complete on the statue, and Angelo was injured.

There had been no further disturbance since the attack on the first night of the Giant's progress, so when the violence erupted in the square that hot night in July, I was no longer on my guard. I was thinking only of what Grazia had told me. And that was my undoing.

It was past midnight and Angelo and I were sleeping on the hard platforms. His splint had come off and his arm had mended but it was still not strong and looked as white and wrinkled as if it had been soaked in a bath for weeks. Grazia had gone, slipping away as quietly as she had come, back to the palazzo on Via dei Servi.

The guard on the statue had been relaxed and when the first small stones fell I woke up groggily wondering if it was raining!

'Devil take them!' said Angelo, struggling awake. 'Why now, after all this time?'

'Stay down,' I said. 'And wrap your cloak around your head.'

I peered out from between the wooden bars and my blood froze.

The square was full of *compagnacci*!

Not a handful of boys with stones like last time but something more like a small private army, armed with swords and daggers and muskets. If they stormed the unguarded statue, it would be the end for David and for Angelo and me.

And then a kind of miracle happened.

Another body of men entered the square from all the roads around it, surrounding the *compagnacci*. The *frateschi*! I could see several of my republican friends among them. There was a moment of complete stillness while the two sides glared at each other.

And then the battle erupted like a thunderstorm in the summer night.

I did not want to cower inside the wooden castle like a craven. I had my daggers and my fists and my blood was hot. I was tired of all the months of pretending. I would protect the statue with my life and fight shoulder to shoulder with the other republicans.

'*Palle! Palle!*' shouted the *compagnacci*, hurling themselves on their opponents.

'Marzocco, Marzocco!' roared the *frateschi* back at them, invoking the name of Florence's lion, another potent symbol of the Republic.

It was a pitched battle.

Casting a last regretful look at my image and my brother, I leapt from the scaffolding, landing in the middle of the fray.

'Marzocco!' I screamed till my throat hurt and threw myself at the nearest man in purple and green.

CHAPTER TWENTY-ONE

A Sweet Room in Hell

The first man went down without my drawing my dagger; my fists were enough. But my blood was up and I didn't really care what I did to defend the statue and the man who had made it. All those years of work and the final exhausting stages of getting it here from the workshop and up on the plinth were not going to be lost at the last minute to a mob of *compagnacci* – not if I could help it!

Looking up to check on the 'castle' I saw several pro-Mediceans climbing the wooden structure.

Roaring, I plucked them off like bits of fluff from a velvet jerkin, hurling them on to the tiles of the piazza. I had never felt such strength as coursed through me now. And then I felt a hand grip at my leg: someone had hold of it and was dragging me down from the scaffolding with a strength to match my own.

It was Antonello de' Altobiondi.

'Serpent!' he hissed, putting his hands around my neck as he forced me to my knees. 'You were a guest in my house!'

It would have been useless to tell him that my affair with his wife had been over before she married him – even if I could have spoken. When men are jealous of each other in that way, they take no notice of times and dates.

And I knew what he was feeling. Hadn't I felt the same way about him when he married Clarice?

'You needn't think your bastard will get anything more from me,' he went on, his face as purple as if he were the one being deprived of breath. 'I'm sending him to a convent to be looked after by nuns. There he can learn that the only way to keep a woman chaste is to lock her up.'

The pressure was intolerable and only the thought of Davide being wrenched away from his mother kept me from succumbing to the dark. He released his grasp just a little, enough for me to get a bit of air. He wanted me to hear more.

'As for his mother, she will go to a convent too but another one. Clarice will never see either of her sons again. Cipriano will be brought up by nurses. He shall inherit my name and my estate – not that little mongrel you got on his mother!'

This was too cruel. Not only were innocent children to be punished by being wrenched away from their mother. The mother herself, who had never swerved from her husband's bed, would lose both boys at a stroke, one of them still a baby. Not to mention her two little daughters by her first marriage. It didn't bear thinking of.

I flexed my thigh muscles and heaved with all my might, throwing Altobiondi to the ground. Air rushed into my chest, causing me to choke and cough, but I whipped my dagger out of my belt and would have finished him off on the spot.

But just then two figures hurled themselves on us.

It was the brothers Donato and Giulio. I left Altobiondi to them, not caring if he lived or died. I had something more urgent to do even than fighting Mediceans.

He had talked in the future tense, as if his sentence of exile hadn't yet been carried out on Davide and his mother, so I ran from the battle in the square, dodging blows and curses and feeling torn in two. If I found he had hurt the boy in any way, I would return to the fray and run him through the heart.

Silently I begged forgiveness of my brother for deserting him, as I ran down the Via Porta Rossa towards Via Tornabuoni. I knew that what he had made should endure longer than both our lifetimes. Knew too that if he lost his life tonight the world would be deprived of many more masterpieces.

But I couldn't help it. Flesh and blood might not endure like marble but Davide's flesh and blood was made of mine. He was my masterpiece and I had to save him first. He should not go to the grey sisters if I could stop it.

I reached the Palazzo Altobiondi out of breath and still coughing from the assault on my windpipe. I rested for a moment at the doorway and saw that the big oak door was ajar. The house was in confusion, with no servants on duty. I could hear the sound of women wailing on a higher floor.

I took the stairs two at a time and burst into Clarice's chamber. She was sobbing with a frightened Davide in her arms, Cipriano whimpering in a crib at her side. And she was surrounded by weeping women. But when she saw me she cried out.

'Gabriele! My husband knows everything.'

'I know,' I said. 'He found me in the piazza.'

'He found you and you live?' she asked, wiping her eyes on her sleeve.

'As you see. But I don't know whether he lives or not,' I said. 'I left him in the hands of two *frateschi*. I don't care whether he lives or dies. I would have finished him if my friends hadn't come along.'

I knelt by her side and tried to soothe little Davide, who was terrified by all the uproar and had no idea what was going on. I stroked his hair.

'There, there,' I said clumsily. 'Clarice, let me take him. I can take him to my parents in Settignano and they will look after him. Then you may be able to see him again.'

'Oh, take me too,' she begged. 'Don't let me be sent away.'

What could I do? I was sure my parents would welcome and look after my child but what could they do for a gentle-woman like Clarice de' Altobiondi? And what of her new baby? Or her little daughters? It was all hopeless.

She saw that in my face and began sobbing afresh. She saw that I would take my son but she would still be separated from both her boys and her girls.

I had arrived in a white-hot rage but now that feeling of power was ebbing away from me and being replaced by an overwhelming sadness. Whatever I did would lead to more sorrow, but I had to do what little I could in such a desperate situation.

Now that I was calmer, I took in more of Clarice's situation and saw that the women who had been trying to comfort her with their sympathetic tears were not all servants; some were well-dressed and obviously of her social class. I was seeing some of the women's network in action.

To my amazement, I suddenly realised that one of them was Simonetta!

Seeing that I had recognised her, she managed a damp smile. Of course, the women's network wasn't based on politi-cal allegiance; a supporter of Savonarola would put her shared womanhood before her republican views when it came to helping a sister who was pro-Medici.

But that meant that Simonetta knew about my relations with Clarice and I could have wished she had not. Still, I couldn't worry about that now. When I looked up again, she was not there. Perhaps I had imagined her?

I took Clarice's hand.

'Let your women bundle up some clothes and his favourite possessions,' I said. 'Time is short. If I'm to save Davide from the nunnery, I must take him away tonight.'

There was a sound behind me. I knew from the expression on Clarice's face what this meant but I turned round anyway.

'You are taking him nowhere!' said the figure of nightmare in the doorway.

Altobiondi was covered in blood; it streaked his face, hair and clothes. But he was on his feet and holding a sword towards me.

'I will kill him rather,' he said. 'After I have dispatched his father.'

He lunged towards me but I jumped back and as I did, someone hit him over the head with a chair. Before I could do more, Clarice had in one swift movement put the child aside, taken the dagger from my boot and fallen on her husband.

There was a horrible gurgling sound as she slit his throat.

And then an even more terrible silence in the room. I noted that it was Simonetta standing behind the body, the wrecked remains of a chair in her hands.

Altobiondi was dead. But I couldn't begin to count the ways in which we were still in danger.

Clarice sank to the floor, almost insensible, the dagger dropping from her fingers. At that moment, Davide began to scream.

The battle in the piazza raged all night before the Watch got the combatants under control. But it was a while before I heard the full story of what had happened after I left. And then the news was very bad.

Donato was dead, killed by Altobiondi, and his brother wounded. There were losses on both sides, several dead and injured, but although the *frateschi* had lost one of their best men, the *compagnacci* had lost their leader.

The story was that Altobiondi, fatally wounded in the square, had managed to stagger home to die in his wife's arms; it was considered very romantic. I believe ballads were written about Clarice's tragedy.

I didn't care about that. But all the women in the room were prepared to swear that his death had happened in this way. I, of course, had not been there.

Simonetta had seen to that, taking charge of a situation that none of the rest of us could handle. She organised servants to take Davide away and make him a drink of warm milk and honey, with nutmeg grated on the top. Others were to take Clarice and wash her hands and the dagger; her dress could remain stained.

Only when this had been done and the knife returned to me, was another servant sent to call the Watch. Meanwhile, Simonetta smuggled me out of the house.

'Where can you go?' she asked. 'They may look for you at your brother's – or at my house.'

We didn't know then how things had gone in the square. It was possible that all the houses of known faction leaders would be searched.

'But I did nothing to him,' I objected. 'He was the one who nearly throttled me.'

'Your clothes are stained with his blood,' said Simonetta. 'And someone might have seen you fighting in the square. It would be best for you to lie low for a while.'

She was right. For a moment I couldn't think where it would be safe to go but then I thought about Leone. I couldn't go to Visdomini's house, since he was another prominent *compagnaccio*, but there was no reason I shouldn't shelter with his pet painter.

Leone lived on the other side of the river. I ran quickly down to the end of the Via Tornabuoni and across the Santa Trinita bridge. I stopped halfway and leaned against the wooden parapet, overlooking the peaceful waters of the Arno. My head was throbbing.

What I had seen and done and heard that night would stay with me for ever. But somehow or other, the terrible fate in store for Clarice and her sons had been avoided. Suddenly, I was shaking in all my limbs. My throat was sore and my whole body ached. I felt like an ancient man with the ague (and, of course, now I know what that feels like!).

It took me some minutes to steady my breathing and to be capable of walking again. Only a few hundred yards behind me, the officials would be examining Altobiondi's corpse.

What could the future possibly hold for me or for any of the people who had been in Clarice's chamber that night? I couldn't think beyond getting to Leone's house. Wearily, I heaved myself off the parapet and staggered onward into the Borgo Santo Spirito. I was glad that the streets were empty and no one greeted me by calling out the name of the statue that night.

I made my way towards the bulk of the great church where my brother had once cut up dead bodies. It seemed eerily appropriate on that night of carnage.

Leone's house was in an alley near the church; I rapped on his door and was never so pleased to see anyone as when he opened it himself. He looked appalled at the sight of me – in fact, it took him a few moments to recognise me.

'Gabriele, is that you?'

'More or less,' I said. 'Can I come in?'

I almost fell through the doorway and just managed to get myself into a chair before I collapsed. Leone bolted the door and fetched some wine and a bowl of warm water.

'Do you want something to eat?' he asked, bathing my cuts and bruises.

I drank eagerly but the wine stung my throat.

'I'm very hungry,' I said, 'but I've been half strangled. I don't know how much I could manage.'

'Who nearly strangled you?' he asked, bustling about sousing bread in some milk.

I supped it down like a two-year-old.

'Altobiondi,' I said.

The city was in chaos for several days while I lay low at Leone's. When I first woke up in his house, I had lost an entire day. The physical injuries and the shock of seeing Clarice kill her husband in front of our son combined to shut my senses down into a deep sleep that lasted twenty-four hours.

I awoke still stiff and sore but rested in my body. I was anxious to know what had been happening and went in search of news and food. Leone was in his kitchen.

'Ah, at last,' he said when he saw me. 'I thought you would never wake!'

'Is there anything to eat?' I said.

'Your throat is better then?' he asked, fetching bread and honey and a cup of wine.

'Still a bit tender,' I said, massaging my neck. 'But I'll manage. I feel as hollow as a cast bronze.'

'Not a man of marble, then.'

'All too mortal, I'm afraid.'

'Can you tell me now what happened?' he asked. 'I could make very little of that jumble of words when you turned up the night before last.'

That was when I knew I had lost a day.

I told him everything I could remember, even though it meant admitting my relation to Clarice and the boy.

'It was good of Grazia to warn you,' he said.

'How is she?' I asked. 'Have you seen her? I am confused about the days. Did you go to your studio yesterday?'

'Yes, though it was not easy getting through the city. The piazza is stained with blood and there are armed men on every street corner.'

'Did you see the statue? Is it safe? And was there any sign of Michelangelo?'

He held up his hands. 'I haven't answered you about Grazia yet,' he said. 'I did eventually get to the Visdomini house and it was in an uproar. Ser Visdomini had been arrested for causing an affray. His wife was in a terrible state. Grazia was trying to calm everything down and keep the household running.'

'Did she ask about me?'

'I told her you were with me and she was relieved. You are lucky that she cares so much.'

I sensed rebuke in his words. I knew Leone did not think I had treated Grazia well; and privately I agreed with him.

'I'm glad she is all right. What is the rest of the news in the city?'

'Well, the statue is unharmed. It is being guarded again. And Michelangelo is there with it – he doesn't leave it night or day, they say.'

'He must be worried about me too. Could you take him a message from me?'

Leone nodded.

'What are they saying about Altobiondi?'

'That he was badly wounded in the piazza and just managed to reach home before he died.'

'Is there any news about Clarice or little Davide?'

He shook his head.

But it wasn't long before I heard about them. I had a visitor after Leone left. I was at first scared to open the door but the knock had been so faint that I did not think it would be an officer I saw when I lifted the latch.

It was Simonetta; she had come across the river on her own, in spite of all the dangers in the city, to find me at the painter's house.

I clasped her hand, really pleased to see her.

'Tell me what's been going on, please. I've been going mad, hiding out here and not knowing. How is Clarice? And the boy?'

'She was still frantic when the Watch came but they understood that to be only natural,' she said. 'They took the body away and the funeral will be tomorrow. Since then she has been calmer – her women tell me she has been sleeping a lot.'

'Me too,' I said. 'And Davide?'

'I have been each day to see him,' she said. 'He is recovering well. I think perhaps small children don't always remember the thing that has frightened them.'

'I do hope so,' I said. 'It was a thing of nightmare.'

'Remember he didn't see his mother strike the blow,' said Simonetta softly. 'Perhaps in time he will believe what everyone else does – that his father was killed in a fight in the piazza.'

Hadn't she heard Altobiondi say he was not Davide's father? Or was she just being tactful?

'It is good of you to go and see them,' I said. 'Will you let Clarice know where I am? I dare not go near the Palazzo Altobiondi until after its master is in the ground.'

'You need clean clothes,' she said, looking at me. 'Yours are all stained with blood.'

'I have nothing to change into here,' I said, shuddering as I remembered the fountain of blood pulsing from Altobiondi's neck. 'But Leone is going to see my brother the sculptor today. He will bring me some.'

'It's best not to be seen in the street till you can burn these,' she said, touching my sleeve.

Then she sat in a chair and put her face in her hands. I realised how much she had been through in these last days and she probably hadn't slept. Davide might forget what had happened that night, but she had seen it all.

Leone did bring me fresh clothes but they were the now hated livery of the pro-Mediceans. Still, Angelo had chosen the black suit given to me after Piero's death so I looked sober enough. But I did not dare attend Altobiondi's funeral in the cathedral.

Suppose he had told his friends – those that weren't still in the Stinche – about me and Clarice? They might take revenge on me for that even if they didn't suspect me of any involvement in his death.

But I did go to the square and see my likeness peering out from his wooden castle.

The worst of the bloodstains had been scrubbed from the terracotta tiles of the piazza, but to me the square still rang with screams and the clash of steel on steel. More than before I wanted to leave the city. Yet I still had so much unfinished business there.

The guards didn't recognise me in my black velvet but Angelo poked his head out from the scaffolding when he heard my voice.

'Gabriele!'

He jumped down and hugged me to his chest.

'I am glad to see you well,' he said. 'Come up.'

I was too finely dressed to work on the statue but I could see he had managed to make some progress on his own. No one knew the details of that marble as well as my brother and I did.

'I see you can use your arm again,' I said.

He held it out and flexed the muscles in his forearm.

'You and Antonio did a good job,' he said. 'And no one ever knew I had been hurt. I shall always be grateful for that.'

'I'm sorry I left you when the battle broke out,' I said, suddenly feeling tears building up in my eyes.

'Don't worry. Leone explained it all to me. He's a good man, that painter.' Angelo patted my arm. 'You have nothing to reproach yourself with.'

'If only that were true. But I see you are not at the funeral.'

'I had no reason to go,' he said. 'Altobiondi was no friend of mine. From everything you have told me the world is well rid of him. It was you I was worried about.'

'I seem to have got away with it,' I said.

'Got away with what? From what I heard you did nothing except defend yourself and that is not a crime, even in this lawless city.'

'No one must ever know it was Clarice,' I said quietly. 'I would take the blame if anyone ever said she had done it.'

'Well, let's hope it never comes to that,' said Angelo.

But we had reckoned without Andrea Visdomini.

CHAPTER TWENTY-TWO

I Once Was What You Are

I was once again staying at Lodovico's house now that the city was calming down. Even Angelo came back to sleep there since the statue was under constant guard. I hadn't dared to be seen at Clarice's house and nor did I show my face at Visdomini's. He could think me dead in the fray if he liked. I knew he had been released from prison but I never expected to see him again.

I was very careful about being seen in the city. Angelo had given me some time off and the only time I went out in public was to Donato's funeral, which took place the day after Altobiondi's, in the church of Santa Maria Novella.

It was Angelo's favourite church in the city and yet I had never been in it. I knelt, feeling full of remorse as the coffin was borne in. Donato's parents and brother followed behind, Giulio with his arm in a sling.

If I hadn't been fighting with Altobiondi, the brothers would not have come to my rescue. But who was to say they would have survived that night unscathed without my involvement?

My eyes were drawn back again and again to the fresco of the Trinity on the left-hand wall of the nave. My neighbour in the pew told me it was by that same 'Big Tom' who painted the Adam and Eve I had so admired in the church south of the river. That was the day Angelo had talked to me about being republican and the importance in this city of knowing what side you were on. Those days seemed impossibly lost and far away now.

Under this painting was another of a skeleton lying in its grave, with the inscription: *I once was what you are and what I am you also will be.* It made me shiver. Donato was well on his way to becoming what the skeleton was. I was aware of my strong bones inside my limbs and the shape of my own skull. Big Tom was right and he too had been long in his grave and was like the painted skeleton now.

After the funeral, Giulio came up to speak to me.

'I'm glad Altobiondi got what he deserved,' he said. 'You saved me a job. He was the one who killed my brother and cut my arm to the bone.'

'Not me,' I said, but Giulio just patted me on the elbow.

Those days I constantly took out my hoard of money from under my mattress and counted it. By the time the David would be ready to shed its wooden castle, I wanted to be ready to go home.

It was Gismondo who alerted me to the new danger I was in.

He came home out of breath. 'Quick, Gabriele, you'd better hide yourself. The Watch are coming to arrest you.'

'What for?' I asked. I couldn't believe they were catching up with me so many days after the battle.

'The murder of Antonello de' Altobiondi,' said Gismondo.

I didn't stop to find out more. I took my money, bundled up some clothes and made my escape through the back yard, with Gismondo hurrying me the whole time.

'Tell Angelo I've gone back to Leone's,' I told him.

I took a long detour through the maze of little streets in Santa Croce and crossed the river by the Ponte alle Grazie. There was no sound of running feet behind me.

My heart was heavy at the thought of having to go back into hiding. I was sick of this hot and sticky city, with its violence and its secrets, its factions and its vendettas.

I wanted to be up in the clean air of my hilltop village, cutting stone by day and cuddling my girl at night. But if I was to survive to live that life I had to lie low now.

Leone was shocked to see me again so soon and – something else – he seemed . . . embarrassed. I couldn't think why. But he welcomed me warmly enough, especially when I told him I was on the run from the city Watch. I used some of my money to send out for a roast chicken and a big carafe of wine. I didn't want to abuse the painter's hospitality.

We were picking over the chicken bones when there came a thunderous knocking at the door.

Leone looked at me in alarm. I gathered up my things and was about to make a run for it when I heard a familiar voice calling Leone's name.

'It's all right,' I said. 'It's my brother.'

Angelo came in like a bear; he had run all the way from the piazza as soon as he heard the news. Leone poured him a cup of wine and he tossed it back in one gulp.

'That's better,' he said. 'You heard what's happened?'

'Only that the Watch want me for Altobiondi's murder,' I said. 'Gismondo told me.'

'Well, it seems Visdomini was not happy with the explanation given out for his friend's death. He has witnesses who saw you fighting in the square and another who will swear you were in Altobiondi's palazzo the moment he died.'

I groaned. Who could have seen me there? One of the women? I couldn't have told anyone who had been there that night apart from Clarice and Simonetta.

'But the worst thing is that Visdomini is saying there is

no way a man, however devoted to his wife, can struggle back to die in his own house when his throat has been cut. He is having the body dug up.'

We were silent. The game was up. Once it was general knowledge how Altobiondi had died, the suspects would be those people who were in the chamber at the time. Better they should think it was me than know it was Clarice. Davide could not lose another parent.

Angelo could see what I intended to do.

'No,' he said. 'I won't have it.'

'What else can I do?' I said. But I felt sick. I had been so close to escaping the city.

'We shall get you out,' said Angelo. 'And we'll say you died of your wounds. Your reputation will be damaged but you will survive.'

At least he hadn't told me to betray Clarice to the authorities.

There was another pounding at the door. This time Leone cautiously lifted the latch and peered out. He opened the door wide and let in Gismondo.

'You're still here,' Angelo's warlike brother said to me. 'I hoped you might have left by now. They've put a guard on every city gate. Everyone's been told to stop Gabriele from escaping.'

'And everyone knows what he looks like,' said Leone. 'Everyone in the city has seen his likeness.'

'Then we must change it,' said Angelo.

He looked at me very seriously. I didn't know what he was going to do, at least not straight away, but I trusted him with my life.

And then he smashed his fist into my face.

243

When I came to, I could hardly see. Angelo was sitting with his head in his hands and Leone was soaking strips of linen in cold water and laying them over my face. It eased the pain a little but I knew I would soon have two dramatic black eyes. My nose throbbed. I had felt it break and I guessed it had swollen to twice its usual size – I must look a sight.

Gismondo was bouncing about the room in a state of high excitement.

'You certainly don't look like the statue any more,' he said. 'This might work.'

Angelo groaned. 'I'm sorry, Gabriele,' he said coming and putting his arm round my shoulder. 'It was the only way. But I know how much pain you are in – it was what Torrigiani did to me all those years ago.'

I couldn't speak at first for the shock and the pain. I looked into Angelo's worried face and saw his own broken nose.

'Now we really shall look like brothers,' I mumbled.

'My brave boy,' he said. 'It hurts me to destroy something beautiful. I am in the business of making such things – not breaking them.'

'What's the plan?' asked Leone. 'He is not fit to travel like this.'

'No,' said Angelo. 'Will you keep him safe here? We'll go back and spread the rumour that Gabriele died of his wounds sustained in the piazza a week ago.'

I tried to think how many people had seen me since then.

'I went to Donato's funeral,' I managed to say.

'I shall visit his family,' said Angelo, 'and ask them to keep quiet about that.'

'His brother Giulio thinks I did it anyway,' I said. 'He sort of congratulated me. I don't think he'll hand me over to the Watch.'

'You will stay here till your new injuries have healed,' said Angelo. 'And then we'll get you out of the city with my father's carter.'

And that's what happened. I still remember the pain of my broken nose – the difficulty in breathing which remains with me to this day. They hacked at my hair with a kitchen knife till all my curls were shorn and I didn't shave for nearly two weeks.

So it was a wretched figure who climbed into the cart the day I left Florence for good. I looked like a prizefighter with my battered nose, the yellowish green remains of the bruising round my eyes, my shorn head and my bristly face. I wore a working man's clothes, after a lot of deliberation. Was Gabriele better known in the city as Angelo's stone-carver assistant or as a pro-Medicean dandy?

They decided that it was the association with the *compagnacci* that I had better avoid and they took all my fine clothing away to burn it. I let it go without regret.

During my period of convalescence, Grazia had come to sit with me several times and Simonetta once or twice. They both wept over my changed appearance.

I begged them both, separately, to forgive me for any trouble I had got them into. I shall never forget that the grave and composed Simonetta had felled Altobiondi with one of his own chairs. And Grazia had come to warn me that the man knew of my past with Clarice.

As I got ready to leave the city, I remembered how I had arrived in it three and a half years ago. I had been so innocent and callow; that very first night I had ended up in Clarice's bed. How little I had understood about the ways of the world then. And I had no idea of what the consequences of that first night would be.

'Ready?' asked Leone.

'As ready as I'll ever be,' I said. My voice had changed since Angelo's assault; it now sounded a bit nasal, even to me.

Angelo had already come to say goodbye. He thought it better not to accompany me because of our well-known association.

Since the day he had broken my nose, he had worn black, not because he mourned my lost looks, but in support of the rumour that I had died. I believe the whole of Lodovico's household did it and so high was my brother's reputation in the city, because of the marble Giant, that his feigned grief was believed.

It was weird to think that people believed I was dead. And in a way I was. My old self had died anyway – the Gabriele who was so carefree and unworldly.

I climbed aboard the cart, which had come into the city with a load of fresh vegetables from Lodovico's farm. As well as me, it was taking back some cooking pots and lengths of cloth from the Buonarrotis' shop. I settled myself down as comfortably as I could and faced the journey to the gate in the north-east of the city.

As far as the carter was concerned, I was a farmhand from the country near Pisa, who was seeking work away from the troubles in that region; Lodovico had hired me to work on his own farm in Settignano and my name was Michele. That was all he needed to know and I wasn't inclined to chat to him on the journey.

'Halt!' cried the guards on the gate.

I could feel my heart thudding against my chest. If they stopped us now and recognised me, I would be taken back into the city and thrown into the Stinche. If found guilty of Altobiondi's death – as I had no doubt I would be – they would take me into the courtyard of the Bargello and cut off my head with no more hesitation than if I were a chicken destined for the dining-table.

My mouth was dry. Vanni, the carter, let them examine the sacks containing cloth and pots. I stayed sitting hunched up, an old sack over my shoulders, so that my real height could not be guessed.

'Who's this?' asked one of the guards.

'Michele,' said the carter.

'Michele what?'

The carter looked at me and shrugged.

'Michele Poggi,' I croaked.

'He's hired to work on a farm in Settignano,' said Vanni. 'I've to take him to the Buonarroti place.'

The guard raised his torch to look at my face.

'Ugly brute, isn't he?' he said and waved us through.

And so I left the city I had had such high hopes of – to be a virtual exile for the rest of my life.

1564

I got the bundle of letters out of my chest and spread them on the table. Angelo was a great letter writer. The most recent had been written only a few months ago. The oldest one that had survived came to me in October, three months after I had left the city.

My dear Gabriele,
I hope you are well and not troubled by pain. And that you are getting plenty of work in the quarry.

He constantly harped on the damage to my face, even though the swelling had gone down months earlier.

I send you a length of silk for Rosalia's wedding dress and wish you both a very happy day.

I must tell you that David now wears the modesty garment Leonardo wanted for him! The Signoria got a goldsmith to make him a bronze belt with twenty-eight copper leaves to 'render him decent'. I am glad you weren't here to see it.

I no longer have his earlier letters, where he told me about the revealing of the statue on the 8th of September. It had borne a wreath of gilded laurel leaves on its head and everyone had praised the work, both for the skill of the sculptor and the beauty of the young man portrayed.

Maybe that's why I didn't keep them; I don't remember now.

My mother had cried when she saw me and Rosalia had screamed. I was very different from the lover who had left her years before.

But with time my looks got a bit better. I shaved off the horrible disguising stubble and my curls began to grow back. The bruises on my face healed and all I was left with to remind me of my Florentine adventures was my flattened nose.

Rosalia was kind enough to say I was still a handsome man in spite of it. But I didn't expect her to take me back without a full confession.

She wept when she heard of my treachery and I spared her no details. She was still only eighteen and very lovely; although she had waited for me she had the right to find another, better man to spend her life with.

When we parted that day, I was sure she would turn me down. But the next day she came to my parents' house and, saying nothing, held out her arms to me. I was faithful to her until her death. I have been alone these last fifteen years.

Leonardo never finished his fresco in the Palazzo della Signoria and Angelo didn't even start his. The paint ran on Leonardo's Battle of Anghiari and the Battle of Cascina remained as a large-scale drawing. Angelo was called to Rome by the new Pope in the spring of the year after I left, to do great work as a painter. Leonardo left for France and I never heard of him again.

But I do know he took the portrait of Monna Lisa with him. Angelo had been right that del Giocondo never did get it.

I did see Clarice once more. She brought her two sons to visit me, not long after Rosalia and I exchanged vows in the church of the Misericordia and Saint Mary. I made sure my new wife knew that I had no idea this grand lady was coming when I saw the carriage outside the small stone house I had bought with some help from the Buonarroti family.

Davide was then nearly three and able to walk on his own little legs. The contrast between him and his baby brother, not yet a year old, was marked, each resembling his own father. Cipriano had the dark features of Antonello de' Altobiondi, which it was strange to see on a child, and he was going to have just as big a nose. But I was in no position to criticise noses.

Davide was a beautiful boy, well-made and strong and going to be tall. He was very sweet to his little brother. I gave him the cupid I had made – the only statue I ever did carve – and he seemed to like it, though it was a strange toy for a child.

The two women were very polite to each other but when Clarice had left, Rosalia said to me, 'I had not realised she was so old,' and never mentioned her again.

I knew from Angelo's letters that the Altobiondi case had been dropped and that Clarice was treated with respect as the grieving widow of an important man. Altobiondi's property and money was held in trust for the two boys equally, according to the terms of a will he made soon after his marriage, and Clarice had the use of his rents for her lifetime, which made her a wealthy widow (she still had property from her first husband too).

I imagine she lived comfortably with her four children until her death twenty years ago. I heard she never took another husband.

Davide and Cipriano remain good friends, from what I hear. I am a grandfather to three boys and two girls who will bear the Altobiondi name, because, of course, Davide does not know of my relationship to him. But I do know that he is a great patron of the arts.

About Visdomini and his household I heard little. Except for the news in one of Angelo's lost early letters that Leone was to marry Grazia! He had developed a fondness for her some time earlier but apparently never thought he stood a chance as long as I was around. I had no right to do anything other than send them both my best wishes for a happy life together.

Another even more unexpected wedding took place between Simonetta and her brother's friend Daniele. I felt worse about that because I knew how bloodthirsty he could be. I hoped he would be kind to her and to any children they might have but I would selfishly have preferred it if she had carried out her suggestion of joining a convent.

The de' Medici were restored to rule in Florence and Piero Soderini deposed eight years after I left the city. But it was Giuliano, Lorenzo's third son, who became ruler, not the Cardinal. And the following year when Angelo's hard taskmaster Pope Julius died, Giovanni de' Medici was elected as Pope Leo the Tenth.

When I knew that the sensuous and self-indulgent man I had failed to kill was now leader of the Church, I wondered if I had done the wrong thing. But later his cousin Giulio became Pope Clement VII so a Medici would have sat on the papal throne in Rome eventually.

Everything the *compagnacci* had hoped for had come to pass. I thought of my old *frateschi* friends in Florence and how disappointed they must be but the story wasn't quite over yet. The de' Medici were driven out again in 1527, only to be restored finally four years later.

That last time, Angelo had to hide in a church lest he be arrested and executed as a dangerous republican!

The family have been ruling in the city for well over thirty years now and I don't expect to see them toppled again in my lifetime. But they have welcomed my brother's body back like the great artist and Florentine he is. I shall go down once more into the city in a few days' time to see him buried.

My grandson Davide will take me. He is the son of our daughter Lisa, the first of five children my Rosalia bore me.

I shall take a look at the statue in the Piazza della Signoria while I'm there, for old times' sake. He had his arm broken during the riots of '27 – the last triumph of the *frateschi*. But it was repaired and I'm told it's as good as new.

I don't need to fear the law any more: no one would recognise me as that strapping young man now.

But if you want to know what I looked like during the years of my adventures in the city, you can go and take a look at Michelangelo's statue of David, the shepherd-boy who became a king.

If it is still there.

Historical Note

The years 1501–04 were very turbulent ones in the city of Florence. The de' Medici family, in the form of Piero de' Medici, had been exiled from the city in 1494 and a Republic established.

For the next four years the city fell under the spell of the fanatical Dominican friar, Girolamo Savonarola. He was responsible for the gathering up and burning of all luxurious items, including works of art, in the famous Bonfires of the Vanities in the Piazza della Signoria. In 1498, he was himself burned in the same place, after being hanged with two of his companions.

Florence was then riven by warring factions, who were either pro-Republic – some of them still pro-Savonarola – or pro-Medici, who would have liked to reinstall the ruling family.

The historical leader of the *compagnacci* was the beguilingly named Doffo Spini, but I have made it Antonello de' Altobiondi because of the storyline I wanted to create for him. And I have dressed them in purple and green and the *frateschi* all in black. I believe I invented this particular Ridolfi and Bellatesta, though those were well-known pro-Medici family names in Florence at the time.

Gabriele del Lauro is a completely invented character. It is true that Michelangelo lived for a time with his wet nurse, who was the wife of a stonemason in Settignano but sadly nothing is recorded of her name and family. I set out to discover what a young man, looking as David looks, might experience if he entered Florence in 1501. The historical setting is as accurate as I could make it but all Gabriele's actions, thoughts and character traits are fiction.

Michangelo was initially pro-Medicean because of the patronage of Lorenzo the Magnificent, but after Lorenzo's death favoured the Republic.

The statue of David really was stoned on the first night of its removal by the four young men named but I am solely responsible the injury to the sculptor's arm and for the battle in the piazza.

The Sangallo brothers really did devise the structure for moving the statue though.

(I am convinced by the ideas of Saul Levine about the change in design of the model for David.)

List of Characters

Gabriele del Lauro, a stonecutter from Settignano
Rosalia, his first girlfriend
Clarice de' Buonvicini, a Florentine widow, later married to Antonello de' Altobiondi
Michelangelo Buonarroti, * the sculptor
Lodovico Buonarroti, * his father
Lionardo, Buonarroto, GiovanSimone and **Sigismondo (Gismondo) Buonarroti,** * his brothers
Antonello de' Altobiondi, leader of the pro-Medicean faction in Florence
Daniele, a *fratesco*
Gianbattista, a *fratesco*
Donato, a *fratesco*
Giulio, Donato's younger brother by two years, a *fratesco*
Fra Paolo, Dominican friar, a *fratesco*
Simonetta, Gianbattista's sister
Giuliano da Sangallo, * a sculptor, architect and military engineer (1443–1516)
Antonio da Sangallo, * his younger brother, architect (1453–1534)
Andrea Visdomini, a young aristocrat
Maddalena, his wife
Grazia, their servant
Leone, a young painter, whose patron is Visdomini, not connected to Leone Leoni (1509–1590), a Mannerist sculptor

Arnolfo Ridolfi, a pro-Medicean conspirator

Alessandro Bellatesta, a pro-Medicean conspirator

Leonardo da Vinci, * the painter and inventor (1452–1519)

Salai, * his assistant

Piero Soderini, * Gonfaloniere of Florence, his appointment made permanent in 1502

Fra Girolamo Savonarola, * A fanatical Dominican friar at the San Marco monastery, who preached against the excesses of the de' Medici family. He was effectively the ruler of Florence from 1494–1498, when he was executed (1452–1498)

Francesco di Bartolomeo del Giocondo, * a silk merchant

Lisa Gherardini (Monna Lisa), * his wife

Fra Angelico, * also called Beato ('blessed') Angelico. Fresco painter and Dominican friar at the San Marco monastery in Florence (1395–1455)

Sandro Botticelli, * painter and one-time follower of Savonarola. Also known as *il Botticello,* 'the little barrel' (1455–1510)

Vincenzo di Cosimo Martelli, * one of a group of young nobles who stoned David on 14th May 1504

Filippo di Francesco de' Spini, * another of these young nobles

Raffaello Panciatichi, * another of these young nobles

Gherardo Maffei de' Gherardini, * another of these young nobles

* = historical figures

Glossary

arrabbiati	'The enraged ones' – anti-Savonarola faction in Florence
Arte della Lana	The Guild of Wool Merchants, responsible for the Duomo
bottega	A workshop
braccio (pl. *braccia*)	A measurement of about 22 and 7/8ths inches, according to Charles Seymour, but variable
compagnacci	'The bad or ugly companions' – aristocratic pro-Medici faction in Florence
condottiere (pl. *condottieri*)	A leader of a band of mercenary soldiers
fanciulli (sing. *fanciullo*)	Literally 'children', specifically the boys who carried out Savonarola's wishes
fratesco (pl. *frateschi*)	'A follower of the friar' (Girolamo Savonarola)
gonfaloniere	The chief magistrate of the city
lizzatura	A method of sliding marble down a row of planks
natura morta	A 'still life' in art
Opera del Duomo	The workshop for work on the cathedral

Operai del Duomo	Officials of the Opera del Duomo
paneficio	A baker's shop
picchiapietre	A stonecutter
piagnone (pl. *piagnoni*)	'A weeper' – impolite name for a follower of Savonarola
practica	A public inquiry
scalpellino	Another word for a stonecutter
Signoria	The seat of government in Florence
vernaccia	A dry white wine

Acknowledgements

Many thanks to my dear Florentine friend, Carla Poesio, for reading the text and putting me right about beer. Also to my quasi-Venetian friend, Michelle Lovric, for doing the same but without the beer. Living near Oxford as I do, I am always so grateful to be able to use the Bodleian, Taylorian and Sackler Libraries and this time I was also able to look at Michelangelo drawings in the Ashmolean Museum.

Among the many, many books and articles I read, *Michelangelo's David: A Search for Identity* by Charles Seymour Jr (1967), Saul Levine's 1984 article about Michelangelo's lost bronze *David*, and Frederick Hartt's *David by the Hand of Michelangelo* (1987) were the most influential. Absolutely invaluable was R. Barr Litchfield's *Online Gazetteer of Sixteenth Century Florence* (2006).

And I never attempt to write any historical novel without the assistance of the indispensable London Library, of which I am a happy Country Member.